Review

The time of World War II, when everything still hangs in a balance, yet the Allied victory may be near, is captured in all its hopefulness and terror. It is as if the author had lived through these times. -www.readerviews.com

Louisa's outspoken but humble and pious personality provides the perfect point of view for anecdotes of small-town life during war. *Copper Star*'s plot builds in conflict and excitement, and its tender romance warms the heart.
-Historical Novels Review

Fisher's book is a gem in more ways than one. For once the romance angle is beautifully created and developed. A wonderful book that is highly recommended for all readers.
-www.roundtablereviews.com

It is apparent that Fisher has studied the craft of writing extensively and knows what she's doing. The book is written in a literary style. The characters are well developed, the romance is very real and present, and the faith message is expertly woven in. This author is one to watch. ~Armchair Reviews and Dancing Word

I read this and envisioned a WWII movie playing out before me. The characters are so real, you are actually there. This is a must read for everyone of regardless of faith. -Karen Find Out About New Books

Endorsements

"Fisher has a knack for sweeping us up in the small triumphs and tragedies of her characters, which echo in surprising ways the often overwhelming dramas being played out in the world around them." -From David Kopp, executive editor of Multnomah Publishers

"We are thrilled that our history coincides so beautifully with your story." -From Barbara Hecht, President of John Tracy Clinic, Los Angeles, California

"I just couldn't put down your book. I kept saying just one more chapter...I loved it!!!! I feel like I'm getting to know a new family and have a window into their life. I don't want to stop getting to know them now. I want to find out what happens to Louisa!" -Linda Danis, author of the bestselling *365 Things Every New Mom Should Know*

"*Copper Star* is an intriguing and altogether believable story woven with heartwarming characters who first touch and then linger in your heart." -Debora M. Coty, author of *The Distant Shore*

Copper Star
Suzanne Woods Fisher

Vintage Romance Publishing

Goose Creek, South Carolina
www.vrpublishing.com

Suzanne Woods Fisher

Dedication

This story was inspired by the life and death of Dietrich Bonhoeffer (1906-1945)

"Heaven's gain was earth's loss." -Louisa Schmetterling

Suzanne Woods Fisher

Prologue

On a blazing hot summer day in Copper Springs, Arizona, the four of us stood in the church cemetery, staring solemnly at a headstone, each one of us lost in our memories of the person who lay before us. I was amazed at how powerful the connection had been for each one of us, with that cold body lying beneath the freshly dug grave. Two of us connected to it with a bond of love, two of us with a sense of responsibility.

I had arrived in America only seventeen months ago, and it seemed as if the entire purpose of my coming to Copper Springs pointed to this fateful moment. As if this was why I had been sent here in the first place.

Never, though, in my wildest imagination, could I have imagined the turn of events that occurred, especially in the last few months, which turned this town upside down. Copper Springs would never be the same.

This is the story of how I ended up in a dusty copper mining town in Arizona after a thrilling but dangerous stint with the Resistance Workers in Nazi Germany and how my journey took me to this gravesite.

And to the very heart of a family.

Chapter One

I had lost track of which day it was. I glanced at a newspaper that a passenger left on the seat. Under the February 2, 1943 date, the headline proclaimed boldly: "Germans Surrender at Stalingrad." A good sign, it seemed, that today of all days was the first big defeat of Hitler's armies. I smiled. This war couldn't last much longer.

The conductor gracefully maneuvered down the aisles despite the jerky movement of the train. "Next stop, Tucson, Arizona!" he bellowed. I picked up my small bag and prepared to disembark, wishing I could borrow some of his confidence for what I was about to do.

I stood at the top of the platform steps, looking for a man who resembled the tattered picture I held in my hand. The picture was over ten years old, and Dietrich's descriptive skills left much to be desired. "He's sort of tall but not really. Average build. Dark hair, I think. Don't worry. He'll find you."

Dietrich was right. Like *always*. There was only one man standing at the station, and he looked similar to the man in the photograph. In the picture, though, he was laughing, young and carefree. The man standing on the platform looked serious, hat in hand, waiting to fulfill a promise he had made to his longtime friend from seminary days to sponsor me, a complete stranger, a German refugee on the lam.

I took a deep breath, whispered a silent prayer, and stepped down from the train. My long journey had just come to an abrupt end in this dry, dusty copper mining town in Arizona.

"Reverend Gordon?"

Slowly the man nodded, tilting his head, a puzzled look on his face.

"I'm Louisa. Louisa Schmetterling. I hope I didn't keep you waiting."

We shook hands. Then came an awkward pause. "Did you have a pleasant trip?" he asked politely, still looking a little surprised.

"Yes, it was fine," I lied. Why did he keep looking at me as if he was expecting someone else?

Just as another train came roaring into the station, we pulled away in Reverend Gordon's 1937 Hudson Custom Eight, a big black box of a car, and headed southeast on the two-lane highway out of Tucson toward Copper Springs. We passed a vast, harsh landscape of cactus, strange looking trees with gnarled trunks and spindly arms, and jutting spires of rusty red rocks. Everywhere were sharp angled rocks. I felt as if I landed on another planet, void of any trace of green.

Still, I should have tried to hide my disappointment. I've never been good at masking my feelings. It's one of my worst faults.

The Reverend noticed the look on my face. Quickly, he pointed out in what I would call a voice of quiet pride, "it may not seem like much, but this state is known for copper; even our state flag has a copper star in the center. Before the turn of the century, these copper mines created boomtowns overnight. During the Depression, they almost turned into ghost towns. Now, though, the War has created a huge demand for copper, and the mines have soared back into production. Mines near here are supplying almost three million pounds of copper a day. It's a very important commodity to help win the war."

I nodded at him enthusiastically, as if I understood. The truth was that I knew very little about this place I had just arrived in and even less about the man sitting next to me. All that I knew for certain was that Robert Gordon and Dietrich Bonhoeffer were in seminary together years ago. I tried to recall the few details Dietrich had told me: He said the Reverend had been raised here, that his father had been a minister, and he was married and had a child.

"Reverend Gordon?"

"Robert. Call me Robert."

I smiled. "Robert, there's something I need to discuss with you. Something Dietrich wanted you to know. I don't know how much he might have told you about our...I mean...my...situation." I had practiced this speech for the last five-hundred miles, yet I was still stymied for words.

"No." He glanced over at me. "Dietrich only told me he needed a safe place for someone to wait out the war."

"I didn't want to leave Germany, but I didn't have much choice. I had to flee. The Gestapo—a secret police force in Germany—was closing in on us...on me." I looked over at him, noticing that now he looked a little stunned.

He cleared his throat. "May I ask why?"

"Well, for quite a few reasons."

He shot a sideways glance at me that silently broadcasted, "who have I just invited to live in my home?"

Who could blame him?

Where should I begin? At the beginning, I supposed. "First of all, my father was Jewish. The Jewish people are under great duress from Hitler. And it is getting much, much worse for them."

He nodded, understanding. "A few years ago, I saw Dietrich in New York. He was quite distressed about the deteriorating situation in Germany. That's when he asked me if I would ever consider sponsoring someone. I've heard some reports about what is happening to the Jews in Germany. It's a terrible thing. You don't need to explain anything else."

Oh, but I did. I had never told another living soul what I was about to divulge, but Dietrich, a straightforward and uncompromising man, felt Robert deserved full disclosure, despite my objections. "There is still another reason that I had to flee. We've been part of the Resistance against the Nazis."

Another furtive glance cast in my direction. "We?" he asked. "You said 'we'."

"Yes, I did. My involvement has to do with Dietrich. And his brother-in-law, Hans, who is an official in the Abwehr...the German Military Intelligence Organization. They both are working in Hitler's War Offices." I could tell this was new knowledge for him, and this was only half of what I needed to say. I felt a little sorry for him, knowing what was to come.

"Go on," Robert said, listening intently.

"Dietrich has been part of a plot, with a few others, who are working within the German government to assassinate Hitler. Actually, more than one. And I played a role—a small one. But each plot has run aground. Hitler is the luckiest man in the world. It's as if someone orchestrates his luck."

Someone evil.

"And the Gestapo is close to arresting those involved. Dietrich insisted I leave Germany immediately. False identification papers had been prepared for me, and, before I knew it, I was heading across the border to Switzerland."

I paused to gauge Robert's reaction as he took in this information. "It would be understandable if you have second thoughts about inviting me into your home." I looked over at him, carefully watching his face, trying to squelch the anxiety churning in my stomach.

We drove along for quite a while in silence. It was obvious he had no idea that Dietrich had been involved in Resistance Work, much less so, assassination plots. To be fair, it was a shocking piece of information. A pastor, a dynamic, deeply devoted man of God, plotting to kill Hitler.

Robert furrowed his brow and bit his lower lip in thoughtful silence. An eternity later, he turned to look at me. "Louisa, why do you think Dietrich asked me to sponsor you?"

"I guess...I guess I don't really know. He said you were friends in seminary together."

"Yes, we were. And I think I know why," he answered decidedly. "I think he trusts me. You are welcome to stay with us as long as you need a home."

I searched his eyes, finding sincerity. Outwardly, I smiled. Inwardly, I felt the first sense of sheer relief since...well...I couldn't remember how long it had been. Months, perhaps. The truth was, I really didn't have a back-up plan of where to go or what to do had this man not extended the invitation to stay at his home.

As we crossed over one more hill, I saw a small town clinging perilously to the side of a mountain, as if defying gravity. The town looked as if it cascaded down a hillside of jumbled rock. Robert parked in front of a wood-framed church building covered with white peeling paint, belfry topping the tapered steeple.

"Here's the First Presbyterian Church of Copper Springs. That's my church. And my father's before me. And over there is the parsonage. Your home, too, for now," he added. "My office connects the two."

I turned to see where he was pointing. The house was an old bungalow with steps leading up to a covered porch. It, too, had peeling white paint. The roof of a covered breezeway connected the church and the parsonage with a small room. Through the window I saw bookshelves lining the walls. Robert's office.

In front of the house was the neglected remnant of a garden. I couldn't help but think back to the beautiful gardens of Germany. Germans prided themselves on their fine gardens.

Robert held the screen door open for me as we walked inside the house. In the center of one wall was a massive stone fireplace flanked by two large bookcases on each side, filled with thick books bearing important sounding titles. The afternoon sunlight filtered through the trees in front of the large picture window, causing shadows to dance on the wall.

Immediately, I loved this front room. It held a wisp of saintliness.

A tall, plain woman entered the room, wiping her hands on her apron. Her peppered hair was twisted up in a hard little knot held with two wire hairpins. She had a look on her face as if she had just swallowed a teaspoonful of vinegar.

"Louisa, this is my Aunt Martha. My father's sister. Aunt Martha, this is Louisa. Louisa Schmetterling. Our houseguest."

It might have been my imagination, but he seemed to announce that to her, as if he was closing the subject. "Hello, Frau Gordon." I reached my hand out.

With one arched eyebrow, she cautiously returned my handshake. "*Miss* Gordon, Louise," she corrected.

"Actually, my name is Louisa. With an 'a' on the end."

Her eyebrow remained arched.

"And there is my son, William. He's peeking around the corner."

A small, serious-looking boy poked his head around the door jam to peer at me.

I peered back. "Hello, William. How old are you?"

William stared at me with wordless curiosity.

"He's four-and-a-half," volunteered Miss Gordon, as if it was one word.

Robert picked up my suitcase and offered to show me to my room. I followed him up the stairs. He showed me the bedroom that he slept in, a bunkroom for William, and Miss Gordon's room. There was a bathroom with a claw foot bathtub, a shower curtain circling around it, a toilet and a sink. Down at the end of the hall was the room where I was to stay. It had a small bed, a night stand, desk and chair, and a bureau.

Robert pointed to the window. "The best view from the house is out your window."

I looked out the window and saw a sheer wall of rusty red rock. The knot in my throat was rather sizable. His words struck me as a metaphor. The end of the road.

* * *

I slept in the next morning. Well, I didn't really sleep in. I stayed in bed hours after I woke, because I couldn't quite figure out what to do with myself. Plus, I was more than a little intimidated by Robert's aunt. And the bed felt heavenly. It had been weeks since I had last slept in a real bed. Finally, I dressed, went downstairs, and found Miss Gordon in the kitchen.

"I was beginning to think I should send William up to make sure you hadn't expired in the night," she said dourly as she handed me a cup of coffee.

"The house is so quiet. Where is everyone?" I asked.

"It's nearly noon! Robert is a busy man; he went to the church hours ago."

"Where is William?"

"Right behind you."

I looked behind me and saw him, crouched on the rug in the parlor, coloring with Crayola crayons on a sheet of paper. I went over to him and asked if I could color with him. He didn't respond, so I sat down next to him, picked up the purple crayon, and started to draw.

I thought he must resemble his mother, because he didn't look anything like his father. William had sandy blond hair with a pronounced cowlick in the center of his forehead and big blue eyes with thick blond lashes. Robert's and William's eyes were the only obvious resemblance they shared. But it wasn't the color, it was something else. Something behind their eyes.

I wondered about his mother. There was no mention of her last night by Robert or his aunt. There was no evidence that another woman lived in this home. Not even a family photograph.

"Do you like to color, William? I do."

Miss Gordon whisked back into the kitchen as William and I colored. *Ah, relief.* The woman made me nervous. She did all of the right things, such as getting me fresh towels for a hot bath last night, but she carried an air of general disapproval.

I offered to help Miss Gordon around the house, but she refused my help. So I invited William to go on a walk with me and show me around.

"He won't talk to you," she offered without elaborating.

"William, come show me the town?" I waved to him to come. He cocked his head, looked at me, and jumped up to join me. I took his hand, and we started our tour of Copper Springs.

The streets of Copper Springs were laid out in a haphazard way, wiggling here and there, as if no one had anticipated a town would eventually emerge. Telephone wires criss-crossed the streets, hanging like strings from abandoned kites.

The buildings were just as erratic as the streets. New, stately buildings looked out of place next to small, hastily built and badly sun-worn storefronts. Residences were curiously tucked in between business buildings. And there were staircases, from the street, leading up to teetering cottages on the precarious ledges of the hillsides.

"William, imagine anyone carrying groceries up fifty stair steps to their home!" His blue eyes appeared suddenly larger, as if he was seriously considering the notion.

Only a few buildings looked as if they intended to be around for a while. The red brick bank, an obviously young building, had a Roman temple portico in front. Over the columns there was a bold proclamation: The First National Trust of Copper Springs. "Now there's a name people can have confidence in," I said to him.

We passed by one lonely public telephone box. Gazing at the telephone box filled me with a sudden wave of nostalgia. Oh, the many times I had stealthily slipped into a similar box in Berlin, heart hammering, to deliver a message of a plot or to let someone know information had been conveyed. A strange part of me missed the thrill, the excitement, even the danger, of being part of Resistance Work. Now, I thought with an absurd twinge of self-pity, I didn't even know a soul in America to call.

Robert called to us as we walked back past the church. "I was just going home for lunch. Did you rest well?" he asked. Absentmindedly, he took William's hand, swinging it back and forth as we headed home.

"Yes, I really did. I just got up, I'm embarrassed to admit."

Miss Gordon had lunch waiting on the table. Meal preparation seemed to be her main preoccupation. Well, that and thoroughly sterilizing the house, as if the King of England was due any moment for an inspection.

I tried to adjust to the family patterns in the next few days without getting in her way. William seemed to have the same strategy. He spent much of his day up in his tree house or in his father's office.

"Robert, do you have any idea of where I might be able to find a job?" I asked, during another quiet meal. I would need to find a job to fulfill immigration requirements, though I was also eager to start a savings account for my return trip to Germany as soon as the war was over.

Robert frowned. "I've been asking around town the last few weeks, but there doesn't seem to be anything available. I'm sure something will turn up."

"Someday, if you're not too busy, would you show me around the countryside?"

Miss Gordon promptly answered for him. "There's a government ban on pleasure driving. Gasoline is rationed. There's a war on, you know."

Did I *know* that there is a war on? Did I *know*? How *dare* she patronize me! She had yet to ask me a single question about the world that I came from. It was as if my past didn't exist for her, only the fact that I interrupted her world now.

Noticing my barely swallowed indignation, Robert quickly interjected, "Aunt Martha, Louisa is well aware there is a war going on. And I hardly drove the car in January. I have plenty of my gas allotment saved up." He turned to me. "Yes, Louisa, William and I can show you around tomorrow, Saturday afternoon. Why not? Maybe we'll take you to the copper pit," he added, a pleased look spreading across his face.

"To a...pit?" I asked, disappointed.

"Well, not just *any* pit. A copper pit," Robert answered. "It's a crater. It's where ore is mined to be melted down into copper. Any town in Arizona worth its weight in salt has a copper pit."

Weight in salt? Copper pit? *What* in the *world* was he talking about?

* * *

The next afternoon, I was reading in my room, hiding from Miss Gordon, when Robert knocked on my door. "Ready to go, Louisa? William is waiting for us. Oh, by the way, I'd like to put your passport into the lock box I have at the bank. Do you mind? Just for safekeeping."

"No, I don't mind," I answered, surprised Robert had even thought about it. At times he seemed so preoccupied, I wasn't always sure he remembered I was here.

This family didn't seem to really talk to each other or even look directly at each other. They issued directives. "Aunt Martha, I need my ministerial robes washed and ironed for the Stollen funeral on Friday." "Robert, the basement window is stuck again." "William, go wash up for dinner."

I was finding I had little to say, as well, which was a notable change for me. My father used to say I was blessed with the gift of conversation. It was his polite way of asking me to be quiet.

We climbed into Robert's car. William jumped into the back seat, hard at work chewing a big wad of bubble gum.

Robert described the town with evident pride. "Copper Springs is a town with an interesting history. It's a mining town. There have been fortunes made and lost here, though you wouldn't know it to see it. The town is only about seventy years old. People live simply, but many of them have become quite wealthy recently from the mines."

We stopped in at the bank. William and I waited while Robert was escorted into the vault by a bank teller to put away my passport.

Then something curious happened.

William watched his father disappear out of sight and then he took off, looking intently for someone or something, but staying carefully out of view of the other bank tellers. He slipped into an empty office and then slipped right back out, hustling to his place next to me as Robert re-emerged out of the vault, acting as if he never left my side. I was the only one who noticed.

We climbed back into Robert's car and drove down the main street to get to the highway, passing by a row of modest homes. One house clearly stood out from the others in its grandeur. "Who lives there?" I asked, pointing to the two-storied brick house with copper sheeting on the roof over the dormers' windows. The yard was green and well-manicured; it was the only grass lawn I'd seen in this dry and arid town.

"That's the Mueller's house. Friedrich Mueller runs the bank. And owns half the mines around here. Say, he and his wife are from Germany. You might enjoy talking to them. Now there's the tavern." He pointed to a rundown building. "Just stay clear of it on Saturday nights." He glanced my way. "In fact, stay clear of it. Period. Not the place for a lady. This town can have a tough element. Seems like someone is always getting hurt in a fight or shot up on a weekend."

Finally! Some intrigue to this sleepy little hamlet.

"And over there is our combined beauty salon and barber shop run by Rosita and Ramon Gonzalves," Robert continued. "Ramon is the town barber, but he's fighting in the Pacific, so Rosita cuts hair for men in town, just while he's away. We're all hoping he'll return soon. Rosita only knows how to cut men's hair in one style, so we pretty much all have the same haircut."

So *that* explained it! His haircut *was* odd, slicked back with a heavy-handed dose of pomade hair gel.

"Let's see. There's the post office."

I looked in the direction he pointed and saw a tiny little building with a flag above the door. On either side of the door were two large war posters with earnest looking soldiers facing forward. One poster said: "Do with less so they'll have enough." And yet another pleaded, "Be patriotic, sign your country's pledge to save the food." I would. I'll eat less, starting today. I would do anything I could to help America win this war.

"And over there is the library." He pointed to a tired looking old wooden building with a cheap metal roof tucked between Rosita's salon and Ibsen's General store.

"A library?" I did *not* expect a provincial town like Copper Springs to have a library. "William, we can go together to pick out books." I looked eagerly at him in the back seat, but he was gazing out the window.

"I thought you might enjoy it. I noticed you were browsing through my bookshelves. Most of mine are theology books from seminary; rather dull, even for me. We could get you a library card." He glanced over at me. "Too bad there aren't any books in German. There used to be; we have a lot of foreign miners in the area. But after war was declared, the Library Committee voted to remove the books."

I looked sharply at him, reminded of the censorship of anything Jewish in Germany. "All of the books published by Jewish authors were burned in Germany," I noted.

Robert had an expression on his face as if he wasn't sure what to make of that comment. Deftly, he changed the subject.

"How are you getting along with Aunt Martha?" he asked as we drove out of town into the open and barren desert.

Oh no.

How should I answer that? I chose my words carefully. "I've noticed your aunt is firmly convinced her opinion should be tacked on to every remark."

Robert grinned. "Well, she's an acquired taste."

I looked over at him as he drove. I couldn't decide if he was handsome or not. Nor could I determine his age. I knew he was younger than Dietrich at thirty-seven, but older than my twenty-three years. I guessed he was in his thirties, but he seemed older. Or, at least, he acted older.

He had once studied alongside Dietrich Bonhoeffer at one of the finest seminaries in this country. Dietrich had spent a sabbatical year at Union Theological Seminary in New York City in 1931. The two men met there and became fast friends. I knew Dietrich felt a great warmth toward this man.

Certainly, Robert could have served in many churches. Why here? In this provincial little town? I would have liked to ask him more, but there was something about the Reverend that made a personal question formidable. I wondered how Dietrich, who enjoyed a good laugh as much as a debate on theology, could have struck up such a deep friendship with this formal, quiet man seated next to me.

Soon, we arrived at the copper pit. Overwhelming in its size, this pit was a gaping, open wound in the earth. It looked as if someone had tried to chisel an amphitheatre of terraced steps with a blunt instrument. In the center was an ominously dark cavity.

"Not pretty to look at but a very important asset to this region," explained Robert. "William! Be careful! Stay back from the edge." Robert waved his hands to motion William to stay back. William was picking up rocks and throwing them down in the center of the pit. I couldn't even hear the rocks hit bottom.

Robert was quite knowledgeable about copper production. As we walked around the pit, he described the process to me. "The rocks you're looking at are actually copper ore, a low-grade copper. Underground mines tend to have a higher grade of copper ore. We have those, too," he added with pride.

I tried to look fascinated.

"The copper ore is then crushed and ground," he continued. "Then comes the floatation process, where water is added to the ground ore. Chemicals are added that coat the copper minerals and float them up to the surface. The copper mineral is dried off and sprayed with acid." His eyes sparkled. "Still with me?"

Lifting my eyebrows, I nodded, feigning interest.

"The copper continues along in a process where another chemical is added to remove all but the copper from the waste materials. Those are called 'tailings.' And that waste is actually recycled into other useful products."

Now my interest was piqued. "So tailings could be called a 'redemptive process'?"

His face grew serious. "I guess...you could call it 'redemptive'." He tilted his head to one side, looking pleased. He launched back into his description of the mechanics at the smelter, but I was having a hard time following him; he didn't seem to notice. It was the most animated I'd seen him be.

He continued to educate me on copper: "After that, it's refined in a fire, and what's left is 99.9% pure copper. It's poured into molds and sent off to the market to be used for just about anything and everything you can think of: coins, batteries, electrical wirings, automobile engines, airplanes, weapons. You name it. In fact, you came to America through Ellis Island, didn't you? I'm sure you saw the Statue of Liberty. She's all copper." He seemed so proud that I would have thought he handcrafted the Statue of Liberty himself.

Now I understood why Robert remained in Copper Springs. He loved it.

On the way back, William fell asleep in the car, leaning against the window. "You speak English very well. Better than a lot of the miners around here. You don't even have a very thick German accent. How did you learn it?" Robert asked.

"Every German school child learns English from kindergarten on. I had a British teacher in gymnasium who was emphatic over proper diction." I looked over at him. "But I find common expressions to be confusing. This morning, I offered to wash the breakfast dishes and your aunt told me that having me in the kitchen was like putting a milk bucket under a bull."

Robert tried, without much success, to hold back a grin. "She meant that she'd prefer not to have anyone else in the kitchen. She's rather...territorial...about her kitchen." His face broke into a smile. "Don't Germans use expressions?"

"Not like Americans. Germans are literal and precise. They idolize perfection. Their idea of it, anyway." I shuddered in disgust, reminded of the Nazis.

"What's a kindergarten?" he asked. "And what does gymnasium mean? Around here, it means a place to shoot hoops."

"Kindergarten means 'garden for children.' That's what we call the first year of school. Gymnasium is another word for school." I looked at him. "Are hoops a type of bird?"

For the first time, he laughed out loud. "I meant basketball. You know, a big ball that kids throw through a hoop. A basketball hoop."

I ignored his amusement. "Will William start school soon?"

Robert's features turned solemn as he glanced back at William. "Well, he will need to wait for a while." For a long moment he was quiet and then said, "You probably already realized this, but William is deaf. 'Profoundly deaf,' the doctor said."

I had guessed as much. William's silent demeanor, coupled with Miss Gordon's wild hand motions, was hard to ignore. Yet I was amazed that Robert and his aunt had sidestepped this issue with me as if it was something to be ashamed of. "There's certainly nothing wrong with his mind," I said.

Robert turned his head sharply toward me. "What makes you say that?"

"He's obviously very intelligent. I can see it in the way his eyes watch what's going on around him. Have you noticed how he feels vibrations to detect when someone is approaching? I saw him do it last night when I was coming upstairs. He puts his hand on the floor and then seems to know who to expect coming up the stairs, just by recognizing the specific vibration."

He looked blank.

"Surely you've noticed how your aunt stomps her feet when she wants William to come in to the kitchen from the parlor. It's the same idea."

"Well, it's just...a complicated situation with William."

"How so?"

"The doctor felt that there might also be some additional problems."

"Was this doctor a specialist?"

"Well, no, just our town doctor. Who, by the way, is a very good doctor. He delivered William. In fact, he delivered me," Robert said defensively. In a milder tone, he added, "He felt that William's withdrawn behavior indicated some degree of retardation."

"Isn't it possible he could be withdrawn because he's been upset about his mother?"

Robert shot a look at me that made me realize I hit a nerve. Not that I knew anything about William's mother. Still, I could tell I had crossed a line. In a softer tone I asked, "have you considered taking him someplace for more testing?"

"What's the point? When he is older, he'll be able to attend the Southwestern School for the Deaf. They'll be able to teach him properly."

"But you're his father. You can't hand him over to a school and expect it to work miracles. He could be learning to communicate now while he's still so young."

"I would never consider sending him away at such a young age. For now, he's fine."

"I'm not talking about sending him away. I'm talking about you and your aunt, and even me learning how to communicate with William. The sooner the better. I met a family on the train with a deaf child, a little girl about William's age. They told me about a new clinic in Los Angeles that is encouraging early intervention with children as young as William. Children even younger. Imagine what it would be like for him to have words formulate in his mind and to be able to communicate. It might not even be that hard to learn. I've noticed you and your aunt already use gestures to communicate with him."

"Gestures are different from sign language," Robert answered, irritation growing in his voice.

"But this family on the train didn't use sign language. Their little girl had a box around her neck, with ear phones, and they were actually teaching her how to read lips and how to talk. They said that there is a window of opportunity for a child to understand speech."

"That opportunity will come in time, and he will be taught properly by professional teachers. Not by his father who is not."

"Perhaps this isn't my place to say—"

"That's right." Tersely, he cut me off. "It isn't. Thank you, Louisa, but this is really none of your concern." *Slam!* The door was closed. Silence loudly filled the car.

He was right. This really *wasn't* my business. I had just met this family. What was I doing? Trying to change the way they lived their life? Trying to act as if I knew everything? I could hear my father's voice echo in my head: "Have patience. You have very good ideas, but you must have patience with people. Let them come to their own conclusions."

Oh Lord, would I never get it right?

After a few minutes of palpable discomfort between us, I said apologetically, "Sometimes I think living in a country at war has left me with a feeling of urgency, as if everything has to be done right now, or the moment will be lost. Of course, you're right. The time will come for William."

Robert gave me a conciliatory half-smile.

Then I just had to say it. I just couldn't keep my mouth closed. "But, Robert, would you object if I tried to learn how to communicate with William?"

He shot me an aggrieved look. "I have a feeling it wouldn't matter if I did."

This was *not* going very well. I'd only been in Copper Springs a few days, and I was already irritating him. It had taken months before I irritated Dietrich.

We stopped for a snack at the Prospector's Diner near Bisbee. The outside of the diner was a large, steel railcar, with big neon lights on top. Inside, there were stools by a counter and booths with bright red vinyl cushions. I found it entirely charming. I hoped the lingering awkwardness of our conversation in the car would dissipate in the cheerful atmosphere of the diner.

A weary looking waitress came up to our table, snapping gum in her mouth. Her hair looked like yellow cotton yarn, bleached one too many times. "Cup of joe?" she asked.

"Yes. No cow. For you, Louisa?" Robert asked.

"Pardon?" My eyes were wide with confusion.

Robert smiled. "Would you like a cup of coffee? With cream and sugar?"

I nodded, even though I preferred my coffee black.

Then the waitress turned and hollered to an overweight man in an undershirt with a white cook's cap on his head and half an apron tied about his round belly who stood behind the counter. "Hey, Vern! A pair of drawers. One no cow. One blond with sand." She turned back to us and blew a bubble from her gum. "Anything else?"

"I'd like to order one Eve with a lid on. In fact, put a hat on. Hmmm, let's see. One Black and White for my son. How about something for you, Louisa?" Robert asked.

I shook my head. I was starving from the long hike around the pit, but I couldn't understand a word of what he was saying. The waitress seemed to know exactly what he meant.

She went to get our coffees from Vern and brought them back, slamming then down on the tabletop without spilling a drop. Soon, she returned with a piece of apple pie with ice cream on top for Robert, and a chocolate soda with vanilla ice cream for William, who started licking the spoon with a pleased look on his face.

"Is that what you ordered?" I whispered to Robert.

"Whatsa matter, dollface? Did ya just roll off the turnip truck?" the waitress asked me.

Turnips?! Never one to ignore mockery, especially when I was its object, I scowled darkly at her.

"No, she just hasn't been to a diner before," Robert answered for me, amused and kind.

I raised an eyebrow at him. "You're enjoying this, aren't you?"

He grinned, humor lighting his eyes. "Here, Louisa, share my apple pie with me. I can't eat the whole piece," he offered, handing me his fork.

After taking a bite, I said, "sehr gut! This pie is delicious! It tastes like Apfel Strudel."

"I'll say. I'm all for rationing and doing my part for the war, but I sure do miss sugar. Aunt Martha keeps us on a strict diet."

The rude waitress brought over some crayons and a tattered coloring book for William, but I wouldn't look up at her. I was still annoyed with her for questioning my intelligence. I took my intelligence *very* seriously. Too seriously, my father often remarked. I picked up a crayon and helped William get started coloring a page.

"Louisa, I never really learned how you had met Dietrich," Robert said, stirring his coffee.

"Oh, I've known the Bonhoeffers since I was a child. My father is," I paused, "my father was an excellent piano tuner. The best in all of Berlin. He even tuned the concert pianos for the Berlin Symphony. The Bonhoeffers are a very music minded family. Father worked at their home frequently and took me along with him. They were very kind to me. They all play the piano, though Dietrich is probably the best musician in the family. He plays the cello and the violin, and can sight read any kind of music, no matter how difficult. He is a big man, yet he has such delicate hands. Perfectly designed for the piano. I think he can reach an octave and a half." I looked down with dismay at my own small hands. I had trouble stretching comfortably to a full octave.

"Did you know that Dietrich has been here? To Arizona," Robert casually mentioned, as if it was an everyday occurrence.

"Really? No, I didn't know." I looked at him, expectantly, hoping he would elucidate. He didn't, so I added the prompt, "when?"

"At the end of the year he spent in New York at the seminary, he drove all of the way out to Mexico with a friend. They stopped in Copper Springs for a few days while they passed through. That must have been in 1931."

So Dietrich had been to this dry, forsaken land. Why would he think that I could live here? My conscience started stinging; I silently rebuked myself for being ungrateful. What was the *matter* with me? This man was kind enough to provide shelter for me, a total stranger, because of his friendship with Dietrich, and I was complaining about the landscape.

But I missed the country of my childhood, and its seasons, sights and smells familiar to me. Oh, the *colors* of Germany. Velvety lawns, trees the color of dark jade. So many shades of green!

I had to stop this train of thoughts. Did I miss the sound of the Nazi boots as they goose-stepped through town? Or screeching police sirens as they hunted out innocent people in the night? Hideous shrieks of "Heil Hitler?"

It worked. Arizona was already looking better to me.

"Did you know that Dietrich is engaged to be married?" I asked Robert. "To a lovely woman named Maria. She's young, very young, but quite well suited to him."

"You're kidding me! I thought that maybe you and he, well, I just thought..." His cheeks became flushed as he looked down at his coffee cup.

"Pardon? Dietrich? And me? Oh no!" I laughed at the thought. "He's like an uncle or a brother to me."

Just then, we heard the woman sitting in the booth next to us shriek, "mouse! There's a mouse under the table! It tried to bite my ankle!" Other people started to jump up as the rude waitress ran to the woman's booth with a broom to swat the mouse.

Suddenly, Robert sprang into action, as if accustomed to this scenario. In one deft move, he scooped William up from under the table. William held a feather in his hand and an enormous grin on his face. Robert tossed two dollars for our bill on the table and nodded his head towards me, indicating we should leave. Fast.

We got in the car and Robert headed back on the highway towards Copper Springs. "See what I mean about his intelligence?" I said smugly.

"Intelligent? Or mischievous?" he answered, but I noticed he was grinning.

No sooner had we arrived at the house but Miss Gordon marched out to greet us, eyes blazing. "William! Go wash up for supper." She scrubbed her hands together as if she held a bar of soap.

Obediently, William hustled inside.

"Robert, I expected you back hours ago. Mr. Mueller stopped by, mad as hops. He says that William stuck bubble gum on his office chair at the bank, and it ruined his favorite pair of trousers. Now, Robert, I know that man would complain if he was hung with a new rope, but if William really did put bubblegum on his seat—"

"That's impossible! Mueller wasn't even in the bank when we were there. And William was with me...or with Louisa the entire time. Unless..." Standing on the porch steps, he turned back to me. "Louisa, did you see William put gum on a chair in the bank while I was in the vault?"

Now that I thought about it, William *wasn't* chewing gum after we left the bank.

Just then, William came outside after washing his hands. He looked at Miss Gordon, who glowered at him. He looked at his father, who eyed him with suspicion. And then he looked at me, wide-eyed.

"No, Robert. I did not see him do that," I answered in truth.

"Well, there you have it, Aunt Martha. Mueller just doesn't like kids. He blames William for everything. I'll talk to him tomorrow..." Robert's voice faded away as he and his aunt went into the house.

I slowly closed the car door, stopping for a minute to watch the waning sunset. *Lord, thank you for bringing me here and providing safe keeping for me. Please watch over and care for those I love in Germany.*

I felt a small hand reach for mine. It was William's, wet and soapy. Together, we stood and watched the sun go down.

"Going, going, gone!" I looked down at him and smiled. He looked back up at me with luminous eyes.

Chapter Two

Come Sunday morning, I attended the service at Robert's church. It was the first time I had been inside the building. Humble, like its exterior. I inhaled the consoling fragrance of old wood, lemon oil, and beeswax. Along the sides were rows of hardwood pews, with a center aisle that led up to the steps that ended at Robert's wooden pulpit. Behind Robert's pulpit sat the choir, like plump pigeons on a telephone wire.

Above the choir was the feature I liked the best: A beautiful stained glass window of a figure of Christ, hands outstretched, and the words below it: "Come unto me all ye that labor and are heavy laden, and I will give you rest." The window was situated so that the eyes of the congregation were drawn to the Christ figure. As the sun hit the window during the morning service, it splayed the colors of stained glass into rays like a rainbow. Someone had planned that well.

The pews were half-filled with an assorted sundry of faces, as oddly diverse as the town buildings. Mexicans with sun-kissed skin, Eastern Europeans with pale skin and dark circles under their eyes, even two tiny elderly Chinese ladies. Later, I learned that these two ladies' parents had emigrated from Canton, China, to work on the Southern Pacific Railroad in the 1800s. Oh, it felt a *welcomed* contrast to the bestial ethnic cleansing of Hitler's Germany.

We sang a few hymns, accompanied by a portly woman on the organ whom I soon learned to be the judge's wife. To my enchantment, an elderly man whistled, loud and in tune, a perfect accompanist to the hymns.

Robert dismissed the children for Sunday school in the fellowship hall right before his sermon. William didn't make any motion to run off with the other children, but I did notice he had been casting covert glances at all of the small boys within view, a look of longing on his face.

Then came Robert's sermon. Dry and dusty, just like Arizona.

He had more enthusiasm giving me a lesson on copper than he did while preaching the word of God. His theology was sound, but something in his delivery was lacking. Conviction? *Yes.* That was it.

Perhaps I expected too much. I was accustomed to ministers who preached like Dietrich, who spoke to the heart of his congregation. I never left church after a sermon of Dietrich's without feeling inspired.

Next came a baptism. Robert invited a beaming young couple with a dimple-chinned baby to come up and join him next to the baptismal font. Robert held the baby in his arms, introduced her to the congregation, and asked the proud parents a few questions of their intent to raise this child to know and love God. He looked surprisingly comfortable with the baby as she peered solemnly at him.

As Robert lifted the lid of the baptismal font, he jumped back, startled. A large greenish-brown frog leaped out. The mother screamed, the baby cried, Robert looked stricken, and the congregation howled in laughter. The judge's wife jumped up off of the organ bench and ran to change the water in the baptismal font. Someone else chased down the frog. Miss Gordon glared at William from her seat in the choir loft as he slunk low in the pew, a rather culpable look on his face.

During the announcements, Robert introduced me. Why hadn't he warned me? I could feel my cheeks burn as all eyes turned to me. Afterwards, a few church ladies came up to greet me, curious about the new houseguest at the preacher's home.

A dangerously handsome man with a closely trimmed beard worked his way through the clump of women. "Fräulein Louisa, allow me to introduce myself." He took my hand and didn't release it. "I am Friedrich Mueller, and this is my wife, Hilda."

Standing next to the man was a tiny woman who looked as if she might jump if I spoke to her. I had a fleeting impression of a large proud peacock with full plumage displayed, standing next to a small brown sparrow. I smiled politely at the woman and turned to her husband, pulling my hand out of his tight grasp. "Grüss Gott. Where in Germany are you from, Herr Mueller?"

"Nowhere important. And you, Fräulein? Where are you from?"

There was something oily in his voice. I didn't trust this man. "From Berlin, Herr Mueller."

Robert came up and told me, wearily, that he was ready to go. On the walk back to the house I asked him if he knew where Herr Mueller had lived in Germany.

"Berlin, I believe. He's been in Copper Springs for over a decade or so. Came for the mines. And he owns the bank in town."

"Odd. Most people are quite proud to tell you that they are Berliners. It's a highly cultured city. Herr Mueller didn't seem to want me to know he was from Berlin."

"Why does that seem odd?

"A Berliner named Heinrich Mueller is head of the Gestapo."

"Louisa, this is America," he said, giving me a fatherly sideways glance. "You don't have to feel suspicious of people here."

Perhaps he was right. Mueller was a common German name. But I still felt uneasy.

* * *

As long as I stayed out of Miss Gordon's sight, she seemed to mind me less. Taking William on outings pleased her; at last I had found a way to make a contribution to the household.

Each afternoon we walked to the library and went straight to the children's department. I picked out a few picture books, sat next to William and read to him, pointing to the pictures. He peered at the pages with such rapt attention that I wondered if anyone had ever read to him. Miss Gordon was busy with her housework and Robert was preoccupied with the church. I glanced fondly down at William's little blond head. He and I were going to be good friends. We needed each other.

I asked Miss Bentley, the librarian, if she could find any books on deaf education for me and if she could locate the address of this new clinic in Los Angeles that the family on the train had mentioned to me. She promised to contact the traveling libraries and see if she could find the information.

I wanted to learn more about what options William might have. I would worry about Robert's reaction to my research project later. For now, I was just gathering facts. Certainly, he couldn't object to fact-gathering.

One morning, Miss Gordon asked me to pick up her groceries at Ibsen's General Store, so off William and I went, grateful for an excuse to get out of the house.

Rosita Gonzalves, an olive-skinned, well-padded Mexican woman with fruit earrings that dangled down to her shoulders, bustled right up to us as we came through the store door. "Hola, Louisa. ¿Como estas? Hola, Guillermo," she stroked William's head, obviously familiar with him. "I am Rosita. I live two doors down from Father Gordon."

I thought I had noticed her as she walked past the house now and then. "How are you, Rosita?" I couldn't help but stare at her earrings. Bananas, grapes, strawberries, all hanging in a cheery row. They reminded me of my father's fishing lures.

"Today, I am very sad. It is your hair. Your hair makes me sad. We *must* do something about your hair."

I put one hand on the lone, fat braid hanging down my back, wondering what she meant.

"Is too...too...antique," she rued.

Oh, *that.*

Rosita was probably right. The more accustomed I became to modern American fashion and hairstyles, the frumpier I felt. American women wanted people to look at them. In Nazi Germany, it was prudent not to be noticed.

As Rosita chattered on, my mind wandered to a story Dietrich told once about his twin sister, Sabine. In 1938, as anti-Jewish regulations started to escalate in Germany, all Jews were required to carry the letter "J" in their passports. As a result, many Jewish families made a last-minute dash for freedom before it might be difficult to leave the country.

Sabine's husband was a believing Jew and, like me, would be affected by those new regulations. They decided to leave Germany before the borders were closed. I would never forget Dietrich's recollection that Sabine wore a long, brown suede jacket to placate the German officials. I understood it perfectly.

Reluctantly, I asked, "What do you suggest, Rosita?"

"A bob. All of the Hollywood movie stars have a bob now. You are young and pretty. You should not look so antique. You come into my shop, and we fix you up. Maybe we find you a boyfriend, sì?" She winked and smiled a wide, toothy grin.

No thank you to the offer of finding me a boyfriend, I thought to myself. But the bob, that I might consider. First, I had to find out what a "bob" was.

William and I took the long way home and walked past the school. The children were having recess. I watched William's face as he stared at a group of boys playing kickball. He looked so wistful, longing to be included. Just to be a normal boy. Suddenly, one of the boys blasted the kickball out of the schoolyard. It bounced in the street and landed on the ground near William. He picked it up as a boy ran up to him to retrieve the ball.

"Hey, you're the preacher's dummy that don't talk. Thanks, dummy," sneered the boy, as William smiled benignly and handed the ball back to him, unaware of what the boy was saying to him. I recognized the boy from church last Sunday.

When the boy returned to his circle of friends, he told them something, then turned and pointed back toward William. The group of boys laughed, mercilessly, before returning to their game. I looked protectively at William, but thankfully, he hadn't noticed the boys. He was already walking ahead of me, kicking a can up the street.

In a flash of blinding insight, I understood why Robert was so reluctant to let his son face the outside world.

After dinner each evening, I made a habit of going out on the front porch to watch the sunset. It dropped behind the steep rock hills so quickly that the light changed dramatically. I had never seen such beautiful sunsets, filled with rose and yellow-tinged hues. The night falls in Arizona were long and peaceful. William often joined me, slipping his hand into mine.

"William, do you know that you have early sunsets here? The sun hides behind the hills. Look, watch carefully! Going, going, gone." And the sun disappeared, leaving us surrounded in pale, purple twilight.

* * *

Every Wednesday night at seven o'clock, Miss Gordon promptly marched off to choir practice. I felt like celebrating when she left the house. Tonight, I took the chess set down from the mantel over the fireplace and took it over to William. I showed him each piece and told him their names. I was teaching him how to set the pieces up for a game when Robert came in from his office and noticed what we were doing.

Interest piqued, he sat down on the davenport next to William and started to play the game with me. I checkmated Robert in just three moves. In clearly an unexpected defeat, he sat there, stunned, frowning at the board, while I took William up to bed. When I came down again, Robert was still on the davenport next to the chess set.

"Give me another chance?" he asked.

So we played again. This time, he paid closer attention. It took a few more moves, but I was still able to checkmate him.

"How did you *ever* learn to play chess like that?"

I laughed. "My father taught me."

"He taught you well." He leaned back on the davenport and crossed his arms against his chest. "Where are your parents now?"

I picked up one of the chess pieces and held it in my hands. "My mother died long ago, many years before the war. My father was murdered by the Nazis."

Robert's grey eyes grew large. I couldn't tell if he wanted me to elaborate or if he wasn't sure he should ask anything more; he continued to look directly at me.

"Hitler ordered all Jews to wear a large yellow star on their jackets to identify them. My father had worked for the Berlin Symphony but, back in 1933, all Jewish musicians were fired from the symphony and the opera. That's when my father relied more heavily on tuning private pianos and one of the reasons he refused to wear that Star of David armband."

I picked up the rook from the chess set, holding it in my hands. I needed time to say this without emotion. Robert waited patiently for me to continue.

"My father didn't want to bring attention to himself or to his clients. He needed the work. Jobs were extremely scarce for Jews. Most were on welfare assistance. However, posing as a non-Jew was an act punishable by death. One night, the Gestapo stopped him in the street."

Someone had informed the Gestapo about my father's identity, but that was another story.

I replaced the rook on the chess board and looked directly at Robert. "The Gestapo shot him. Right then and there. They left his body on the street as a message to other Jews who might be tempted to hide their identity. Soon after, I went to Dietrich and joined the Resistance Movement."

A heavy silence hung in the air.

"I thought you had said you had heard stories about the atrocities of the Nazis."

Robert shifted uncomfortably on the davenport. "Well, yes, but nothing like that. Is there no justice in the legal system?"

I gave a short laugh. "Justice? No. Vengeance, yes." I looked down at the board. "I'm sorry. We were enjoying a challenging game of chess, and I brought up unpleasant things."

"Actually, you were enjoying a game of chess; I was losing quite badly. And I'm the one who is sorry, about your father."

I glanced up at him. His eyes held genuine concern. For the first time, I thought he might be a good pastor after all.

* * *

Most evenings after dinner, Robert worked in his office unless he was called out on church business. People in the town, even those who weren't churchgoers, seemed to count on him for their various crises. Some serious, some silly. Nonetheless, they looked to him for support, wisdom, and guidance.

One night, William had gone to bed early, and Miss Gordon had a headache, so she, too, had gone upstairs. Robert came in to the kitchen to get his car keys, and I asked him if I could go with him. I wanted to see more of the area and I had taken William on as many walks through the town as I could possibly discover on foot. He hesitated, but agreed.

"Where are we going?" I asked as we climbed in the car.

"To Mrs. Drummond's. She's been ailing, and I promised her I would get by this week. Not sure she'll last much longer."

Mrs. Drummond lived quite a ways out of town on a small goat ranch in a well-loved, weather-beaten house. As we drove up, noisy roosters greeted us, mistaking our headlights for a rising sun. A pleasant looking woman opened the door to us.

"Hello, Rev'ren." The woman eyed me with curiosity. "Hello, Miss."

"Evening, Betty. This is Louisa Schmetterling. How is your grandmother feeling tonight?" Robert's voice was kind.

Betty's eyes were locked on me. I smiled to reassure her. "Hello, Betty," I said.

Eyes still locked on me, she answered, "oh, not so well, Rev'ren. Her feet are swollen up something fierce."

"Who is it, Betty?" called a wrinkled voice from the front room.

"It's the Rev'ren, Gran." Adding in a loud whisper, "and he brought a lady with him."

"Come in here, Reverend. Bring your ladyfriend so I can see her," called the wrinkled voice. We walked into the front room. Someone had moved Mrs. Drummond's bed into this room; I think she didn't want to miss anything. The furnishings were scarce and modest, but the room was cared for and clean. On the four poster bed perched a small, frail woman with bright, curious eyes. Instantly, I liked her.

"Mrs. Drummond, this is our houseguest, Louisa."

"Hello, Mrs. Drummond." I walked over to her bedside to shake her gnarled, misshapen fingers.

"Is she a German?" she asked Robert, peering at me over her spectacles.

"Yes, she is," he answered.

"Is she a Nazi?" She looked me up and down.

"No, Mrs. Drummond, she's not a Nazi."

"Well then, good. I approve. Come closer, Louisa. You're such a pretty girl. I didn't think Germans could be pretty." She winked at me. "Sit down here next to me." She patted the bed. "Tell me how Martha is treating you. I've known Martha Gordon since she was a girl. Even as a child, she looked as if she'd just been starched and ironed."

I burst out laughing and quickly covered my mouth, glancing guiltily up at Robert, but his eyes were smiling.

"I can tell we're going to be good friends, Louisa," warbled Mrs. Drummond.

How ironic! The first person in America who chose to befriend me, just for being me, not out of any obligation, was on her deathbed.

Robert wondered if he could do anything for them before we left, so Betty asked if he would help her move some firewood in from the barn. I stayed in the front room with Mrs. Drummond. It was a nice change to hear someone chatter away. Conversation didn't go beyond the day's necessities in the Gordon household.

On the other side of Mrs. Drummond's bed was a beautiful, old upright piano. It looked to be the only really valuable furnishing in the house. When I complimented her about the piano, she invited me to play, but I hesitated. I hadn't touched a piano since the day my father had died.

I went to it and sat on the bench, gliding my hands gently over the keys. Without even consciously intending to, my fingers found their place and started to play my father's favorite piece: Beethoven's *Moonlight Sonata in D*. The piano was old and slightly out of tune but had a lovely mellowed tone. Many fingers before mine had polished these ivory and ebony keys.

Lost in the music, I closed my eyes and let memory take control. I thought of my father, yet without the pain that doing so usually evoked. When I finished, I sat quietly for a moment, then turned back to Mrs. Drummond. Robert stood in the doorway. I hadn't even heard him come in. I felt my cheeks flush with embarrassment. "I'm out of practice."

"It's time we headed back home. I'll come again soon, Mrs. Drummond," he said, without a word about my playing. He took Mrs. Drummond's tiny hands in his large ones and prayed a tender prayer for her.

The car ride back was quiet, but companionably so. Finally, Robert broke the silence. "First chess and now piano. I had no idea you were so talented."

"Well, I'm the daughter of a piano tuner. It would be a disgrace not to be able to play a tune or two."

He glanced over at me, raising an eyebrow. "A tune or two?"

I looked out the window, unseeing. "I studied classical piano at University. But that was a lifetime ago."

"Is Beethoven your favorite composer?" Robert asked.

I shot a look at him, impressed that he had recognized *Moonlight Sonata* and knew the composer was Ludwig Beethoven. "No. No, I think Felix Mendelssohn is my favorite composer. Are you familiar with him?"

"Didn't he compose *The Wedding March*? From *Midsummer's Night Dream*?"

"Yes! The very one." I hadn't expected Robert to be knowledgeable about classical music.

"Every preacher knows that melody. So why is Mendelssohn your favorite composer?"

"He's considered to be the 'Mozart of the 19th century.' His music is very graceful and lyrical. Even spiritual. He's mostly known for his organ and choral music, but he was also a painter and spoke five languages. Most people don't know that he was a Jew who converted to Christianity, but his music was banned in Germany because he had Jewish blood."

I gazed out the window and looked up at the sky. I had never seen a night sky like the one in Arizona. It seemed as if I could reach out and touch the stars. Tiny jewels on black velvet. I pointed to a bright star. "That one is so bright that it doesn't even twinkle."

"You're right. It shimmers. Miners call it the copper star," he explained. "There's an old legend that the first miners followed that star until it led them to the copper mines." He gave me a sheepish grin. "Truth to be told, it's really the North

Star. It's positioned along the axis of rotation of the earth, so it never seems to move. It always appears fixed above the North Pole. So, if you're ever lost, look for the copper star, and you'll know your course is due north."

We rode along in silence for a while until I said, "it's hard to believe we're standing under the same sky as my friends in Germany are. All over the world, people look at the same moon and stars and sun." Somehow, I didn't feel so far away when I looked at the night sky.

"Louisa, when did you last see Dietrich?"

"A few months ago in Berlin."

"When you last saw them, how was he?"

"Weary." I looked out the window at the stark desert. The moon cast shadows on the mesquite and sagebrush. It looked eerily beautiful. Then I noticed rows of lights. "What's that? Over there," I pointed.

"Where? Oh." He saw the lights, too. "That's one of Mueller's copper mines. His biggest, in fact."

"Why are there so many trucks heading out? Do miners work at night?"

"They're probably heading over to the smelter. It's up north, near Tucson, close to the railroad."

But the convoy didn't head north. It was heading south. Toward Mexico.

* * *

A few days later, Robert drove out again to see Mrs. Drummond and invited me to join him. She must have sent word to him that she wanted me to come, because I doubted he would have thought of it on his own.

This time, I played hymns for her. She especially loved Bach's *Joyful, Joyful, We Adore Thee*. I wished that I could play more than German composers given that her country was at war with mine, but those were the only composers we were permitted to study at University. Still, I felt renewed and refreshed after playing for her. Music could do that. It wasn't limited by language, culture, or a world at war.

Mrs. Drummond died in her sleep the next week. At her funeral, a wave of grief washed over me, surprising me with its intensity. I had only known her a few weeks, but I had been blessed by her. I had lost my first friend in America.

In her will, she left the church one thousand three hundred and twenty-five dollars to be used for whatever the Reverend felt was most necessary. Her life savings. The choir members felt they needed robes but the elders insisted the church and the parsonage needed a new roof and a paint job. Herr Mueller, head of the finance committee, proclaimed the money belonged in the bank, drawing interest. It became quite a heated controversy in the First Presbyterian Church of Copper Springs.

Being a choir member with considerable influence, Miss Gordon used every moment at home to stress to Robert the need for new robes. I found it somewhat entertaining to see her campaign so diligently. It was the most conversation I'd heard between them, but I could tell Robert was wearying of the constant badgering. She was unrelenting.

"I might have a solution," I offered at dinner one evening.

They both stopped eating and looked at me.

"I used to work for a seamstress during my summer holidays. I could make the robes. Then you would have enough money for the repairs."

Robert looked delighted. "Louisa! That's a fine idea! That would solve both problems. How about it, Aunt Martha?"

She glared at me. "We want Christian choir robes, not something made from a..." She stopped herself from finishing the sentence.

It slowly dawned on me what she intended to say. "A what? Please finish your sentence. Do you mean you don't want something made from a German? Or a Jew?"

"Both," she answered, radiating waves of disapproval.

The sharp words hung suspended in the air, waiting for someone to act.

I pushed back my chair from the table, went up the stairs and firmly closed the door to my room. Fighting back hot tears, I flopped down on the bed and buried my face in a pillow. How *dare* she treat me like that! *What* had I done to deserve that? Hearing that bitter tone in her voice brought up a stinging set of feelings.

My silent diatribe was interrupted by the buzz of a fierce discussion going on downstairs. Curious, I got up and went to the radiator. My room was directly above the kitchen. I unscrewed the cap and found that if I held my head right above the radiator pipe, I could hear their conversation as if I was in the same room as them.

"I insist that you apologize to her," I heard Robert say. "I won't tolerate rude remarks like that. I won't tolerate prejudice in my home, either."

"But Robert, she's a...Jew!" Miss Gordon pronounced the word as if it were dirty. "You never even told me. I only found out because she told me so herself."

"Why should that matter? She's a guest in my home."

"You also never mentioned this houseguest was going to be a young woman."

"I didn't know myself until she stepped off the train. The papers I received said 'Louis Schmetterling,' not 'Louisa.' The typist must have left the 'a' off."

Aha! That explained the baffled look on Robert's face when he met me at the train station.

"Just how long will she be here? I thought this was going to be short-term."

"As long as she needs a home. Probably until the war is over."

"It just isn't fitting for a minister to have a young woman as a houseguest. People will talk. Lord knows they already have plenty to talk about."

Irritation rising in his voice, Robert snapped, "I don't make my decisions based on town gossip."

"Well," sniffed Miss Gordon, "if you ask my opinion, I think you are getting a little too friendly with her."

"I don't remember asking for your opinion," Robert said curtly.

Then there was silence. I heard the dishes clink as Miss Gordon returned to her dishwashing.

After a moment, I heard Robert's voice softly imploring, "Aunt Martha, you haven't even given her a chance. She helps you with William. He seems to like her. Haven't you noticed that he seems happier lately? Please. Just give her a chance."

Carefully, I screwed the top back on the radiator with a greater appreciation for Robert. And an even lesser one for his aunt.

Chapter Three

The day following the incident in the kitchen, I took William to the library. Partly for his sake, partly for mine. It gave me needed distance from Miss Gordon.

I loved everything about a library, any library. I had to admit that this old rickety building in Copper Springs was a dire disappointment. Nonetheless, as I walked through the doors, I inhaled deeply. The dusty smell of books held such promise, like a pink bakery box tied with a string.

William enjoyed our ritual, too. As soon as we entered, he ran to our special corner of the library, next to a cracked and dirty window that let in some natural lighting, which gave us the added bonus of watching people walk down the street.

There wasn't much to do in Copper Springs.

Today, as I watched William's blond head peering out the window, I wondered again about his mother. I had yet to discover a single clue about what happened to her. Not one. Even the townspeople seemed to have taken an oath of silence on the subject of the Reverend's wife. No one uttered her name. There was no sign of her in the house—not a picture, not a trinket, not even a recipe card with her handwriting on it. I knew; with the air of a burglar, I had checked.

I had even searched for her grave in the cemetery by the church one afternoon. There I found Robert's parents, side by side, but no sign of Robert's wife, though I didn't even know a name to look for, other than "Mrs. Gordon."

My curiosity was one of my worst faults. I knew it wasn't any of my business and, clearly, no one was going to fill me in, but I couldn't help but wonder what had become of this

49

woman. My latest musing was that she had died in a tragic and horrible accident, so heartrending that no one could speak of it. And surely the Reverend was still so bereaved he couldn't bear to have any memory of her. Well, so I imagined, anyway.

"Louisa!" Rosita had burst through the library doors, spotted me, and hurried over to say hello. Her eyes swept over my hair, and a frown flickered over her face. "This is my daughter, Esmeralda." A spitting image of her mother, the girl looked to be about nine or ten years old. "My husband, Ramon, he is in the Army. He is fighting the Japanese now."

I enjoyed Rosita, even if she was intent on improving me. She had a way of making one feel as if everything would come out the way it was intended, all for good.

"I don't go to that church of Father Gordon's because I am very Catholic," she offered, without being asked. "But that priest of yours, he is a good man."

"Actually, he's not a priest," I explained. "He's a reverend, Rosita. In the Presbyterian Church, the minister is called a reverend."

She wasn't listening. She gathered up Esmeralda like a hen gathering her chick, and left to check out her books. "You come to dinner to my house soon, okay?" she added as she hustled toward the door.

I looked for the local history section to read up on Copper Springs. It was a young town, at least in the eyes of modern Europeans. The Apache Indians had managed to live for centuries in the nearby mountains. I read that they poetically called the mountain ranges "islands in the sky."

Legend had it that their chief, Cochise, was buried in the mountains nearby with his favorite horse and dog. I recognized the name Cochise as the county in which Copper Springs resided. I learned that copper was discovered in the 1870s, which brought countless fortune hunters, escalating the territory disputes between the settlers and the Indians.

As William and I checked out books, Miss Bentley handed me an old, weathered book on sign language she had received from the traveling library. "And here is that address you wanted, Louisa," she said as she handed me a slip of paper. She looked victorious, like a hunter returning with game.

Then, suddenly, I felt someone stand close behind me.

"Guten Tag, Fräulein," said Herr Mueller.

It didn't surprise me that he was one of those men who stood too close to a woman, crowding her space, either dense or delighted about making her feel uncomfortable.

"Good day, Herr Mueller." I stepped away from him and turned to sign my name on the check-out slip.

"I see that you have the Reverend's kleiner Dumkopf with you. A tragedy, no?"

I spun around on my heels to face him, temper flaring. "Nein, Herr Mueller. Wilhelm ist nicht ein Dumkopf!" I grabbed William's hand to march out of the library, but William wouldn't budge. Just as I turned to look at William, wondering why he wasn't coming, I saw him spit on Herr Mueller's shoes.

Without a doubt, I knew there was nothing wrong with William's mind. I just had to find a way to reach into it.

The following Sunday, as we were having supper after the church service, Miss Gordon said, "That was a wonderful sermon today, Robert. Wasn't that a wonderful sermon, Louise?"

"Yes, it was fine," I lied. "And there's an 'a' on the end of my name. It's Louisa," I explained for the hundredth time.

"Just fine?" she asked, almost combatively. "I suppose you've heard better sermons in Nazi Germany?" Her lips pursed together in that downward, disapproving look that was now quite familiar to me.

"Aunt Martha, what is on this bread?" Robert said, grimacing, looking at the bread as if it were poisonous. William tried a bite and spit it out, dramatically.

"Oleo. We're supposed to use it now instead of butter. You'll soon get used to it." She turned back to me. "So..."

"Aunt Martha," interrupted Robert. "Louisa is entitled to her own opinion."

I was grateful he didn't press me. Robert's sermon was as lacking in flavor as the oleo.

Later that evening, after Miss Gordon went upstairs to bed, Robert came into the house from his office. For a long while, he searched for a book in the parlor bookshelves, but it was obvious something else was on his mind. Finally, he sat down on the davenport where I was curled up reading.

"Tell me the truth. What did you think about my sermon?"

Oh no.

I searched carefully for my words. "I...um...I thought you had good points. It was all biblically accurate. I just..."

"You just...what?" he persisted, leaning forward.

I hesitated, hunting for painless adjectives. Well, I told myself, he did *ask* for my opinion. "I just felt as if you didn't encourage the people to see how God is at work in their lives. To depend on Him in their everyday activities."

Without expression, he leaned back on the davenport.

"It's one thing to believe that God is in His heaven. It's another thing to believe that He is also here, closer to us than our own breath. I believe God is seeking each one of us, if only we have the eyes and the heart to see Him. Isn't that the question everyone is truly asking? Deep inside? Do I really matter to God?"

He rubbed his chin, mulling over my remarks. After a long moment of silence, he abruptly stood up. "Thank you, Louisa, for your candor. Good night. You'll turn off the lights?"

I nodded. He turned to head up the stairs. Robert kept surprising me. I never expected a conversation like that.

* * *

At church the following Sunday, after Robert gave the Benediction and people stood milling around, chatting, Herr Mueller cornered me against a pew, oozing charm. "Good day, Fräulein Louisa. I'd be delighted to have the pleasure of your company at lunch tomorrow. Come to my house at one o'clock."

Was that an invitation or an order? Just then Robert walked past us, carrying hymnals to the shelves in the back. "The Reverend and I would be delighted to join you," I answered.

Robert stopped abruptly and looked at me, puzzled.

"Herr Mueller would like us to have lunch with him tomorrow," I explained.

"Oh? Well, that sounds fine," he said, though he didn't look like it sounded fine. He looked like he felt trapped. I felt the same way.

Herr Mueller politely nodded to Robert, as if including him was always his intention.

The next day, Robert and I walked over to the Mueller's house right at one o'clock.

"You don't like Friedrich Mueller, do you?" Robert asked.

"Is it obvious?"

His facial expression told me "yes."

"There's something about him that seems rather...disagreeable. You don't sense it?"

"No, not really. Our interaction is always business-like. Well, except for incidents involving William. But this is the first social engagement he's initiated with me. Any idea what he wants?"

I shrugged my shoulders. I didn't want to confess that I had contrived a way for him to attend this particular invitation.

Just as Robert knocked on the door, a maid in a black uniform, complete with crisp white apron, opened it and showed us in. The house's interior was just as elaborate as its exterior. The décor was impeccable, punctuated with priceless antiques, uncommon in a humble town like Copper Springs. Obviously, Herr Mueller had a taste for fine things.

His little brown sparrow wife, Hilda, joined us. We sat down to a flawlessly set table: polished silverware, fine china, crystal glasses. At each of our settings was a single blue hydrangea in a silver bud vase. The maid served chicken salad with capers and peeled grapes along with warm croissants. To top it off, she brought champagne flutes filled with cantaloupe melon balls, sprinkled with balsamic vinegar.

"Reverend, did you notice my beautiful roses out front? They are just about to open their buds, perhaps another day or two," Herr Mueller pointed out with evident pride.

"Yes, yes. They're always the talk of the town," Robert responded congenially.

I was relieved Robert was here. Perhaps the two men would chat, and I could remain invisible, not unlike Frau Mueller. I took a bite of the chicken salad and started to relax a little.

Then Herr Mueller turned to me. "Fräulein, I am curious to know of your impressions of Berlin before you left."

I nearly choked on the chicken. "Pardon? What do you mean, Herr Mueller?"

"There must have been great ebullition in the country after Hitler's latest victories."

I put down my fork. "Quite the opposite! Berliners are suffering from great shortages and rationing; many are sick or starving."

Herr Mueller looked skeptical. "There is also rationing in the United States. We, too, have gasoline shortages, sugar, butter, and canned foods. It is the duty of every citizen to sacrifice for their country during times of war."

"Oh, but it's more than just shortages, Herr Mueller. I think Hitler has been on the defensive for quite a few years, since 1940, when the Luftwaffe took such a beating from the British in the Battle of Britain. Hitler has spread himself over too many fronts. Germany is fighting a losing battle."

I picked up my fork, pushing the chicken salad around on my plate, thinking back to that pivotal year. The German newspapers only reported propaganda, so I had to scour underground news reports for credible updates. Somehow, after six long months of steady bombardment, the little Royal Air Force beat back the attacks of the Luftwaffe. Hitler turned his focus away from Britain toward Russia.

I picked up my croissant and spread it with butter, remembering the joy I felt when it became apparent the tide had finally turned.

With a jolt, I realized I had been day dreaming. "Anyway," I continued, picking up where I had left off, "I think the end is on the horizon for Hitler's Third Reich. Though I doubt he would ever surrender. He will fight to the finish and try to take

Germany down with him. It is like Satan's last gasp in the book of Revelations."

I took a bite of my croissant. Then a peculiar piece of trivia bounced into my head, something that had always gnawed at me. "But would you believe, Hitler has a dog? He is wonderful to that dog. He suffers no guilt about sending millions of innocent people to their death, but he has the ability to be kind to a pet." I shuddered in disgust.

Satisfied that I had thoroughly answered Herr Mueller's original question about the condition of Berlin, I picked up my fork to concentrate on my lunch.

As I started to take another bite of my chicken salad, I suddenly had an odd awareness. Glancing up, I discovered that everyone had stopped eating and was staring at me, their forks held suspended in mid-air. Herr Mueller's face was now drained of color, except for one lone blue vein bulging on his forehead. Even Robert looked at me with an astounded expression on his face. Frau Mueller's eyes darted from her husband to Robert to me.

Something flickered across Herr Mueller's face. Abruptly, he stood up to excuse himself. "Foolishly, I have forgotten a very important business call that I need to make. My apologies, Fräulein Louisa. Reverend Gordon." And just like that, he left us alone to eat the remainder of the meal with his silent little wife.

"That seemed rather peculiar," I said to Robert as we walked back home.

"Which part?"

"Herr Mueller. He seemed upset about my remarks about Hitler."

He stopped. "Louisa, did it ever occur to you that you were answering questions no one was asking? Why did you launch into a monologue about Hitler at the dinner table? That could give *anyone* indigestion. It did me," Robert said, placing a hand over his stomach as he made a dyspeptic face. "And why on earth did you have to say that Hitler was nice to his dog?"

"Well, Herr Mueller *did* ask for my opinion about Berlin." Then, meekly, I added, "and I love dogs."

Slowly shaking his head, Robert said, "You do have a tendency to speak your mind, don't you? It's a wonder you didn't get yourself shot in Germany. I think I'm starting to understand why Dietrich sent you to the other end of the earth."

I looked at him and frowned. It was true. I was far too outspoken.

On Friday morning of that same week, we were eating a tranquil breakfast on a beautiful spring day when Herr Mueller stormed up to the parsonage and banged on the kitchen door. Robert jumped up, alarmed, knocking his chair to the floor.

"Gordon!" thundered Herr Mueller. "That boy of yours! He's at it again. He cut off all of the buds on my roses! Every single one is gone! All that is left are green stalks." He continued to rant and rave, his face reddened with rage. Miss Gordon, William, and I clumped together on the other side of the kitchen, timorously watching the interchange.

"Now, now, Mr. Mueller," Robert soothed, "how do you know William cut your roses? Perhaps deer ate the buds."

"And when was the last time you saw a deer in Copper Springs? *Never!*" he bellowed. "It was your imbecile child. The next time he plays another prank on me, I am calling the authorities and having him taken away. Have I made myself clear?" And away he stomped, marching down the street, green stalks sadly devoid of flowers in his hands.

Robert closed the door and slowly turned back to face us with a very unhappy look on his face. William bolted up the stairs and slammed his bedroom door.

As we sat back down at the kitchen table to finish our breakfast, Miss Gordon didn't say a word and I followed her lead.

It seemed as if this battle between William and Herr Mueller was epic and two-sided. Privately, I was on William's side.

* * *

Miss Gordon made an effort to be kinder after the unpleasant episode in the kitchen about the choir robes. Well, maybe kinder wasn't the right word. Less hostile.

One day I found a package on my bed of four yards of satin and velvet, thread, and her Singer Featherweight sewing machine placed on the floor. Just enough material to make one choir robe. And there was a note attached in her spidery handwriting: "Treat this machine well. They aren't making them now like they used to. P.S. Because of the war."

For Miss Gordon, it seemed a kind of olive branch. It was the closest she could come to apologizing. In turn, I thought decidedly, I was going to sew the most professional looking choir robe in all of Arizona.

I knew the Gordon ancestors were Scottish, but often I thought there must be Teutonic blood somewhere in Martha Gordon's lineage. She was more Saxon than I, running the household like a Swiss clock. The house was painfully clean. Dinner was served promptly at 6 p.m. Bath and bedtime for William at 7:30. She retired to her room at 8:00.

She liked to listen to a soap opera program on the radio called "Painted Dreams." She'd been listening to it for years; I think it was her only vice. That and going to Bisbee to the picture show once a month to see the latest movie. She adored movie stars: Humphrey Bogart, Cary Grant, and Jimmy Stewart. She often talked about their characters as if they were real.

Unlike every German hausfrau, however, as important as the inside of the house was to Miss Gordon, the outside was another matter. She didn't bother with it.

So outside was where I spent my time.

It was such a pleasant afternoon that I couldn't help but want to work out in the garden and see if I could bring it back to life. During my train trip across America, I had seen government posters in the railroad stations that encouraged Americans to have a Victory Garden, to grow their own vegetables so farmers could send more food to the soldiers fighting overseas.

I was eager to do anything to help the Americans win this war. I fought a persistent feeling of frustration that I was useless here. In Germany, despite the danger of working with the Resistance Movement, at least I was doing *something*. Here, I waited. I was just waiting out the war until I could return to Germany. And I have never waited well.

I went into the darkened shed to look for garden tools, lifted up one of the dusty boxes, and opened it. Inside were photographs, clothing, and some books. Out of curiosity, I picked up one photograph and looked at the face. It was of a woman with coloring that resembled William. My heart started hammering. *William's mother!* I peered into the box filled with her belongings. The clothes still held a lingering scent of expensive perfume she must have worn. I held up her sweater to my face and breathed in the sweet smell.

I went over to the window to examine the photographs more closely. Her hair was honey blond, like William's, but shoulder-length and wavy. Her features looked finely sculptured, like delicate porcelain. She was beautiful, with that kind of elegant beauty I envied in some women, so unlike my own ordinary looks. She looked directly at the camera, but I could tell her mind was elsewhere. Probably had a touch of mystery, too, I thought, wistfully. Just the kind of woman I longed to be.

Suddenly Robert's voice startled me. "Put those things away."

I dropped the frame. "I'm so sorry—I was looking for garden tools. Your aunt said I could find them in here."

"The tools are on the shelf above the bench. Please leave those boxes alone." He turned to leave.

"Wait. Robert—shouldn't William have a picture of his mother in his room? My mother died when I was young, too, and I know how much I cherished her picture."

He stiffened his back, turning his head slightly to the side to look back at me. "Louisa, William's mother is not dead," he said coldly, in a tone of voice that made it abundantly clear the subject was closed. He walked back into the house.

Two feelings welled up within me, and I didn't know which one was stronger—being embarrassed to have been caught snooping or being shocked at this latest revelation.

* * *

Polite but cool. That's how Robert treated me after finding me in the shed, prying through the box of his wife's belongings. Mealtimes felt strained between us, though I doubted Miss Gordon even noticed. One evening, I tried to see if I could thaw things out and get a conversation started at the dinner table. "I've been reading an interesting book about the local history of this area. It's about Chief Cochise and the Apache Indians."

"All I need to know about Cochise is that he's a bloodthirsty warrior," said Miss Gordon.

"Actually, the truth is he was known for his integrity, and he kept his word with treaties. Later in his life, he was able to negotiate to get the reservation established near here, to the land where the Apaches had originally lived."

"If the Indians would just stay on their reservation, then there wouldn't be so many problems for them," advised Miss Gordon, insinuating that if she could only run the Bureau of Indian Affairs, things would be much better managed.

"Can you really blame them?" I asked. "Imagine how awful it would be to have the government insist you must go live where they want you to and that you may not leave. How different is a reservation from a relocation camp in Germany?"

My comment caused Miss Gordon's temper to flare. "Oh for Pete's sake, Louise! America is not Nazi Germany. We are civilized here." Under her breath she muttered, "sometimes I think you knit with one needle."

Knit with one needle? How could *anyone* do that?

Robert saw the look on my face and rose to my defense. "Aunt Martha, I think it's good for us to see the United States through Louisa's eyes. She's watched Germany change very quickly. Don't forget Germany was a democracy in the 1920s. Shaky, but still a democracy. There's wisdom in paying attention to other countries' mistakes."

I looked at Robert with wonder. Perhaps he was feeling apologetic for snapping at me in the shed. A good sign, it seemed, so I decided to push him a little further.

"I read something else quite interesting in this book." I picked up the book from my lap and put it on the tabletop. "Did you know that the Indians were the first people in America to use sign language? The tribes spoke such different languages that they needed to find a way to clearly communicate. Their signing was elegant, considered to be a fairly extensive system. In fact, some similarities exist between Indian sign language and sign language for the deaf."

I paused, anticipating a cold reaction.

"Louise, why do you bother filling your head with these things?" complained Miss Gordon.

I ignored her remark. I was really watching for Robert's reaction, though he didn't seem to have one. He kept his head down as he cut his asparagus. Dared I continue? Never one to let the restraint of good judgment stand in my way, I plunged forward.

"Since we're talking about sign language, I sent away to some organizations that help deaf children, and I received back some brochures in the mail today." I thought I had just made a brilliant segue to the topic that I had wanted to bring up all along.

Robert looked up at me sharply. "Louisa, I believe I told you William would be taught when the time was right." Abruptly, he stood up to clear his dishes.

"But Robert, maybe that time is now. From everything I have been reading, time is of the essence to help William. The younger he is, the better. And there is so much help to be had! Do you remember I told you I had met a family with a deaf child on the train? And they told me about a new clinic in Los Angeles? Well, I found out that this clinic offers correspondence courses for deaf children."

Robert picked up his plate and went to the sink.

"And it doesn't cost a penny." I waited to let that sink in. I looked over at Miss Gordon, trying to gauge her interest. I was ready to pull out my trump card. The one piece of information I knew could greatly reinforce my position. Timing was key, and I knew this was my moment.

Strategically, I placed a piece of paper on the table. "The clinic is called the John Tracy Clinic of Los Angeles. John Tracy is the son of Spencer Tracy. You know, Spencer Tracy, the movie star." I cast a furtive glance at Miss Gordon.

"Spencer Tracy?" she gasped. "The movie star? Spencer Tracy of *Boystown*? Father Flanagan?"

Now I had her hooked. *Boystown* was one of her favorite movies. Miss Gordon picked up the paper and started skimming through it.

"Why, yes!" I said, as if I had just made that discovery myself. "The very one. His son, John, was born profoundly deaf, just like William, and his wife devoted herself to teach him how to communicate. In fact, Spencer Tracy provides financial support to this clinic. And Mrs. Spencer Tracy answers all of the letters herself." I slid the letter I'd received from Mrs. Tracy onto the table, close to Miss Gordon. Just as I hoped, she snatched it up and started to read it.

I looked over at Robert. "She's had so much success with John that she started this clinic to help other families. She believes in early intervention with children."

I pulled out another piece of paper from my pocket and started to read a paragraph I had previously marked. "Listen to this: 'First, it's important to make a decision, rather than no decision at all. Hearing impaired children need early language and communication intervention in order to succeed in life. Deaf children are normal children who just have a hearing problem. Their handicap is communicational, not mental'."

There. My speech was complete. I waited patiently, biting my lip, bracing myself for their response. For *his* response.

"You know, Robert, perhaps you should be willing to see what they offer. Just consider looking at the information from the John Tracy Clinic," Miss Gordon coaxed. "I really don't think Mrs. Spencer Tracy would mislead you."

A glimmer of hope. If I got her on my side, I knew I had won the battle. We both looked over at him at the same time.

Leaning his hip against the sink with his arms crossed, Robert tilted his head, arching one eyebrow at me as if to convey that he was well aware of the strategic tactic that I had used to corner him. Then he sighed in resignation. "I have the sudden sense of being squeezed between a rock and a hard place. All right, all right. I'll read the materials."

A door had opened, spilling forth light.

* * *

That night, Robert took out his guitar, and we sat on the porch to listen to him. William climbed onto my lap. It seemed Robert hadn't played the guitar in quite a while because even Miss Gordon looked pleased. He strummed a few songs and then sang a song I recognized. It was an odd song to hear from such an erudite minister, just as odd as when I heard it from Dietrich. "Swing Low, Sweet Chariot" and "Go Down, Moses." I wondered where this kind of music originated, because they were the only two men I knew who played it.

Later, I tucked William into bed, stroking his hair until he fell asleep, whispering a prayer. *Thank you, Lord, for caring about this little boy in the midst of a world at war. Please help us find a way to unlock all that is in the wonderful mind you created for him.*

The following morning, I reached for a juice glass from the kitchen cupboard and asked Miss Gordon more about those songs.

"They're called gospel songs," she explained. "From the Negroes. Robert went off to seminary and made friends with a colored minister from Alabama, Franklin Fisher, while he was there. Robert and that Dietrich fellow you talk so much about, they used to go to church with Franklin in a place called Harlem. That's where he learned those songs."

Miss Gordon seemed to be in a friendlier mood this morning than usual, so the time seemed right to show her the completed choir robe. Quickly, I went upstairs and brought down the robe.

"Miss Gordon?"

She looked up from the sink where she was washing dishes. Slowly, her face softened into delight.

"Why, it's...it's perfect!" She dried her hands and came over to examine every seam. I wasn't concerned. I had anticipated a thorough inspection. "It's better than the Methodists' robes! Why Louisa, you're a fine seamstress. We'll have to show Robert. And the ladies in the choir! They'll be so pleased. In fact, I might run it right over to Mrs. Wondowlowski."

Now I knew I had done well; Miss Gordon rarely left the house except for church, choir practice, or to exchange her rationing coupons at the grocery store. Once in a great while, she would attend a war bond rally or a recycling drive.

When I had first arrived, I asked her what the used tin cans and old toothpaste tubes she saved so conscientiously could be recycled into. "Saving aluminum cans means more ammunition for the soldiers," she answered authoritatively, as if she were in charge of supplying weapons for the military herself.

Martha Gordon might not fully understand the grim realities of war, but she took seriously her patriotic duties and united with the American people in efforts to conserve. If the government asked Americans to recycle, then she would carefully save paper, metal, and rubber. She had remarkable hunting and gathering skills.

At least once a week, I found her at the kitchen table, peppered head bent over, pasting stamps into bond books. Like many Americans, the Gordon family only served red meat once a week, ate cottage cheese by the quarts, was miserly with sugar, traded coupons with other families for favorite products, and tried not to use the car unless they had saved up their monthly gas allotment. The government had instigated such rationing to ensure that the rich could not purchase privileges. Every American was expected to do their part to help win the war.

But, besides leaving the house on an unscheduled visit, another reason I could tell she was impressed with the choir robe—she called me Louisa. *Not* Louise.

So I started to work on the rest of the choir robes. Miss Gordon arranged for the choir members to come to the parsonage for fittings.

As I pinned hems and chalked seams, the ladies chatted amongst each other as if I was invisible. I didn't mind. I thought back to my summers as a teenager working in Frau Steinhart's seamstress' shop, in the heart of the Jewish Ghetto in Berlin. Now I wondered, with a wisp of nostalgia, if that might have been where my shameful habit of eavesdropping got started.

I was waiting for the day when Frau Mueller came in for her fitting; I was planning to use the opportunity to find out more about her husband. When the day finally arrived, I spoke to her in German, hoping to coax her to reveal information.

In her husband's absence, she was quite talkative. She volunteered that they had emigrated ten years earlier from

Berlin. Herr Mueller deliberately chose Copper Springs as their destination before they had left Germany.

He bought up several copper mines in the area during the Depression when prices were devalued. He started the First National Trust of Copper Springs; he had even designed the building himself. He traveled regularly on lengthy trips, often to Mexico, she said, evidently proud of his business success.

Privately, I wondered how Herr Mueller had the foresight to buy up copper mines during a Depression. As if Herr Mueller knew a war on the horizon and gauged the time was right to stockpile.

So spun the wheels in my distrustful mind.

One afternoon, as I was finishing up another hemline, Robert knocked on my door and poked his head in. "Well now I'm especially glad you are making those choir robes, Louisa. I'd hate to have to tell Aunt Martha she couldn't have her robes. Mr. Mueller just informed me the money we were going to use for the new roof and the paint job will have to be used for raised taxes or else the church will go into arrears."

"*What?* Are you certain?"

"Well, I knew our taxes had been raised; I didn't realize by how much. Mueller has always taken care of the church's finances. I've never had reason to doubt him. We never could've weathered the Depression without his financial acumen."

"Did you already give him the money?"

"Yes, I wrote a check this morning."

After Robert left, I turned back to the choir robe in my hand, but my mind remained stuck on Herr Mueller. Somehow, I doubted his story.

* * *

A few days later, a truck rumbled up to the house early in the morning. Gruff voices carried up the stairs. I quickly dressed and went downstairs. Robert was directing the men to move a large object, covered in blankets, over to a blank wall in the parlor. I looked quizzically at Miss Gordon and William, but they looked just as puzzled as I.

Robert's eyes shone with happy amusement. He pulled the blankets off with a flourish. "It's a piano! Haven't you three ever seen a piano before?" He laughed. "It's for you, Louisa. Mrs. Drummond's piano. Betty was in town a week or so ago and told me she was selling off some of her grandmother's belongings. She doesn't play the piano, so I asked if I could buy it from her. Seemed like you should have a piano to play."

This avalanche of kindness overwhelmed me. I couldn't talk. I don't remember that ever happening to me before. Utterly speechless.

He walked over to me, a worried look on his face. "Is something wrong? Don't you like it? I thought you said it had a mellowed tone."

More kindness. Stunned and happy, tears sprang to my eyes. What could I say? Somehow, someway, without ever telling him, I think he understood all that a piano represented to me.

I finally gathered myself together and sat down at the piano bench. I turned on the bench and looked at Robert. "What shall I play?"

"How about that piece you played for Mrs. Drummond, the first night we drove out there?"

So I played Beethoven's *Moonlight Sonata in D*.

It had a magical effect on me. I felt as if I was reliving the sweetest moments of my life, crowding out the horror of the last few years.

On the very last note of the Sonata, as if it was orchestrated, Miss Gordon interrupted my reverie. "Some of us have things to do. Not just play ditties on a piano." She frowned at me. "I suppose I'm going to have to listen to that nonsense all day long."

Ditties. What a remarkable talent she had to spoil lovely moments. I realized I would have to play the piano when Miss Gordon was gone, which wasn't often. Silently, I wished she had more errands to run.

Chapter Four

That afternoon, I began to get serious about preparing my Victory Garden. I pulled up deep-rooted weeds and prepared the soil for planting, tilling in the coffee grounds and egg shells I had coaxed from Miss Gordon.

I recently read in the newspaper that 20 million Americans planted Victory Gardens, and that these gardens produced 40% of all the food that was consumed. Nearly half!

I planned to grow tomatoes, peas, carrots, cucumbers, beans, onions, and a few sunflowers on the far edge, marigolds and zinnias at the other, just for panache.

As I was leaning over, engrossed in my task, I suddenly felt a big, wet, scratchy tongue lick the back of my neck. I jumped up, startled. Looking up at me with his head cocked to one side was a yellow-haired puppy with large brown eyes. My heart melted. He seemed sweet, gentle and affectionate, without trying to nip at me as I petted him. He had no collar, and his ribs stuck out of his dirty, matted fur.

William came around the side of the house and saw me patting the puppy. I waved to him to come over. He looked nervous as I showed him how to put his hand out so the pup could smell him. Soon, William relaxed. Encouraged, the puppy started licking his hand.

Then something wonderful happened. William laughed. *He laughed!*

At that moment, Rosita ran out of her house, waving a broom frantically in the air. "That dog is a big pest! He has been hanging around my backdoor begging for food."

"No, Rosita, wait! Don't chase him away. Do you have any idea whom he belongs to?"

"No one! Who would want him? He's a stray. Just a mutt. He's a pest. Don't feed him or he will never go." She shook her head and went back home with her broom.

I picked up a stick and threw it. The pup scrambled after it on paws as large as dinner plates, proudly returning to us the treasure between his teeth. William threw it next, and we were soon completely entertained by the game. It wasn't long until the puppy was exhausted and crashed down on the grass, tongue hanging out of his mouth, panting heavily. William sank down beside the puppy, rubbing ears that felt like pieces of velvet. I went inside to get a bowl of water for the puppy.

As I was filling up a dish, I was struck with a brilliant idea. *Brilliant!* I had already enrolled William in the correspondence classes from the John Tracy Clinic, audaciously anticipating Robert's approval.

The materials had come yesterday in the mail. I had spent last evening up in my room, pouring over the assignments for correspondence course #1. I was confident I could teach William how to make an association for a word, through lip reading, by using this dog as a cue.

I hurried outside to join William and the puppy. In my eagerness, I took William's hands in mine and placed one of his hands on the puppy. I tapped him on the shoulder to look at me and placed his free hand on my throat to feel the vibrations of my vocal chords as I said the word "dog." He didn't understand, so I tried it again. And again. And again.

I could see in his eyes that he didn't make the connection that there was meaning to the word. Too soon, both the puppy and William lost interest. Thirst quenched, the puppy bounded across the street to continue exploring Copper Springs.

I gathered up my garden tools and took William inside. At least Robert and his aunt hadn't witnessed that futile lesson. This was going to be harder than I thought. I spent that evening re-reading through the correspondence course materials, feeling woefully incompetent.

I had a sweeping empathy for Robert as I could now understand his reluctance to begin this challenging work with William. I was trying to teach a child a spoken language, a deaf child who had never learned that words or letters had an association to an object.

And I felt a needling concern since I was doing this without his father's permission. Or approval.

I lay on my bed, staring at the ceiling, and finally prayed a prayer over the problem before falling asleep.

Lord, you are the author of language. I believe you want William to have a way to express his thoughts, his feelings, and his prayers, and to be able to take his place in this world. Please give me the wisdom to do this. Amen.

The next morning, I came downstairs and went straight to the coffee pot, pouring myself a cup. Robert's head was bent over his sermon notes at the kitchen table, giving them a final once-over before the church service began as Miss Gordon ironed his ministerial robe.

Not long after, William came downstairs in his striped pajamas, sleepily rubbing his eyes. He opened the pantry cupboard, got out his favorite cereal of Cheerioats, then climbed up on the counter to get a bowl. I heard a scratching sound at the kitchen door. No one else noticed; they were preoccupied with their tasks.

I went over to open the door. In leapt that big yellow puppy. He made a wild dash around the room and then happily bounced over to William, paws up on the counter where William sat, to give him an enthusiastic greeting. Giggling, William jumped down and hugged the pup around his neck.

Now recovered from their shock at this unwelcome and boisterous guest, Miss Gordon and Robert sprang into action and started shouting to get the dog back outside.

"Wait!" I yelled, holding one hand in the air. They stopped in their tracks, startled by the authoritative tone in my voice. I went over to William, and, once again, placed one of his hands on the puppy, his other hand on my throat. With great exaggeration, almost as an actress, I said the word "dog." With my left hand, I pointed to the puppy.

And just then a miracle occurred.

In William's eyes, I could see the connection. He tilted his head to one side, looked at the puppy, and uttered a sound. A *sound!* He pointed to the puppy as if to say: Is that what you meant?

I nodded. I said "dog" again, and he said it back to me. It wasn't an intelligible sound, almost a grunt, but to me, all of the music on this earth fell short of that one little attempt at a word.

I looked up at Robert. I'll never forget the unmistakable joy on his face. Even Miss Gordon understood this was a pivotal moment. She started dabbing her eyes with her dishtowel and then went outside to collect laundry, she said, even though none was hanging.

Robert crouched down next to William and practiced right along with him. The three of us, including the puppy, delighted to be the center of attention, sat on the kitchen floor practicing how to say the word "dog."

Too soon, Miss Gordon came back inside and scolded us for neglecting the clock. We had to hurry to get to church, but it seemed the time was ripe to teach William to communicate. Robert locked the puppy in the backyard with water and William's leftover bowl of soggy Cheerioats.

Church seemed especially worship-filled for us that morning. Robert happened to be preaching on the miracles of Jesus from the Gospel of Matthew. 'Ask and it will be given unto you, assured Jesus. For everyone who asks, receives.' Once or twice, I caught Robert gazing at William with quiet amazement.

Just as you promised, Lord Jesus, I asked for your help, and you answered my prayers to help William.

We hurried home after church and spent the afternoon at the kitchen table, pouring over the correspondence course. I explained to Robert and Miss Gordon what I had been studying the last few nights in my room.

The John Tracy Clinic was based on the concept of oral communication. Mrs. Tracy believed deaf children could be taught to communicate with the hearing and speaking world. She had patiently taught her own son to lip read, beginning at the age of three. She felt parents were the key to help a child discover that sounds exists even if he couldn't hear them.

"But what about sign language?" interrupted Robert, looking skeptical. "I assumed that would be the best option. The only option."

"From what I've read, he will always be able to learn sign language. But as far as learning to speak, there is only a window of opportunity while he is still so young. Think of it as learning a language. It's so much easier if you're young."

The puppy interrupted us, dashing around the kitchen table before slurping up water from a bowl near the door. Miss Gordon curled her lips with disgust.

I ignored her and carried on. "And the reason Mrs. Tracy wanted her own son to use oral communication was because she didn't want him excluded from the world. Even though sign language is an official language, it would still mean that William could only communicate with people who knew the language."

I paused as William climbed up on my lap. "And one other thing about sign language...it is supposed to be very difficult to learn it from a book. You have to be immersed in it. I don't think we could teach him without being fluent in it ourselves. He would probably have to be at a special school."

And that meant boarding school.

We read through the correspondence courses that included games and activities, until Miss Gordon announced that her brain hurt, and she went up to bed for an afternoon nap.

"Don't be disappointed, Louisa," Robert said, noticing the look on my face as I watched her go up the stairs. "She's interested. It's just a lot of new information to take in."

"I thought I might ask her if she would be the one to write the letters to Mrs. Spencer Tracy."

Robert burst out laughing. "Yes, that would definitely keep her interested."

There was one more piece of information I needed to present to Robert. "William should be seen by a specialist. He's really never been thoroughly tested, and he is going to need to have some kind of amplification box. I found the name of a doctor in Phoenix who works with deaf children."

Robert looked doubtful. "I don't know what could be amplified when a child is profoundly deaf."

"Couldn't you at least find out? It seems to be an important part of understanding sound."

Robert looked over in the parlor at William. William was doing somersaults on the parlor rug around an enraptured puppy, repeating the same sound he had made this morning in the kitchen. Finally, Robert turned back to me. "Okay, Louisa. Before we go any further with trying oral communication, I'll take William for testing and hear what this doctor recommends. You picked this doctor, so whatever he suggests is what we'll do. Fair enough?"

I smiled. "Fair enough."

And despite Miss Gordon's loud objections, with a rare overruling by Robert, a yellow-haired, brown-eyed puppy became the newest member of the Gordon family. Robert even insisted the puppy be allowed to sleep in William's room. We decided to name the puppy "Dog."

To my surprise, Robert made the call to the doctor in Phoenix without any reminding on my part and set up an appointment for the following week. He and William made the two-day trip, staying overnight with a relative.

I couldn't sit still while they were away, having no idea what the doctor would recommend. Miss Gordon complained I was "fidgeting worse than a dog with fleas." She was right, but I was more than a little concerned that he would be just like the ancient doctor in Copper Springs who recommended that Robert wait until William was older, then send him off to boarding school.

The more I read about Mrs. Spencer Tracy, the more I realized how forward thinking she was. Even though I only knew of her by reputation and through her correspondence, I had confidence in her. Perhaps it was because she was a mother. Perhaps it was because we shared the same name. Louise Tracy.

Robert and William returned back late the next night—so late I didn't even hear them come in. When I woke in the morning, I heard Robert's voice in the kitchen, talking to his aunt. I unscrewed the radiator cap and listened carefully.

"So he gave us this..." With a thud, I heard Robert place an object on the table. "The doctor said everything she had told me, about a short time of opportunity to try spoken language and lip reading. I don't know *how* she knows so much."

With a satisfied smile, I realized I was the 'she' to whom he was referring.

"And the doctor said I was an enlightened father."

"Well, you're a Gordon, of course. It's always been said the Gordons are enlightened," proudly affirmed Miss Gordon.

What?! I nearly said aloud but clapped my mouth shut with my hand. The *Gordons? Enlightened?* I shook my head in disbelief. Who would have possibly ever said that? I finished dressing and hurried downstairs, hoping to be included in the conversation while Robert was in a mood to talk.

He smiled broadly as he saw me walk into the kitchen. "Louisa! I've been waiting for you. Guess what? William is *not* profoundly deaf! He has a moderate hearing problem but not profound. He's been able to hear some things all along. Low sounds, the doctor said. And he gave him this." He pointed to the kitchen table. There lay a hearing aid.

"So it was worth the trip?" I asked, making a valiant effort not to look self-righteous.

He laughed. "Yes. And you have my blessing to carry on." And then, just like that, he left to go to his office, happily whistling, as Miss Gordon went upstairs to check on William.

I sat down at the kitchen table, flummoxed. His *blessing*? Did he just give me his *blessing* to carry on? With *his* son? How could I expect William to develop language when his own father hardly communicated?! A small fire of anger started smoldering within me. I marched over to Robert's office and burst in without knocking, startling him. He was seated at his desk, already engrossed in preparing Sunday's sermon.

"Robert? This is not *my* project. Helping William to learn to communicate is a project for the entire household! This is an enormous undertaking. I can't do this alone!"

Wide-eyed, Robert said nothing and stared at me.

I looked at him in utter disgust and marched out again, closing the door with a decided *bang*.

William hadn't woken yet, so I took the hearing aid and the instruction manual up to my room. Not long afterwards, I heard a timid knock at my door. "Who is it?" I snapped, knowing full well who was there.

Robert walked in, a little awkwardly, and sat down on my desk chair. "You're right," he said sheepishly, chin to chest.

I raised an eyebrow at him but didn't say anything.

"It's just that...from what I learned from the doctor...and from the materials you have...it is going to be an enormous, time consuming work, and someone will have to make this a full-time job." He cast a guilty glance at me. "I just assumed that...since you started the whole thing...you would be the one to take the bulk of responsibility for it."

He raked a hand nervously through his hair. "In fact, as I was driving back from Phoenix, I realized it might be best if you didn't have a job outside of the home. What I mean to say is...if you could consider this to be your job, almost like a tutor or governess. I would pay you, of course." Cautiously, he glanced up at me. Then he hastened to add, "And I will be involved, I promise. I can't speak for Aunt Martha, but I will support this."

"And help? You'll learn to help teach him?" I asked, eyeing him with suspicion.

"Yes. Of course."

I hesitated, just to make him squirm a little. Then I smiled. "I accept the job offer. But I won't accept payment. Consider it a barter agreement. In exchange for room and board."

He held out his hand to shake mine. As I took his hand, I said, "So help me understand how this hearing aid works."

He came over to the bed and picked it up. "It's a Zenith Radionic A2A. First vacuum tube hearing aid. Just came out last year and they're already working on a new model."

I took it from him to look it over.

"From what I understand," continued Robert, intrigued by its mechanical features, "this hearing aid uses a microphone to turn incoming sound waves into an electric current so they can be amplified. Then a speaker transforms the electric current into sound in the ear canal. Voilà! Sound! It won't be the same as you and I hear, but it will give William some awareness of sound."

I watched him as he explained the process. It struck me that he looked a little different after returning from Phoenix. For the first time, I thought he looked like a young man.

"Robert?" I asked, suddenly feeling more than a little overwhelmed. "Do you really think we can do this?"

He sat back down on the chair. "Louisa, the doctor told me something that clinched it for me. He said, 'Language is language is language. You have to get language into these kids.' So, yes, I think we can do this. The doctor said we have nothing to lose and everything to gain." He looked at me with great confidence. "He also said to expect miracles."

Robert, William, and I worked diligently to finish correspondence lesson #1 and started on lesson #2 as we waited for lesson #3 to arrive. The John Tracy Clinic planned for families to have something to work on at all times, so there was a continual overlap of correspondence courses.

Intuitively, William sensed the need to learn to listen, which was the foundation to oral communication. He was never without the hearing aid hanging around his little neck. Soon, we didn't even notice it; it became as much a part of him as the cowlick on his forehead. His ability to concentrate and his determination to learn kept me scrambling to keep up with him. His sounds were unintelligible, but they were the beginning of language.

It was *thrilling!* And *exhausting.*

I worked to bring sounds to his attention all day long. We repeated exercises hundreds of times. Hundreds of repetitions! I fell asleep each night completely worn out but woke up refreshed, reinvigorated by William's enthusiasm.

One day, I tried to engage Miss Gordon in the process. We played a game where I knocked on the door and she would answer it. She tried it once or twice, but she had to exaggerate her behavior to help William understand the relationship between sound and response and said she felt ridiculous.

So we tried it the other way, where she knocked on the door, and I opened it. But again, she said she felt foolish, knocking on her own front door. Then she stopped trying. I knew her well enough by now to know not to push her. Martha Gordon was *not* a woman to be pushed.

"This is no way to live!" she grumbled one day.

I had made up little sheets and taped them on the furniture, the bathroom mirror, and the doors, to remind all of us to acknowledge the sound an object made. "It's just for a little while, while we're trying to teach William. Soon, it will be automatic."

She did not look happy, but she didn't take the signs down either. And when she didn't know I was watching her, I saw her staring at the reminder note on the coffee pot, stuck there to have William smell the coffee and notice the percolating sound it made as it brewed.

Chapter Five

As I climbed out of bed one morning, I found Robert's sermon on the floor next to the door. He had slid it under the door, with a note that said, "Please review and add suggestions." I climbed back into bed with a red pen and read through the sermon. I read it again and again and then I began to scribble my thoughts.

"You've bloodied it with your red ink!" Robert said, laughing, when I placed it on his desk in his office later that afternoon, not at all offended. We discussed my suggestions and even argued, amicably, over a few comments I had made.

"Prayers don't just stop at the ceiling. They are being heard, Robert. God is ready to work in our lives, if we only ask for his help. It's a two-way relationship. An on-going conversation. Don't you believe that?"

"I believe God cares about us, and prayer is a tool to help us cope with our circumstances."

"It seems as if you miss the benefits of prayer with that logic. Prayer can change our circumstances on earth, as much as it can change us. Nothing is too important or too insignificant to leave in God's hands. Look at how Jesus prayed. He prayed about every detail of his life—which disciples to pick, or to multiply fish and bread for the crowd, or even to find a coin in a fish to pay his taxes. No concern seemed too small for Jesus to take to prayer. And he prayed straight from his heart, with confidence that God heard Him."

Robert shook his head in disbelief. "How did a Jewish girl end up knowing so much about Jesus?"

"My mother. She read the New Testament to me as a child; I couldn't help but be fascinated by Jesus. Jesus *is* fascinating. The more you know about Him, the more there is to know. In a way, I'm very lucky to be half-Jewish. I feel a special tie to Christ."

Robert looked directly at me. "I can see how you and Dietrich would have enjoyed each other. God was very real to him. Very close to him."

"And you, Robert? Do you not feel God is near?"

Robert sat upright like a rock. The curtain drew closed. I had pushed him a little too far, once again.

* * *

It became a pleasant routine for Robert, William, and I to go out for a drive or take a long walk on Sunday afternoons. Miss Gordon preferred to have a Sunday nap in a quiet house. When the weather accommodated, we went to a reservoir where William liked to hunt for Apache arrowheads. Today, we sat on the grass, watching William toss a ball for Dog to chase.

"You're quiet today. Anything on your mind?" Robert asked me.

I pulled a letter I had received in the mail yesterday from Dietrich's twin sister, Sabine. Besides Dietrich, she was the only one who knew where I was living. I read the letter out loud, translating it for Robert, describing Dietrich's arrest. His face was stoic as he listened, watching me with worried eyes. "If Dietrich was arrested in April, and there are still no charges, what could that mean, Louisa?"

"I can only guess, but I think it means they don't have any evidence to convict him. Just suspicion. But they could hold him for quite a while. They're probably collecting evidence. I think it's good he is still in Berlin, not moved to a prison or relocation camp, but knowing the Nazis, they'll hold him as long as they'd like." I continued translating the letter to him.

He looked up at me when I finished. "Louisa, that is unbelievable."

Sabine described news of a protest in Berlin. On February 27, 1943, the Gestapo made a "Final Roundup" of Berlin Jews. Hitler wanted to make Berlin free of Jews. Most of the Jews were deported to Auschwitz, a concentration camp, but 2,000 Jewish men had non-Jewish wives.

Those Jews were taken to the Headquarters of the Jewish Community on a street called Rosenstrasse. They, too, were to be deported to Auschwitz, but their wives came down to Rosenstrasse and made a public protest. "Give us back our husbands!" they called, for over a week. 6,000 women cried out on these men's behalf. They wouldn't go home. In an unheard of response, Hitler finally buckled in and released those Jewish husbands.

"Dietrich was wise to send you off when he did, Louisa. Do you realize you would have been rounded up like these Jews had you remained? This happened only a few months after you left Berlin."

I nodded, heavy-hearted. "I didn't want to leave." I carefully folded the letter and put it back in my pocket. "My mother would have been one of those women, protesting, if she was alive."

"If her daughter is anything like her, I have no doubt that you're right."

I half-smiled at that remark. "If only the German people would fight back against Hitler. It *can* be done. The wives on Rosenstrasse proved that."

Robert stood up to skim rocks across the pond. I watched the ripples form in the pond. "Do you think an evil person comes to power like that rock creates ripples? It just overpowers the good people?" I asked.

"Maybe. But look what happens now," he answered. He threw a handful of pebbles all around the area where the ripples were heading out over the pond. Each pebble stopped the rippling effect of the large rock and started a rippling effect of its own, albeit smaller. Little by little, the small pebbles stopped the course that the original ripple has started.

"It just seems, somehow, Hitler was handed a very large rock," I said.

"Yes. Yes, he was. But he can and will be stopped. Each time someone does the right thing, it changes the course of evil."

"Why, Robert," I said, feeling a little cheered up, "that is the makings of a great sermon."

As we walked home in the fading sunlight, a swarm of painted lady butterflies drifted past us. After noticing more than a few of them the last few weeks, I had read up on butterflies in the library. Painted lady butterflies winter in the desert, I learned. As caterpillars become adults in the spring, they migrate north in search of food and places to breed. Scientists placed their numbers in the billions. The billions!

"Did you know that these very butterflies will eventually fly north all the way to Oregon? Then their offspring will fly on to British Columbia by summer before heading back south again in the fall. We'll see them again next winter."

"Can't say I ever knew that," Robert answered pleasantly.

"The name I chose for my passport is Schmetterling. That's the German word for butterfly."

Robert cocked his head in interest. "Why are you so taken with butterflies?"

"I don't know," I shrugged. "Sounds silly. I guess it's such a wonderful example of how something beautiful can come out of something as ugly as a caterpillar. Sort of biblical, don't you think?" I watched one butterfly lilt in front of me and added softly, "My father's name was Louis. That's why I chose Louisa."

Suddenly, Robert had a stunned look on his face. "I don't know why it never occurred to me until just now. Louisa Schmetterling isn't your name, is it?"

Slowly, I shook my head.

"Will you ever tell me what your real name is?"

"Perhaps. Someday."

A gentle river of wind swirled past us. As William chased the painted lady butterflies, Robert looked at me and gently brushed hair away from my face that the breeze had lifted. Then he realized what he had done and looked embarrassed, as did I. My cheeks grew pink, and I turned away to watch William hop and jump as the butterflies scattered.

* * *

Things grew quickly in the Arizona sunshine. One morning I went outside to my Victory Garden to stake my tomato plants, which were already leggy and sprawling.

Rosita came over to visit while I worked. She plopped herself down on the grass and pulled out a piece of paper. "Okay, so now I have made a list of all of the bachelors in this town. First, there is Ernest. Maybe not too cute, but he has a steady job. Muy importante. Next, we have Emileo. He is the Italian boy who works at the hotel. Very handsome, but he is a little too friendly with the ladies, I have heard. One of the good things about my job at the salon is that I hear lots of things. Okay. Next we have Tom O'Riley. He is a miner. He goes to my church. He is a good man. So a little on the old side. Next, there is—"

"Rosita! I am not interested in finding an American boyfriend."

She looked shocked. "Why not?"

"Because I will be returning to Germany as soon as this war is over. Germany is my home. When Hitler is finally defeated, Germany will need all of the help she can get."

"But what if Hitler isn't defeated?"

I looked at her, astounded. "I can't believe you said that! Don't ever, *ever* say such a thing! Rosita, he *must* be defeated. Americans don't understand how evil he is, how dark Germany has become. Hitler has committed terrible, horrible atrocities. Don't even *think* that Hitler won't be defeated!"

Rosita was taken aback by my strong reaction. But I felt surprised at her ignorance, too. At times, I felt so frustrated with Americans. They had committed their country to fighting Hitler, yet so many seemed naïve about the horror of Hitler's diabolical ways. True, most did not know the depth of the terrible atrocities that I was aware of, but after reading the newspapers and listening to the radio for news reports, they had more information than they wanted to admit. Sometimes, I felt as if Americans just didn't want to concern themselves with the suffering of others.

"Louisa, you and Father Gordon and his aunt and William, you all come to Sunday dinner at my house," offered Rosita in a conciliatory tone.

"Oh, Rosita." I sighed. "Forgive me for lashing out at you." I looked at her, chagrined. "Robert's aunt says that if anyone even mentions Hitler's name around me, they end up feeling as if they walked straight into a buzz saw."

Rosita laughed. I felt relieved, glad that awkward moment was behind us.

"About your dinner invitation, I would love to accept for myself, but I'll have to ask the Gordons'. Reverend Gordon not Father Gordon, remember? Maybe you should just call him Robert. I'm sure he wouldn't mind. May I bring something?"

"You just come and bring a big appetite."

I smiled at her. "Okay, Rosita, so who else is on your bachelor list?"

Happily, she chattered away, detailing the positive and negative points of each single man under the age of ninety in Copper Springs, until Esmeralda called to her to come home. After the sun rose high in the sky, it became too warm to work. I went inside to wash up and told Miss Gordon about Rosita's dinner invitation.

"Please give her my apologies," she said.

I turned to look at her. "Is there any reason you are unable to go to Rosita's home?"

"I have too much to do."

"You take a nap on Sunday afternoons."

"Then that is what I'm going to be busy doing." She marched upstairs with the clean towels she had just finished folding.

I knew *exactly* why she was too busy to accept Rosita's invitation.

On Saturday, I baked a cake that I used to make for my father. I covered it with a dishtowel to take over to Rosita's for dinner tomorrow as Robert came into the kitchen to listen to Walter Winchell's commentary on the radio.

"Smells good. Can I have a slice?" He lifted up the dishtowel.

I shook my head. "Ah-ah. Don't touch. I made it to take tomorrow to Rosita's. My father used to call it 'the forgiving cake'."

Robert walked over to get a coffee cup and started to fill it. "Why did he call it a forgiving cake?"

"Because no matter what I did to it, it still turned out well." I filled up the sink with warm, soapy water to clean up the dishes I'd used.

Robert picked up a dishtowel to help dry the dishes. "So are you more like your father or your mother?"

"Oh, definitely, my mother. She and I never seem content to leave things well enough alone."

"Yep," he nodded in friendly agreement.

I frowned at him but couldn't hold back a grin. "My father was the peacemaker in our family. Like you."

He took the last dish from me and dried it, then handed me the dishtowel. "Louisa, do you have any relatives left at all?" he asked, his voice kind.

I glanced over at him. "Well, my father had a cousin in München, in Munich, and she had a little daughter who played the piano like I did. Better than I, actually. They went into hiding a year ago." I had tried to trace their whereabouts, to provide care packages and money to them, but I could never find a single lead. A good sign, I hoped.

I took the dishtowel from him and hung it carefully on the dish rack to dry, just the way Miss Gordon liked it. I looked around the kitchen to make sure I had left it in pristine condition for her. This was the first time she had let me use the kitchen without supervision. Satisfied that it would pass inspection, I said, "Robert, why is your aunt so prejudiced? You're not. Sometimes I don't even understand how you could both be from the same family. You're nothing alike."

"Well, Aunt Martha has never lived anywhere else, never even traveled further than Tucson or Phoenix. She has a set view in her mind of the way people are. It's hard to change, I suppose, at her age." He picked up his coffee cup and took a sip.

"She has such brittle requirements for everyone. Who isn't she against? She doesn't like Mexicans, Catholics, Jews, she doesn't like divorced..."

Robert winced.

I clamped my mouth shut. Up to that moment, up until his reaction, I didn't really know he and his wife had divorced. Even though I wondered about this mysterious woman often and was aware of the damaging effects her absence had created in this family, it had never really occurred to me that she and Robert were divorced. A divorced minister, no less. I felt terrible. I hadn't meant to insinuate anything. Would I *never* get it right? Would I never think before I spoke?

"What I meant is that Copper Springs has a great deal of diversity; she's been around people of different races and cultures all of her life," I said feebly, trying to deflect my thoughtless remark.

He poured the rest of his coffee down the drain. "Well, sometimes that can reinforce stereotypes, too. If all she has ever known about a Russian, for example, is a Russian miner who gets drunk every Saturday night, then that's what she thinks they're all like. Give her time. She'll come around."

He flipped on the radio, and we heard the familiar words of Walter Winchell as he began his commentary with his usual catch phrase: "Good evening, Mr. and Mrs. North America and all the ships at sea. Let's go to press."

Later that night, the house was so hot from the day's heat that we sat on the porch. The parsonage had a swamp cooler in the attic, but Miss Gordon said it couldn't be turned on until it was hot enough to melt butter. I didn't quite agree with her, but she said I didn't know how hot "hot" was yet.

She brought out fresh lemonade for everyone. As she handed me a glass, she pointed to my arm and asked, "What's that?"

She was referring to three small scars, evenly placed a few inches apart from each other in a row on my left upper arm. "Nothing really," I answered.

"What on earth could have made scars like that? It looks like someone came at with you a hayfork."

I crossed my arms, covering the scars, more than a little embarrassed by her persistence.

Miss Gordon reached for my arm. "And they're not so old, either."

She was right. They hadn't completely healed. "Just some battle scars," I said, hoping she would drop the topic.

Now Robert noticed. "Louisa, what happened to you?"

"I got them when I was escaping through France." I took a sip from my lemonade. They both looked at me, waiting for me to continue. I didn't really want to say more; dark memories of Germany left me feeling edgy. But they kept staring at me, waiting for me to elaborate. "I had made it through Switzerland and was in Chamonix, France. They say that is where downhill skiing began. It's a beautiful village. Someday, after the war, you should try and visit Chamonix."

Robert had that look on his face which communicated clearly, without saying a word, to please get to the point of the story.

"So," I hurried along, "there was a very kind farmer who helped me get to Beaune. He transported me in a hay wagon. Beaune is a medieval town, another beautiful French village.

We passed by some German soldiers sitting on the roadside. I was hidden under the hay in the back of the wagon. The soldiers stopped the farmer's wagon and poked a pitchfork through the hay, just to make sure no one was there."

Miss Gordon gasped. "How did you keep still?"

"Sheer terror. Fortunately, the pitchfork hit my arm, and the soldier thought he had hit the bottom of the wagon, so he let the farmer pass on."

"He could have put out your eyes...or worse," she noted.

I gave an uncomfortable laugh. "I am sure he would have preferred to have done just that, rather than to have let a German refugee get away. But...you are exactly right. It could have been much worse. For the brave farmer, too. I was one of the lucky ones. A narrow escape, yes?" I stood up to go get William from Robert's lap and take him upstairs to get ready for bed.

William's bedroom was directly over the porch. The windows were open to let the breeze in, and as I tucked him into bed, I could hear Robert and his aunt talking about me down below. I knew I shouldn't have listened, but it was just too tempting.

"Can you imagine? I marvel she never mentioned it. She chatters like a magpie about everything else," said Miss Gordon.

"Not about everything. You have to ask her about her life in Germany; she doesn't bring it up. I think it was harder than we could ever know," added Robert. "Did you know the Nazis killed her father?"

"*What?*" Her voice sounded filled with disbelief.

"Aunt Martha, have you ever even asked her about her family? Did you know she studied classical piano at the university? Or that she worked with the underground to fight Hitler?"

It was true. She had never shown any interest whatsoever in my background. *Good for you, Robert!* I wanted to call out through the open window but didn't.

"I'm amazed she wants to return." Robert's voice broke the quiet.

"What do you mean, she wants to return? When?"

"As soon as the war is over."

Miss Gordon set her glass down. "Must be why she listens to those gloomy news reports so often."

"Probably so. She has a map of the world up in her room. She marks the progress of the Allies with dressmakers' pins as they infiltrate Europe."

I heard Robert refill his glass of lemonade as Miss Gordon said, "I thought she liked it here. She seems happy enough."

"I don't think it's about being happy here. I think she feels that she belongs in Germany."

"She's wrong. That was then and this is now. She's lucky to be in America."

Robert gave a short laugh. "Well, if you feel that way, why don't you treat her a little more kindly?"

"I treat her just fine. Same as anyone else. Well, it doesn't matter. That war isn't going to be over anytime soon."

That's where you're wrong, Miss Gordon. I could almost smell Hitler's defeat.

* * *

After church on Sunday, I pleaded with Miss Gordon one more time to join us for Rosita's dinner, but her mind was made up.

Rosita had prepared an elaborate feast, with foods I had never seen nor heard of, flavors and textures that were completely new to me. Tamales in corn husks, nopales or cactus leaves, empanadas in pastry dough, enchiladas verde. We lingered around her dining room table for a long time after the meal, enjoying café con leche, while William and Esmeralda played checkers together.

Either Esmeralda seemed to be able to understand William's attempts at words or they had worked out a way to make their intentions understood to each other. They were good companions. I hadn't realized that Robert was fluent in Spanish until he and Rosita carried on a long conversation. It would have been a logical assumption, though, living just a few miles from the Mexican border.

Maybe it was better that his aunt didn't come. Robert looked relaxed.

Once or twice I caught Rosita watching us, with a curious look on her face. She followed me in as I took the dishes to the kitchen. "I think that Father Gordon, he is sweet on you."

I practically dropped the dishes in the sink.

"Rosita! Please don't say that. He is just a kind man." I peeked quickly into the dining room, hoping Robert hadn't heard her. Rosita was not going to leave my marital status, or lack thereof, alone.

"I am not so sure about that," she said in a cloying sing-song voice.

Just then, there was a knock at the front door. Robert, closest to the door, went to answer it. Miss Gordon was standing there along with Ernest from the telegraph office holding a yellow Western Union telegram in his hand, a solemn look on their faces.

"Robert," Miss Gordon said soberly, "Ernest has some news to deliver for Rosita and wanted you to be there when she received it."

Rosita came to the door, smiling, and then, as if in slow motion, as she seemed to grasp the meaning of why Ernest was at her door, her countenance changed completely. She collapsed into Miss Gordon's arms.

To her credit, Miss Gordon seemed to know just what to do in such a crisis. I certainly didn't. "Help me get her inside, Louisa."

As we sat down on the sofa, Miss Gordon calmed Rosita. "You need to listen to what the telegraph has to say, dear, so hold your tears."

Ernest handed the telegraph to Robert, who read it to himself and then explained it to Rosita. Ramon, Rosita's husband, had been badly injured in the battle of Attu.

"Rosita," Robert started gently, "it describes a little information about his condition. His injuries were compounded by the bad weather. He suffered from frostbite." He paused. "Ramon's legs were both amputated at the knee."

A heavy silence filled the room. Rosita hugged herself and began to rock back and forth.

On the radio, just last night, I had listened to reports of an important battle going on over a small Japanese-occupied island called Attu, in the Aleutian Islands. The U.S. military was alarmed that the enemy might use Attu and other neighboring islands as a staging area for attacks on North America, plus an enemy presence on American soil was an embarrassment. The radio announcer described the battle as a difficult campaign, made even more difficult with the bitter Alaskan cold. The island was now fully back in American hands, but at terrible cost. Over 2,100 American soldiers were injured, 500 killed, trying to save this little island, much of the casualties from exposure to the cold.

Hauntingly, I recalled hearing the news correspondent say that grown men were heard crying out for their mothers.

Robert went on to explain that apparently Ramon was now on a hospital ship but would eventually be sent home. At that point, Rosita broke down and wept loudly as Miss Gordon held her.

"You just remember that he is alive, dear, that's all that matters," Miss Gordon soothed.

I eyed Miss Gordon with the beginning of admiration. That no-nonsense way of looking at life, which so often made me bristle, was now just what Rosita needed to hold on to, giving her the handles to grasp this terrible news about her husband and not let it overcome her.

Robert walked Ernest to the door, then he and I wordlessly cleaned up the dinner dishes. Just thirty minutes earlier, we had been enjoying each others' company, lingering at the table after a pleasant meal. The war had reached in to this home and altered all of that. How quickly life could change.

* * *

Not long afterwards, Rosita and Esmeralda took the train to San Diego to meet Ramon as the hospital ship docked and to stay near him while he was in the rehabilitation facilities.

While they were away, Robert organized a work crew of volunteers from the First Presbyterian Church and from St. Mary's Catholic Church to make adjustments to the Gonzalves' home to accommodate a wheelchair. It was a one-story home so modifications were manageable. Robert, Ernest from the telegraph office, Judge Pryor, Tom O'Reilly, the mining supervisor, and a handful of others built a ramp over one section of the porch stairs. They added a railing in the bathtub, moved furniture to allow for a wheelchair to pass by easily, and made other adjustments.

I brought hot coffee over to them mid-afternoon and found Robert hammering away at a little ramp he had built over the front door stoop. He had his shirt sleeves rolled up, denim work jeans on, and his hair wasn't slicked back. Now I understood the rationale behind the heavy dose of pomade hair gel. His hair looked like a thatched roof.

It was a very different look from the usual Robert, who wore a necktie to the breakfast table. Privately, I had often wondered if he slept in a necktie, too. I didn't think he even owned a pair of work pants. I watched him for a minute before he realized I was there.

He looked, well, rather attractive as a carpenter.

He glanced up at me, and for some ridiculous reason, I felt my face grow hot. "I brought hot coffee," I said, lifting up the thermos.

He stood up and stretched. "Perfect timing. I'm ready for a break." He looked at his hands and rubbed the areas where blisters were forming. "Guess I haven't been using a hammer as much as a pen lately."

"It's kind of you to do this for Rosita." I poured a cup of coffee from the thermos and held it out to him.

He took a grateful sip. "I'm really doing it for Ramon. If I know him like I think I do, he won't want help from anyone. He's an independent type of man. What the Mexicans call a 'macho man.' A man's man. A gaucho."

I looked at him, puzzled.

"You know, a cowboy. He used to ride in the rodeos over in Bisbee. He was kind of a local legend in his day." He took another sip of coffee. "I've even been wondering if we couldn't do some things to help make his barber shop accommodate a wheelchair. I know the men in this town want to get him back on the job. Rosita is a very nice lady, but she can't cut hair if her life depended on it. Ramon is really the talent behind the shears."

He put down his coffee cup and picked up his hammer, looking at it thoughtfully. "So I've been thinking about ways to make barbering easier for a man in a wheelchair. Maybe lower the seats and mirrors." He glanced over at me. "What do you think?"

"What do I think? I think, well, I think you're an extraordinary kind of minister," I said, and quickly went inside to take the coffee thermos and cups to the other helpers.

When Ramon, Rosita and Esmeralda returned to Copper Springs, Ramon was given a hero's welcome, complete with a town parade. It seemed as if all 874 members of the town showed up for the parade. The men of the town, especially, seemed eager to shake Ramon's hand and ask him when he planned to be back at the barber shop.

I felt a little worried that the makers of pomade would notice a dip in their sales soon.

Judge Pryor declared the day "Ramon Gonzalves Day" and presented him with a flag of Arizona. Rosita could not have looked any more proud of her soldier husband, dressed in full uniform with a purple heart pinned to his chest, sitting proud in his wheelchair on the makeshift platform.

I knew America had been wounded by Pearl Harbor, by the tragic loss of over 2,000 soldiers, and by being unprepared for an attack by the Japanese. I knew most Americans felt it was their patriotic duty to fight the evil dictators of Germany and Japan.

But a little part of me, a cynical part, I'm ashamed to admit, wondered if Ramon's missing feet were the first time the town of Copper Springs understood that a world at war had far deeper consequences than rationing sugar and missing your favorite barber.

Chapter Six

The next day, Miss Gordon asked me to take lunch over to Robert in his office because she was washing and waxing the kitchen floor and didn't want anybody walking on it. The floor was tiled with black and white small tiles, hard to keep clean. Her bane of existence was that floor, scuff marks being a particular nemesis.

"And take that flea-ridden mutt with you, too. If I don't watch him every minute, he starts chewing on the parlor rug," she groused.

I waved to William to catch his attention so that he would look directly at me, and slowly said, "Come! See Dad."

Robert looked pleased when we arrived at his office door; he was ready for a break. "Oh, so Aunt Martha is wrestling with the floor again. Glad to be away from it!" he said cheerfully when I explained the basket on my arm. "Looks as if she wants you and William to picnic with me; she packed enough for the three of us." He cleared his desk, picked up William and put him on top of it, cross-legged, as I pulled up a chair. Dog sprawled contentedly at Robert's feet.

"What's the title of this sermon?" I asked, grateful to see that Robert must have visited Ramon's barbershop this morning. Ramon offered to give Robert a haircut as soon as he saw him, before the long line-up of men with haircuts in need of desperate repair began. He said it was his way to thank Robert for organizing the wheelchair accommodations made to his house, but I suspected it was probably because he was appalled at the state of Robert's hair under Rosita's watch. Gone was the slicked-back look, lathered with pomade.

"What do you think of this sermon title? 'Lord, I believe. Help thou my unbelief!' The text is from the Gospel of Mark, when a man seeks help from Jesus for his son." He glanced up at me. "Think it would catch attention?"

"I do." I sat down, watching him as he placed something into William's hand. I knew that sermon was for him. *He* was that man talking to Jesus.

Robert had given William two pennies to compare. One of them was made of copper, one made of steel. Responding to a shortage in copper, the government had just started to replace copper pennies with steel ones. After William had finished examining the pennies, I said, "something wonderful happened today."

Robert glanced my way with mild interest.

"William said 'mmmmm.' He meant 'more'! I understood exactly what he was trying to say! He wanted more milk, and he used a word to tell me!"

He tried to suppress a grin without success. "Louisa, how in the world did you survive as a Resistance Worker when you show your emotions as plain as a roadmap?"

I frowned. It was true. I couldn't hide a thing. "They never let me talk to anyone," I admitted. "The only two jobs they would give me were surveillance and eavesdropping. Dietrich often said I had a lethal curiosity."

Robert burst out laughing. Bored by the lack of attention, William wandered into the sanctuary. He liked to find bulletins Sunday church-goers left scattered in the pews and make paper airplanes of them, sailing them airborne around the sanctuary. As Robert watched him go, he said, "it's a miracle to see what is happening to William. I hope you know how grateful I am."

"The credit belongs to William. He's an amazing boy."

I started to unpack our lunch when Robert asked, "Any new word about Dietrich?"

I shook my head sadly.

He leaned back in his chair. "Louisa, I still can't understand when Dietrich became involved in assassination attempts. When I knew him, back in seminary in 1931, I remember he was very concerned about the direction Germany was heading. There had been an election that had brought socialists to a majority power, and I recall how upset Dietrich was about that election."

"Did Dietrich ever tell you about the radio address he gave the day after Hitler became chancellor?"

Robert shook his head.

I sat down across from him. "He was giving a speech on true leadership, warning the Germans of the dangers of absolute obedience. Suddenly, he was cut off the air. Right in mid-speech! It was one of the first times the government suppressed free speech." I looked at him cynically. "A portent of what was to come."

Robert tilted his head. "But how did Dietrich go from being against war to actually participating in plots to assassinate Hitler? It's hard to understand. I thought Dietrich even leaned a little toward pacifism. I'm not saying the world wouldn't be a better place without Hitler in it, but to actually assassinate him? It's just, well, it's hard to believe."

"It wasn't an easy decision for him. Of course, Dietrich wasn't going to actually be the one to assassinate Hitler. But he was willing to be totally involved despite what it might cost him personally. I think he assumed that, after the fall of Hitler, it might mean the end of his career as a pastor. He was even willing to risk that, to lose his reputation. He wasn't afraid of anything. Just last year, we all realized we were being watched.

Dietrich's mail was censored, and his telephone was tapped. He became more vigilant, but he didn't make any change in his activities. He was fearless."

I tucked my hands under me, thinking back on those last few tension-filled days I had spent in Germany. "It was different for me. I couldn't sleep. Or eat. One morning, Dietrich handed me an envelope to deliver, and my hands shook so much I dropped it. I bent down to pick up the envelope, looked up at him, and we both realized I was done. I couldn't handle the pressure anymore. That very afternoon, they whisked me off to Switzerland."

Everyone knew I was a danger to them as well as to myself.

As I fell silent, Robert said reassuringly, "Louisa, you did more than most. You can't blame yourself."

Maybe not. But I would never forgive myself for not being more courageous or more faithful. Or both.

Robert interrupted my private flagellation. "But I still don't understand how Dietrich went from resisting Hitler to planning to assassinate him."

I stood up and took the napkins out of the basket, handing one to Robert. "After he worked so hard to keep the Church free of the influence of the Nazis, he realized it was becoming an impossible situation. At first, they tried to use the German courts to overthrow Hitler. After Hitler invaded other countries, they tried to get the People's Court to declare him insane. That effort collapsed, and it became clear that war was inevitable."

I smoothed out William's napkin and placed it on Robert's desk, like a placemat. Then I did the same for me. I was stalling for time. I still felt quite upset about Dietrich's arrest; it was difficult to talk about him. I fought a dreadful premonition of what might be in store for him.

"And so..." Robert prompted.

I looked at him. "So...Dietrich faced the question of which was the greater guilt-tolerating Hitler or removing him. He finally decided there are situations in which a Christian must become guilty, out of love, to help those who are suffering. There's a passage in the New Testament in which Jesus warns his disciples that they who take the sword shall perish by the sword. Dietrich felt those words had spoken to his own heart. It was about that time that he agreed to help in an attempt to actually assassinate Hitler."

"What happened next? Was there another plan?" Leaning forward with his elbows on his desk, he was listening to me with intense concentration.

"Oh, yes, a number of them. Another time, Hitler was on his way to the Russian Front, and one of the officers in Hitler's entourage was asked to deliver two bottles of brandy back to Germany to give to a General as a celebration for his anniversary."

I unwrapped William's peanut butter and jelly sandwich and placed it on his napkin. "The package actually contained a bomb. Hitler's plane took off but later landed without incident. The Resistance Workers scrambled to retrieve the package. Somehow, the detonator had failed to ignite."

I put some cut carrots next to William's sandwich so he would be sure to eat them. He avoided all vegetables with the exception of potato chips.

"Yet another time, Hitler was scheduled to be at a military exhibition. A young officer had two plastic bombs in his pocket and was planning to approach Hitler, set the fuses, and explode the bombs. But Hitler suddenly changed his plans and left after being there just a few minutes."

I handed Robert a sandwich wrapped in wax paper and picked up one for me. I sat down and opened it slowly. Then I looked solemnly at Robert.

"When I left, the Gestapo didn't know all of the details, nor did they know all who were involved, but we knew suspicion was growing. With all of his contacts and connections, Dietrich helped Jews to escape through Switzerland, as he did with me, paying their expenses out of his own pocket. It's occurred to me that they might have traced a trail leading to him. I've wondered if that's why they've arrested him."

Suddenly, Dog stood up, hackling and growling. A door clicked shut.

"Did William go back to the parsonage?" Robert asked.

I stood up and went over to the office door that opened to the sanctuary, but there was William, carefully placing paper airplanes in the large Bible on Robert's pulpit. I turned and looked back at Robert in alarm. "Is Jackson here today?" Jackson was the church janitor.

"No. He only comes on Fridays."

Could someone have been listening to us? And why?

* * *

During church on Sunday morning, I looked around at the faces, many of which were becoming familiar to me. Elder Ray MacNeil stood to read Scripture from the pulpit Bible. He opened up the Bible, took a deep breath to begin reading the text, but then abruptly stopped himself. One by one, he pulled out paper airplanes William had hidden.

He gathered the airplanes, turned to Robert, and said, "Reverend, I believe these belong to you." The congregation erupted in laughter; I looked over at William as he looked at me with wide eyes. Neither of us dared to steal a glance at

Robert's aunt, who was, no doubt, glaring down at us from the choir loft.

Robert's sermons saw a definite upturn after he let me edit them. Every single week, we would argue agreeably about my comments, he would sigh in exasperation, but many of my suggestions would be woven into his sermon by Sunday morning.

The pews were a little less empty. I overheard two ladies at Ibsen's store one day when I was picking up a few things for Miss Gordon. "So I'm going to try that Presbyterian Church next Sunday. Have you noticed the titles out on the marquee in front of the church? This next week's is: 'What Are You Going to Do?' And last week's was 'Are You Sure?' About *what*? That's what I want to know."

The other lady leaned over and whispered loudly, "you know all about that preacher, don't you? You don't? Sure you do. Remember what happened to his pretty wife? *Such a shame.* You don't know? Well, you won't hear it from me. That Martha Gordon made it clear to everyone in town she would personally draw and quarter anyone who uttered a word about the preacher's pretty wife. She *would*, too. But you've seen his little boy, haven't you? That little blond boy one who doesn't talk? *Such a shame.*"

What *about* his pretty wife? I wanted to interrupt to ask but didn't. *What* could have been such a shame? I was dying with curiosity to know more about this mysterious woman, but out of respect for Robert, I knew I shouldn't ask.

I had lived in the Gordon household for six months; I had learned quite a bit about Robert. I knew he loved his coffee, and I had learned, by experience, he didn't like to talk in the morning until he had his first cup. He stayed up late at night to read and study. He would drop anything to help someone. It seemed as if at least once a week, most often late on Saturday nights despite the demands of a busy Sunday morning church service, there would come a persistent rapping on the door, and Robert would dutifully head out to solve the visitor's problem, without question or complaint. A few nights ago, he was asked to stop a fight between two miners who were drunk and threatening to kill each other.

People tended to view a minister as someone who belonged to them, day or night. A parsonage wasn't respected as a home but considered a twenty-four-hour- a-day office. It often occurred to me, were it not for his aunt's cold countenance, many more than drunken miners would be knocking on the parsonage door in the wee hours.

But there was much about Robert that I didn't know nor did he make easy. He was a man typical of his generation: He guarded his emotions and kept his opinions to himself, veiled by a gentleman's exterior. It took patience and persistence to try and have him be more forthcoming about personal details. Usually, I had to have a reason to find out more information.

It was only when we celebrated his birthday one evening that I learned he was thirty-four years old. His age surprised me; he seemed older. Another time, after I had wandered through the church cemetery searching without success for his wife's grave, I noticed his parents' deaths were separated by only a few days. When I asked him about them, he told me his parents had both died from an influenza epidemic that swept through the town when he was away at seminary, more than ten years ago. Forty-four people in the town died from that epidemic—not uncommon in those days.

"It's so sad to think your parents' deaths could have been prevented with this new medical miracle." I pointed to the newspaper headline. Just this year, in 1943, the first antibiotic, penicillin, was finally made in mass production and was now available for large scale use. It was having a significant effect on the battlefield by rapidly conquering the biggest wartime killer: infected wounds.

"Yes, that thought occurred to me."

That was all.

Another time, I was playing the piano with the pedal on mute one evening so I wouldn't disturb Miss Gordon when Robert came in to the parlor and sat down to listen. When I finished the piece, he asked what I had been playing.

"It's called *Two-Part Invention* by Johann Sebastian Bach," I answered. "The left hand, the bass cleft, plays a melody, and the right hand, the treble cleft, echoes it. Here, listen." I played a few measures for him. "I had a teacher at University who said the two-part invention symbolized an ideal marriage. Each hand had its work to do, but together, they complemented each other."

He gave a short, cynical laugh. "Is there really such a thing? A perfect marriage?" Then, abruptly, he got up and left.

I watched him go and thought about his missing wife. His wife might be gone, but her absence loomed large.

One evening, as we cleared the dinner dishes, I said, "Robert, I was just thinking..."

"Uh oh," he winced. "I'm starting to brace myself when you start a sentence with those words."

I ignored that remark. "I'd like to learn how to drive a car."

"Not a bad idea."

This conversation was going better than I had expected. "When could we start?"

"Wait. You mean, my car? My Hudson?" His eyes were wide with alarm.

"Well, yes, of course."

"But I love that car."

"I'm not going to *hurt* it," I said with disgust. "I just want to learn to *drive* it. Think about it. I could run errands for your aunt or for you. It would be a very good skill for me to have."

Robert put his hand to his forehead to think for a moment. "Well, then, Aunt Martha, I think you should teach her."

That was a twist. Miss Gordon able to drive a car? A buggy and horses—now *that* I could picture.

"Your thoughts are written on your face, Louisa. I'll have you know I am an excellent driver. I taught my own brother, Robert's father, how to drive. You don't know everything, I hope you know," she said.

I coughed to cover a smirk. "I would never doubt you, Miss Gordon. So would you be willing to teach me?"

"Perhaps, someday."

"Perhaps someday soon?" I asked.

She frowned. "I can see I'll get no peace about the matter. Saturday then."

Saturday couldn't come soon enough. That afternoon, Miss Gordon found me out in the backyard, throwing a ball with William and Dog. She shook the car keys at me and said, "Let's be off."

She didn't have to tell me twice. I dropped the ball, grinned at William, and headed to Robert's car.

"In the driver's seat. Be quick about it!" she said bossily.

I sat behind the wheel as she explained the meaning of the instruments on the dashboard. Every *single* one. She spoke authoritatively and with great detail. I knew enough not to ask questions, but I missed half of her lecture due to the excitement I felt at becoming a driver. That, and I was distracted by the sight of Robert watching us from the parlor window, looking as if he was about to be ill.

Miss Gordon described the odometer, the speedometer, the heater, the windshield wipers, and finally, the pedals on the floor. I had been so accustomed to staccato orders from her that I had no idea she could talk for so long.

"Now, the one on the right is the gas pedal, you gently push it in to go faster. The one in the middle is the brake pedal, and the one on the left is the clutch. You press it in, all of the way to the floor, and release it slowly as you shift gears." She pointed to the gearshift, described the purpose of each gear, the point at which I should shift gears, and how to downshift.

I tried to listen to her, but I couldn't wait until I could turn the engine on—the first time in my entire life that I had turned a key to a motor. Finally, the moment had come. She had exhausted herself of all automotive information. She braced herself and said, "proceed."

I turned the key and nothing happened.

"Press the gas pedal. The engine needs fuel."

So I turned the key again, and the engine roared to life. What a *thrill!* And we hadn't even left the driveway.

"Okay, now we are going to drive down the street in first gear."

I concentrated on shifting the pedals slowly and carefully but forgot to look at the street as the car lurched forward. A boy on a bicycle swerved wildly around us to avoid getting hit, and Rosita ran to get Esmeralda from the front yard and take her inside. Nonetheless, I had the car moving forward.

"Other side of the road, Louisa! Quick!" I swerved the car over to the right just as a car came around the corner. Down the street I drove, in first gear, as the engine started to sound like it was whining.

"Now listen to that sound. That high pitch means the engine is working too hard and needs to be brought into second gear. Shift again."

I did what she asked, but the engine made a hideous grinding sound. I hoped we were out of Robert's range of hearing.

"Make it smoother! You're grinding gears. It should be a smooth movement between pedals, like dancing."

Dancing? I could *not* imagine Martha Gordon dancing. I shot a look over at her, and again she read my mind.

"I'm not a Baptist, Louisa. Presbyterians do dance. Watch out!"

I looked back at the road and realized I had drifted the car toward the middle. I overcorrected, and we both leaned heavily to the right. "I'm going to get better at this," I promised. "Don't you worry."

Her forehead was starting to show beads of perspiration. "Let's head out of town before you kill someone."

The next hour flew quickly. I thought it was a wonderful first attempt. As we pulled back up to the house, a bit jerkily, I asked Miss Gordon if we could plan for another lesson next Saturday. She groaned and said, "Lord knows I'm not a miracle worker." She got out of the car and went straight up to bed. We didn't see her again until the next morning.

Robert walked around his car, giving it a thorough inspection to check carefully for any dents or scrapes. But he had a look of happy amusement in his eyes, I noted, irked, as we ate a meal of cold leftovers for dinner.

* * *

The next morning, I wasn't sure if Miss Gordon had fully recovered from giving me a driving lesson, but she was up early, coffee was brewing, and breakfast was underway.

"Feel better?" I asked.

She only raised an eyebrow at me and continued to set the table.

Robert was sitting at the table with coffee in his hand, reading through his sermon notes. He glanced up at me. "Louisa, tomorrow afternoon I want to take you and William back to the copper pit. I have to run an errand out that way and thought it would be fun to see it again."

Fun? I winced. For me, the copper pit and fun just didn't belong in the same sentence.

So on Monday, Robert drove us back to that gaping hole in the earth. He wanted to show us the process of how they extracted the ore when the workers were there.

Like the first time, I feigned interest. "Robert, why do you like copper mining so much?"

"I don't know," he said, rubbing his chin. "I find it fascinating. I worked at the mines when I was a teenager to save up for college. I even studied metallurgical engineering in college. I wanted to run a mine someday, but my father wouldn't hear of it. He was determined I would carry on the ministry."

I wasn't going to let this rare moment of openness pass without getting a few questions in. "Is that how your family ended up in Copper Springs?"

"My grandparents emigrated from Scotland back in 1872. My grandfather had worked in coal mines in Scotland and was able to get a job here in Arizona. My father and Aunt Martha were raised right here in Copper Springs. And then my father went to seminary, built the First Presbyterian Church and the parsonage, too. Later, I picked up where he left off."

"You didn't feel a call to the ministry?"

He gave a short laugh. "No, not really. Only my father's call."

I tilted my head and looked at him. "Are you sorry?"

He gazed at the pit as he answered. "Sometimes. Sometimes I am. I'm not sure I'm as good a minister as I might have been at running a mine."

"But, Robert, you're a wonderful minister," I said, meaning it. Robert's sermons might be lackluster, but he was a true shepherd to his flock.

In a charming way, his cheeks flushed as he kicked a stone on the ground.

Just then, a group of B-25 bombers flew overhead. Because of Arizona's perpetually sunny weather, the military had built airstrips in the desert to test planes. Robert picked up William to point out the planes, and the three of us watched them circle the sky, mesmerized.

We stopped again at the Prospector's Diner in Bisbee. Just as we were heading to the door, I spied the rude waitress inside. "Wait." I put a hand on Robert's arm as he held the door. "Before we go in, tell me what you want to order."

"Why?"

"Please? Just tell me now, and let me do the ordering." I already knew what William would order. Robert cocked his head slightly, bemused, but went along with my request.

Inside, the rude waitress asked if we wanted to sit at a booth or a counter. "The gallery," I said imperiously. She led us to a booth, and we slid into it.

"Dollface, whatcha gonna have?" she asked, chomping on her gum.

"A pair of drawers. Blond with sand for him. Draw one in the dark for me. For the boy, paint a Bow Wow red and add bullets. A Jack Benny for the gentleman, a splash of red noise for me. Oh, and add dog biscuits."

The rude waitress looked at me without expression for one long moment. Then recognition slowly flickered in her eyes. Without even flinching, she turned back to holler a word-for-word repeat to the cook, Vern, of what I'd ordered.

"Please tell me that you didn't memorize diner lingo just in case we came back here," Robert said, shaking his head in disbelief after the waitress left.

"Perhaps. Perhaps I did just that," I said airily.

"How in the world did you learn it?"

"I read an article about it in a magazine at the library."

"Happy, now?" he asked, arching an eyebrow, a touch of sarcasm in his voice.

"Yes, actually, I am," I said smugly.

Not much later, the waitress brought back our orders and placed just what I had ordered in front of us.

"Thanks, Soup Jockey," I said, grinning.

William started in on his hot dog, slathered in ketchup, with a side of baked beans. Robert looked down at his grilled cheese and bacon sandwich. And I crumbled crackers on top of my tomato soup.

The waitress returned to refill our coffee mugs. Before leaving our booth, she looked right at me and said, "Dollface, if you're ever looking for work, come on back and tell Vern that Wilma sent cha."

"Ah, vindication," I said as she left to wait on another table.

Robert just shook his head, grinning. "Louisa, God broke the mold when He made you."

"Pardon? How so?" I stopped stirring my coffee and looked up at him.

"You're just one of a kind." He reached over to help William pour even more ketchup on his hot dog.

I frowned at him.

"I meant it as a compliment. Do you remember the first time I took you and William to the copper pit and you called the tailings of the copper process 'redemptive'?"

"Yes. I also recall that you looked at me as if you thought I was peculiar."

"It was a peculiar comment, but I did find it intriguing. I've thought about it since."

"Now you're teasing me."

"I mean it. Not many could find something theological about copper waste."

"I just think it's interesting that in God's economy, nothing is wasted. Sometimes, I think my life is like copper tailings. I hope it is, anyway."

Robert seemed pensive after that. We finished our meal and as we walked back out to the car, I asked what I'd been wishing for all afternoon. "Let me drive on the way home?"

He looked apprehensive but held the keys out to me. "But I just love this car," he said.

"Oh, Robert, you of all people know you shouldn't love inanimate objects. For heaven's sake, you're a minister," I scolded, as I pried the keys out of his tightly gripped hand. With a twinge of horror, I realized I just sounded *exactly* like Miss Gordon.

He still looked worried. "Please remember that they don't make Hudsons any more."

"Why not?" I jumped in to the driver's seat before he could object.

He helped William climb in the back. Then he slid into the passenger seat next to me. "Because of the war. Every resource has been diverted to support the war effort. They're not making any new cars." He turned back at William, pointed to me, made a steering motion with his hands, and then grimaced. "Hold on tight, William. Louisa is behind the wheel."

William laughed out loud.

I scowled at him. "That is *not* a message of confidence building. And stop looking so worried. You're making me nervous, too."

After I had trouble shifting the car from first to second gear, he only let me drive the highway section in fourth gear. He even made me put it in neutral rather than downshift as I pulled over on the highway to switch seats. And he held on to the door handle the entire time, as if gripping it for dear life.

After we switched places, he said, "Not too bad, Louisa, but remind me to get my gears checked out this week in case you stripped them."

That evening, Miss Gordon had one of her headaches and retired to her room early, so I tucked William in to bed and went downstairs to clean up the dinner dishes in the kitchen. I turned on the radio to hear the latest news at the top of the hour.

I was happily humming to myself as I rinsed the last dish, until I heard the a reporter say, with enthusiasm, "Today, November 18, 1943, the British Royal Air Force conducted a successful air raid over the city of Berlin."

Suddenly, in my mind, sprang up images of that beautiful city being bombed, a city I had grown up in and knew intimately. I thought of the house in which I had been raised, the school I attended, the practice room in University where I had played the piano hour after hour. I thought of my friends and neighbors—Deidre, my best friend from school, the

Bonhoeffers. Then I thought of my parents' bodies, buried next to each other in the cemetery near our Lutheran church.

The images actually caused a physical reaction and made me feel as if I might faint. I grasped the sides of the counter for support.

Robert had been reading in the parlor and heard the news report on the radio. He came in to the kitchen, clicked off the radio, and held me close to him, wordlessly.

Chapter Seven

As the months passed, I felt more comfortable living in the Gordon household, except for one topic that was *verboten*. Off-limits. A topic I had bumped into a couple of times and had stepped quickly back as if I touched a hot stove.

William's mother.

I knew she had been raised in Copper Springs, but no one ever mentioned her name. I couldn't find out who her parents might have been; I didn't even know her maiden name. If Mrs. Drummond had lived longer, I think she would have told me the full story about the mystifying Mrs. Gordon. Robert and his aunt certainly had no plans to inform me. Even Rosita, who kept nothing to herself, was close-mouthed. I tried to hint to her once about William's mother, but she only shook her head and said, "oh, such a pity."

What? What was *such* a pity? What had *happened* to this woman?

One afternoon, I crawled up in the tree house to find William. Miss Gordon wanted him to come inside to clean up for dinner. "I hope you appreciate this, William, because I'm afraid of heights." I swung my legs over the ladder and sat down beside him.

William had a box of his mother's belongings from the tool shed. He was looking through the box and held up a wedding picture of his parents. They looked young and happy and hopeful. Even Robert's eyes looked different. Now, his eyes carried a trace of pain.

"Dad? Box?" I asked, trying to keep my words as simple as possible, patting on the box so he would know to what I was referring.

He nodded.

Robert impressed me. I knew it was not easy for him to share this box with William.

Then came a shock. William said, in sounds that I was starting to comprehend but doubted anyone else could have, "go. Man."

'Go. Man.' What could *that* mean?

I asked William to repeat himself. Patiently, he did. Again and again.

'Go. Man.' Could that mean what it sounded like? Was it possible that she had *left* with another man? I hoped it wasn't true. What kind of a woman could abandon her husband and child? William deserved better. And Robert? He was so proud; I knew he would never want anyone to pity him, but I felt so sorry for him. It was a horrifying thought—a minister whose wife ran away.

Later that evening, Robert asked me to play a game of chess. "Tonight, Louisa, I think I am going to beat you." Indeed, it was taking me longer to checkmate him. I was reluctant to break the lighthearted mood he was in, but it was seldom that we had time alone together without Miss Gordon, who was now at choir practice, hovering nearby.

"William told me two words about his mother today." I waited to see his reaction. "I didn't ask him; he just volunteered it," I rushed to add. I expected to see the familiar stiffening of his back to let me know I had crossed an invisible line.

Tonight, though, he surprised me, looking at me with keen interest. "What did he say?"

I told him the two words William had said to me.

He leaned back in the davenport and crossed his arms against his chest. "I wasn't sure how much William remembered about her. He was such a little guy when she left." He was quiet for a long moment.

There was so much I wanted to ask him, but I knew I had to go slow. He would shut down if I asked too many questions. I watched him select his words with care. Then he took a deep breath and looked up at me.

"Her name was Ruth. She grew up in Copper Springs, as did I. But she had big dreams and wanted a more exciting life than being the wife of a country parson. I believed my life belonged here. I still do. I knew she was unhappy; I thought after William was born she would feel more settled, but motherhood made her feel even more trapped. Especially with William's handicap."

I remembered reading a magazine article once that described how some animals would reject their young, most common among caged animals. Scientists could not explain why; it seemed appalling and unnatural. *Just like Ruth.*

"She left one day. I got home from work and found William asleep in the tree house. Her wedding ring was on my pillow. No note. William and I, well, we were both in pretty bad shape. After that, I invited Aunt Martha to come live with us. I really needed her help, caring for William, keeping the household intact."

I listened carefully, hoping he might say more. He didn't, so I finally asked a question I had wondered about for months. "Robert, did William make any sounds before his mother left?"

"Yes, some. As a baby and a toddler, he cried. Cried quite a lot, actually. He laughed some. After she left, though, not a sound. Until Dog showed up, anyway," he said with a half-smile.

"Does Ruth have any family left here?"

"No, she only had a mother. She never knew her father; he left before she was born. Iris, her mother, died, soon after we got married. I often thought things might have worked out differently if her mother had lived. If she had known William. Iris had a way of...helping Ruth remain steady...and when she died, Ruth lost that anchor."

Dare I ask him one more question? I just had to. "You never heard from Ruth again?"

He took another deep breath and exhaled. "The last I heard from Ruth was when I received a package of signed divorce papers her lawyer in Phoenix sent to me. I sent them back to the lawyer, signed in return, just as she wanted. I don't even know where she is." He paused and gazed at the crackling fire. "Or with whom."

We sat in silence for a long moment. Then I said, "Do you remember the first chess game we played? When I told you about my father? And you said you were sorry. Now I'm the one who is sorry."

"Louisa, don't you despise those Nazis who killed your father?"

"I realized I could not have hatred and Christ living in my heart. One would have to go; they couldn't exist together. I chose Christ."

He stood up and walked over to the fireplace, putting one hand on the mantel. "You make it sound so easy."

"It's not. I think forgiving someone who doesn't even care if you forgive them is the hardest thing in the world. There are many mornings when I wake up and the bitterness has seeped back into my soul like a toxin. Then I have to start all over again to re-forgive the Nazis in Germany. Only with God's help am I able to do so."

I watched him for a while. I could tell he was lost in his memories, so I stood up to say good night.

"Louisa?" He kept his head down. "Pray for me?"

"Of course."

* * *

William and I were in the library one afternoon when I recognized someone whom I had seen a few times before. At first, I thought she was a child, head bowed earnestly over a picture book, but when I watched her more carefully, I realized she was a young woman.

Tiny, delicate, yet she already looked world-weary. Like the times I had seen her before, she sat alone in a corner in the children's area, looking intently at picture books. Obviously, she was hoping to go unnoticed, but her hair made her hard to ignore. Bright red curls. As William settled into his routine of gathering books, I went over to her.

She didn't notice me, but I heard her sounding out words. "Go g-e-t the b-b-a-ll," she whispered to herself, her finger running along the simple text.

"Hello." Without meaning to, I startled her.

She looked up at me and quickly started to pack up to leave.

"Don't leave. I wanted to introduce myself. I'm Louisa." I held out my hand to her.

She looked at me as if she had never known been offered a hand before. Then, without looking at my eyes, she shook it. Her hand felt so fragile, like it might break if I squeezed too hard.

"What's your name?" I asked.

"Glenda."

"It looks as if you're teaching yourself to read. That's hard work."

Again, she lowered her eyes. Her cheeks began to turn pink.

"Please don't be embarrassed. I think it's wonderful! In fact, I wondered if I could help you. William and I—that's William over there—come here nearly every day at this time."

"No. Thank you for the offer, ma'am. That's not necessary."

"Actually, Glenda, you'd be doing me a favor. William is deaf, so I'm working on ways to teach him to read. If I could help you, too, then you'd be giving me some practice. I could really use the practice. I'm new at this."

That strategy worked. The three of us sat in the corner and went over a few picture books with simple vocabulary. For William, I said the words and had him repeat them back to me. For Glenda, I helped her sound them out. William watched us carefully, noticing the differences. I wondered how long it would be before he was reading. His mind was like a dry sponge, thirsty for water.

Glenda glanced at the library clock and got up to leave. "Thank you, Miss Louisa."

"Glenda, we'll be here tomorrow. Same time, same place."

She gave a quick nod as a small smile crossed her face.

William and I stayed a little longer before going up to the desk to check out our books.

Usually friendly, Miss Bentley, the librarian, had her lips pressed tightly together. "Do you know who that girl is, Louisa?" she whispered disapprovingly.

I knew.

"Her name is Glenda, Miss Bentley, and she's learning to read. Isn't that a wonderful accomplishment? For anyone?" I used a tone of voice borrowed from Robert. It meant: end of discussion.

It became a habit for Glenda, William, and me to meet a few times each week. Glenda made slow but determined progress. One morning, as William ran off to find books, I asked Glenda about her future. I knew she had some plan, but I didn't want to ask her much about her current life. I didn't want to know too much about it.

"I am going to learn to read, and someday I am going to get out of this town and make somethin' of myself," she announced.

"I know you will, Glenda," I told her, meaning it.

"I never meant to be....doing the kind of work I've been doing."

"Of course not," I said.

"My sister and I, we lived out on a farm with our father until he died. Then my sister had a baby, and her boyfriend run out on her, and we had lots of doctor bills to pay. I borrowed some money from the bank, but then I couldn't pay it back. We had a bad year on the farm. The bank took the farm. So Mick at the Tavern, he told me he knew a way I could pay off our bills."

"Where's your sister now?"

Her face grew somber. "She passed on. Got a bad fever one winter. She was always a little sickly." Then she brightened. "But I got her little boy in a home in Douglas. I paid a family to take him in. They're good folk. The man is a preacher. When Mr. Mueller told me that, I knew they'd be the right folk to take care of my boy. But I'm gonna get him back soon."

Herr Mueller?

"Glenda, did you say Herr Mueller helped you find this family?"

"Yes ma'am. He said he knew about this preacher and his wife, living over there in Douglas, no kids of their own. I even got to meet them. Real good folk, Miss Louisa."

"Do you remember their names? The minister's name?"

"Yes ma'am, I do. His name is Sid Carter. I send him extra money as often as I can spare it. For my nephew."

"And what did you say your nephew's name was?"

"Tommy. He's about ten-years-old now."

"When did you last see Tommy?"

"Well, Pastor Carter, he don't let me see him. He thinks it would be too hard on him." Her voice trailed off.

Suddenly Herr Mueller's voice bellowed throughout the quiet library. "Fräulein Louisa! Get that monster away from me!"

I jumped up and ran to find William. He had climbed up onto a bookshelf and was shooting spitwads through a straw at Herr Mueller through the openings between the books. I pulled William down and apologized profusely to Herr Mueller, who was frantically batting his hair to yank out little white balls of spitwads.

I looked around to find Glenda to finish our conversation, but she had vanished. I asked Miss Bentley if she had seen where Glenda had gone, but she told me "no" and that I shouldn't know, either.

There were moments, like this one, when Miss Bentley seemed eerily similar to Miss Gordon. And one was quite enough.

* * *

A few days before Thanksgiving, Rosita came rushing up the porch and rapped on the door. Miss Gordon opened it as Rosita burst through the door and found me in the kitchen, putting away groceries. "Louisa! I have found just the right boyfriend for you!" she interrupted breathlessly, eyes shining with excitement.

"Oh Rosita, please don't do this." I dreaded these conversations with Rosita. She just would not leave this subject alone. She insisted I needed a boyfriend no matter how many times I told her otherwise.

"No! This time, you will thank me. He wears a uniform, Louisa! He is so handsome. He is visiting his relatives for Thanksgiving, and he wants to meet you! I told him all about you!"

I put the iceberg lettuce in the icebox. "Rosita, I told you that I don't want to find an American boyfriend. Please stop hunting men for me."

"Louisa, trust me. He is so handsome that he looks like...a movie star. He is coming to take you on an afternoon drive this very day! So be ready at four o'clock! And wear something bright!" Her face scrunched up with worry. She didn't think much of my fashion sense. She said I had none. "Something pretty. Okay? I have to get back to my Esmeralda. Don't forget! Four o'clock. And you will *thank* me!" She scurried out the door before I could object any further.

Miss Gordon came into the kitchen from the parlor, one eyebrow raised.

"Did you hear that? How dare she!"

"Well, if it's any consolation, he does look like a movie star. A little like Gary Cooper. I saw him this morning at the market. He's a flight instructor over at Falcon Field near Phoenix. He's a nephew of the Johnsons. They're very proud of him."

"But I don't want to go somewhere with a complete stranger. What will we talk about?"

"Since when have you ever been at a loss for words?" was her dry response.

I looked at the clock and realized I had better get prepared for this "blind date" as Miss Gordon called it. I didn't have much to choose from, but I picked out a lace collared shirt I liked and an old blue flowered skirt of Rosita's I had altered to fit. A little before four o'clock, I came down the stairs and asked Miss Gordon if I looked all right.

"Oh, stop acting as if you're heading to the electric chair. It's just a few hours with a lonely soldier."

At four o'clock on the dot, there was a knock at the door. I froze. "I don't even know his name."

"It's Stuart," said Miss Gordon. "Stuart Johnson. Now go. Open the door before he changes his mind and leaves."

I went to the door and opened it. And then I smiled. There stood an extremely good-looking young man wearing a well-loved leather flight instructor's jacket. He had sun-tanned skin, blond-streaked hair, a broad jaw, and deep set eyes. I decided I should be more opened minded to Rosita's suggestions. "Hello. You must be Stuart. I am Louisa."

"Hello, Louisa. Rosita didn't lie. She said you were the prettiest girl west of Texas. Call me Stu. Everyone does. Shall we go?"

Just as we walked down the porch to the car, Robert and William walked up to the parsonage. I introduced them to Stuart but found I couldn't quite look either Robert or William directly in the eye.

How ridiculous, I thought. It's just an afternoon drive. *That's all.*

Stuart headed out of town, seeming to know his destination.

"Where are we going?"

"Thought we'd go sparking. Ever been sparking before?" he asked.

"No. It sounds like fun," I said. "So, Stuart, tell me about your time in the Air Force."

"Stu, darlin'. Folks call me Stu."

"Will you be sent overseas soon? With the Air Force?"

He gave a short laugh. "No, darlin'. I'm a mechanic who works for the Army Air Force. I got my mechanics' license a while back and started working for Southwest Airlines before the war. Then they needed flight instructors over there at Falcon Field, so I went to work for the military. Don't plan to leave anytime soon, neither."

"Why is that?"

"Well, it's my ticket to stay out of the war. It means I can defer my draft. I don't have to fight. I can stay right there up near Phoenix and sit things out."

Pardon me? What kind of able-bodied young man could live with himself by avoiding the draft during a World War? True, Robert had been issued a draft deferment, too, but that was because he was the sole provider and guardian for a deaf child. I knew, from Miss Gordon, that he had agonized over that decision. Stuart seemed proud to have found a way to avoid his duty.

"My job is to train those British pilots how to fly. See now, the Brits aren't very good at this flying business, so we've been training 'em for a while out in the desert. The desert at night with no moon, that is just about as black as anything can get. Most of our accidents happen at night. Flyers become disoriented, and some fly straight into the ground. And ya want to know something else about those Brits? Those big fur collars on their flight jackets that they're so darn proud of— well, they burn like a torch."

Now I was getting *more* than a little irritated. I did *not* appreciate hearing such derogatory remarks about the British pilots. Just the opposite, I felt a great deal of appreciation for the British military and their sacrifices to fight Nazism.

Our blind date began a rapid downhill descent.

Stuart parked the car up on a mesa, a flat table area overlooking a valley. "Now that there is called a tortilla flat. See how the rocks are piled up like tortillas?"

I looked to the right to see where he was pointing, and before I looked back, he had slid over to my side of the car. I moved over to the door as far as I could, but that only encouraged him to move closer to me. He slid one arm behind my head and reached over to kiss me. I pressed one hand firmly against his chest and asked, "Stuart, would you mind explaining to me exactly what sparking is?"

In half the time it took to drive out to Tortilla Flats, we were back home. I stood on the porch and watched Stuart's car zoom angrily away house after dropping me off. As I walked into the house, everyone was in the kitchen eating dinner. Without a word, I got a plate and filled it up at the counter, sat down at my place, offered a silent prayer, and began to eat. Just as Miss Gordon opened up her mouth to ask about my date, I interrupted her. "I'd rather not talk about it."

She and Robert exchanged an amused look. "Well, that's a first," she said crisply.

William glared at me, then pushed back his chair, and stomped upstairs to his room.

After dinner, Rosita knocked on the door, timidly this time. "I saw him drop you off. I saw his car rush away. No good date?"

I closed the door behind me. "It was terrible, Rosita. He didn't plan to take me for a drive! He wanted to 'spark'. Do you know what 'spark' means? Well, now I do." I glowered at her. "And another thing, Rosita, he's avoiding the draft! Can you imagine? And he talked only about himself the entire time!"

Rosita sighed and shrugged her shoulders. "Louisa, you are too picky. There's something wrong with every man I find out for you. Too old, too young, talks too much, talks too little. Most men only talk about themselves, you know."

"Not all men."

"Who, then?"

"Well, Ramon, for one. And Robert doesn't talk about himself very much. It's hard work to get him to talk about himself."

"That is because he is a priest, Louisa," she said knowingly.

"Not a priest, Rosita, a minister."

"It is his job to not to talk about himself."

"That's not the only reason, Rosita. He would be the same kind of person even if he was a...a miner. Robert shows interest in other people."

"Oh." Her eyes started to twinkle. "Oh, oh, oh, oh. Now I see."

"You're misunderstanding me. I only meant that not all men are so...so...consumed with themselves."

"Well, there are lots of fish to fry in the lake. We try again," she said cheerfully.

"No! Rosita, listen to me. You are *not* to try and find me a boyfriend. I am not interested. Do you understand?" I scolded. "It's not that I don't want to fall in love and get married one day. I was in love with someone once."

Her eyes glittered with interest. She sat down on the porch steps and patted the spot next to her so I would join her. "So? What happened?"

I sat down beside her. "War. It divided us." That was one story I did not want to share with Rosita. "Someday, when the time is right, I hope to find someone and even have a family. But back in Germany where I belong."

"But you always say that our future belongs to God."

"Well, yes, but—"

"So maybe God wants you to stay here."

"Oh, no, Rosita, I don't think so. I think God wants me to go back to Germany. I'm sure He does. Germany needs me."

"But maybe God thinks we need you more."

That comment astounded me.

"What about William?" she asked.

"What about him?"

"Does he know you plan to leave someday?"

"Yes, of course." *Did* he realize that? "Well, I guess I don't know," I admitted.

"That little boy loves you. And his own mama is gone. Don't you think it will be hard on him if you just up and go?"

I stared at her, speechless. I didn't know how to answer her. I had never even given it a thought. Of all of the preconceived ideas I had about living in America, it never involved becoming attached to anyone.

"Well...even still, that Stuart...he looked like a movie star, no?" she asked, meekly.

I tried to scowl at her but then we both ended up giggling like schoolgirls. "Rosita, why are you so determined to find me an American boyfriend?"

She leaned her head to one side and looked at me with frank, brown eyes. "If you fall in love and marry an American boy, then you will stay. I don't want to lose you when the war is over."

I put an arm around her and squeezed her shoulders. "You'll never lose me."

She went back home, but I stayed out on the porch, watching the sunset, nettled by her remark about William.

After a while, Robert came out to join me. He leaned against the porch rail, hands in his pockets. "Still don't want to talk?"

"Not really."

He sat down next to me on the porch steps. "Louisa, did that fellow frighten you at all?"

I looked at him, touched by his concern. "No. He just had different ideas about...well, things...than I did." I smiled at him. "Any idea why William is upset?"

"He'll be fine."

"That doesn't answer my question."

He waited for a moment before answering. "I think it bothered him to see you go off with a stranger."

I looked down at my hands in my lap. "Rosita was just saying something like that. She wondered if I had thought about how William would feel when I go back to Germany, especially after..." I stopped myself, realizing what I was just about to say.

"Especially after his mother left? It's true. He has grown fond of you."

I looked at him. "And I of him."

"I know."

"Rosita told me why she's been working so hard to find an American boyfriend for me. She doesn't want me to leave after the war." I glanced down at the ground. "I didn't expect this."

"Expect what?"

"I came to America for safekeeping. I didn't expect...I didn't expect to..." I just couldn't finish the sentence.

"Didn't expect to find people who cared about you? I guess we didn't think about that either when I told Dietrich I would sponsor someone."

"I just hope...I hope I haven't made things difficult for William."

"Just the opposite. You've been part of a miracle for him." He gazed out at the sun, watching it disappear behind a ridge. "Louisa, when you go back to Germany, if you go back, it won't be like when his mother left. Let's worry about that when the time comes."

The sky turned a beautiful rose color.

"Alpenglühe." My eyes locked on the reddish glow on the summit of the mountains.

"Alpenglow?" he asked.

I nodded. "Look! The first star." I pointed to the sky. "I think it's your copper star."

Robert looked up at the emerging star. "Seek him that maketh the seven stars and Orion, and turneth the shadow of death into the morning, and maketh the day dark with night: that calleth for the waters of the sea, and poureth them out upon the face of the earth: The Lord is his name."

"Is that a quote from Scripture?"

"From the book of Amos," he answered with a shy grin. "Always liked that Amos. He earned his living from a flock of sheep. He wasn't a man of the court like Isaiah or an educated priest like Jeremiah. Just a simple shepherd. But when God called him into duty as a prophet, he went. And that man could preach a sermon!"

As he watched the stars appear in the sky, I watched him. Not for the first time that day, I wondered why that awful flight instructor couldn't be more like Robert.

Chapter Eight

On Sunday afternoon, Robert planned to take William and me hiking at Cochise's Stronghold in the Dragoon Mountains north of Copper Springs. Just as he opened the back door of the Hudson for Dog to jump in, Esmeralda ran up.

"My mother and I want William to come over this afternoon; we're baking cookies and want him to join us. Okay?"

Robert looked at me, uncertainty in his eyes. William had never been invited to play at someone's home before.

"I think it would be good for him," I answered.

Reluctantly, Robert agreed. Using a combination of words and gestures, he asked William if he wanted to go with Esmeralda. Before he could even finish, William was running behind Esmeralda back to the Gonzalves' house.

"Esmeralda! Miss Gordon is home, if you need help," I called after her. "Just keep banging on the door until you wake her up!"

She waved back at us. We watched William follow her down the street at a full gallop. Then, as quickly as William disappeared into the house, an awkward silence covered us like a blanket. I was glad I had brought a book to read, tucked in my handbag. We hadn't really done much alone before; our outings always included William. We got into the car. Dog reached his big head over the top of the seat, tongue dripping slobber, as if to remind us that he was here, too.

Robert pushed Dog back. "Well, I guess we should be off, then." He started the car and backed out of the driveway.

We drove for quite a while before arriving at the Dragoon Mountains, an area of jumbled granite domes and sheer cliffs. We hiked along an ancient Indian trail. Half-way up, we found a shallow cave with petroglyphs. Running my hands along the etchings, I wondered what story the rocks would tell, if only rocks could talk.

Finally, we reached a rocky promontory. I let Dog off his leash and let him explore to his nose's content. We walked around the promontory in silence, looking down at the thick tangle of boulders and superb views of the canyon.

"It's so beautiful," Robert said, craning his neck to see into the valley below.

"When I first arrived in Arizona, I didn't think the desert was very beautiful," I confessed.

He straightened up. "Well, you came from a very different place. I think you almost have to have been born here to appreciate its beauty. It's pretty desolate."

I gazed out at the sea of boulders. "Do you think that Moses and the Israelites wandered for forty years in an area like this?"

Robert looked at me, an odd expression on his face. "Louisa, sometimes your comments come like a bolt out of the blue. What on earth made you think of Moses?"

"This book I've been reading." I pulled it out of my handbag. "It's about the Underground Railroad during the American Civil War; the woman who organized it was called Moses."

"Harriet Tubman?" he asked, taking the book out of my hands.

"Yes! You know of her?"

"Every schoolchild in America does. She's a heroine."

"When I was making the journey from Germany to Arizona, I felt as if I was being taken care of by this same kind of Underground Railroad."

He leaned his hip against the rock ledge, arms crossed, facing me with an interested look.

"Getting past the border guards of Germany was a mystery. A miracle, really. Just as a guard was looking at my passport, my false passport, a whistle blew and guards ran toward a frightened looking man and woman. The guard was distracted by the commotion. He stamped my passport and motioned to go ahead. I walked through the gates and was accepted through Swiss customs without any question."

Dog tore past us, chasing a jackrabbit into the scrub brush.

"What happened next?" Robert asked, watching Dog disappear into the thicket.

"A contact met me on the other side of the border, and from there, I was in the hands of kind strangers. Angels of mercy. There was someone to meet me at every juncture: bus station, train station, ferry. I was given rest, food, and shelter. Then and only then was I given instructions about the next leg of my journey. I was even handed the proper currency I would need. I was never told anyone's last name. It had all been organized by the Resistance Workers. I felt like a piece of fragile luggage, being carefully delivered from place to place."

"Weren't you ever afraid?"

"Oh, yes! Many times. Especially through occupied France. Well, you remember the story about the hay wagon."

Robert glanced at my arm.

I covered the scars. "In England, I felt rather protected. But from there, I took passage on a big merchant boat across the Atlantic Ocean. German U-boats had been spotted nearby, and the ship felt like a giant..." I cocked my head at him in a question. "What does your aunt call it—a sitting chicken?"

"Duck. A sitting duck." He tried to stifle a grin but didn't make it.

I raised an eyebrow at him. "Anyway, finally, we reached America. As soon as I was admitted through Ellis Island, I felt like...I finally felt out of harm's way. I wasn't really anxious again until..."

I caught myself and stopped.

"Until when?"

I looked down at the ground. "Until the train pulled into Tucson and I knew you would be waiting for me. Then I felt a little nervous."

Robert had been gazing beyond me at the horizon. He turned his head and gave me one of his straight-in-the-eyes look. "And now, Louisa?"

Something in the way he looked at me made my heart skip a beat.

Just then, Dog came barreling straight at us with the biggest stick he could carry in his mouth, wild-eyed, looking utterly ridiculous and extremely proud of himself. Grateful for the diversion, I grabbed Dog, put on his leash, and we made a dash back down the hillside.

Our enjoyable afternoon came to an abrupt end as we pulled into the driveway. A smoldering Miss Gordon marched out of the house, dragging a contrite looking William behind her.

"Oh no, what has he done now?" Robert asked under his breath.

"You won't believe it! Robert, you just won't believe what kind of trouble your son has gotten into this afternoon!"

Robert said, "Calm down, Aunt Martha. Just tell me what happened."

"I woke up from my nap and went to start dinner. I took eggs out from the ice box and cracked one. The eggs were bad, so I put them on the back porch to take back to Mr. Ibsen. I forgot all about those eggs until Mr. Mueller came banging on the front door. He was covered with those rotten eggs! William and Esmeralda stole those very eggs and ran to where Mr. Mueller was out pruning back his prize peonies. They hid in the bushes and threw rotten eggs at him! I declare, Robert, I don't know *what* gets into that boy."

Just as she finished, Herr Mueller came storming up the driveway. He must have seen Robert's car drive past his house a few minutes earlier. Miss Gordon quickly took William back inside. I tried to get inside, too, and away from the approaching Herr Mueller, but he blocked the path.

Robert and I were cornered against the car. "Gordon!" he bellowed. "It's time you do something with that boy. He needs to be institutionalized before he becomes known as the Village Idiot. He's already a menace to that church of yours. He's an embarrassment to this entire town."

Indignation surging, I stepped forward and prepared to give Herr Mueller a piece of my mind, in German, so Robert wouldn't know to interrupt me, but Robert grabbed my arm and held it tightly in warning.

"I apologize on my son's behalf, Mr. Mueller," he said. "It will not happen again. Please remember he's just a child."

Herr Mueller was in no mood to be mollified. "This time, apologies are not enough. I've had enough excuses! The truth is that you can't manage your own child. You are an incompetent parent! This time, I am going to the authorities!" Mueller spun on his heels and marched back down the street. The only thing that almost got me smirking me was the sight of eggshells stuck on his pants.

Robert threw me a stern glance. "Not a word, Louisa."

The evening meal was a very silent one. Weary from the day's crime, William kept his eyes lowered to his plate and hardly ate. Miss Gordon turned down the offer for clean-up help in the kitchen, so Robert went to his office, William up to his room with Dog, and I slipped unnoticed out the front door and over to Rosita's house.

As I knocked on the door, a tear-stained Esmeralda, lips trembling, answered it. "I am so sorry!" she bawled. "I didn't know how much trouble William would get in." Rosita came to the door behind her, chagrined.

"Esmeralda, please don't worry," I assured her. "Just tell me what happened."

"After we finished baking cookies and played some games we got bored, and Mama shooed us outside. We were just kicking a ball down the street when William saw Mr. Mueller outside working on his flowers. William ran back to his house and brought back the rotten eggs. He threw them at Mr. Mueller. I didn't want him to, but he just kept throwing and throwing the eggs at him. I promise that I didn't throw any eggs." Then, sheepishly, "but I did hold the carton open for him. Mr. Mueller got so mad! His face got red, and he waved his arms and said some bad, bad words," she stopped to take a deep breath, "and then he took William by the shirt collar and dragged him to Miss Gordon and then said more bad words to her."

"Esmeralda, why do you think William threw those eggs at Herr Mueller?"

"I don't know." Then she looked at me from the corner of her eyes. "But that Mr. Mueller is mean."

"That's not a reason to throw rotten eggs at the man."

"Is Father Gordon mad with me?"

"Reverend Gordon not Father Gordon. He's disappointed with William's behavior, but he's not mad at you." I smiled and gave her a hug.

"Will you ever let him come to our house to play again?" asked Rosita.

"Of course!" I hugged her, too, and left to go to Robert's office. Gently, I knocked on the door and poked my head in.

He wasn't working; he was gazing out the window. He frowned when he saw me. "I don't want to talk about it, Louisa."

"I understand. Just let me say one thing and then I'll go."

Slowly, he nodded.

"I'm not excusing William's behavior, but there is some reason that he truly dislikes Herr Mueller." I told him about the time when William spit on Herr Mueller's shoes in the library. And about the spitwads through the straw.

Robert's eyebrows shot up. "For Pete's sake! Why didn't you tell me about those things when they happened?"

"Because there's something about Herr Mueller that makes me want to spit on his shoes, too."

He rolled his eyes. "That's really not very helpful. I need to discipline the boy. He's played tricks on Mueller before. Once he shot a rock at Mueller's backside with his slingshot. Another time he threw tomatoes at the Muellers' windows during a fancy dinner party. I heard about that one for months." He shook his head in disgust.

"William might have a very good reason for doing what he did."

He gave me a look as if I had lost my mind. "And what could that possibly be?"

"I don't know. I really have no idea. And until his language improves, I don't know how we could find out why William hates Herr Mueller so. But I have faith in William. I hope you do, too. Please don't be too hard on him."

He sighed. "You might have a point." He spun around in his chair and looked out the window. "I've been sitting here wondering if maybe the time is right for William to attend the Southwestern School for the Deaf. I had wanted to wait until he was older, but it's apparent he's more ready than I had expected." He spun back around to look directly at me. "You've shown me that." Then, quietly to himself, he said, "I'm just not sure I could bear having him gone."

I drew a sharp breath. It never occurred to me that by teaching William to communicate, it might mean he would be sent to boarding school. I couldn't imagine the Gordon home without William. I didn't even want to consider it. I put my hand on the doorknob to leave but turned to say, "Anyway, thank you for such a lovely day up in the mountains with Chief Cochise."

"Somehow, I think Cochise would have been easier to deal with than Mueller," Robert lamented.

* * *

I had hoped Robert would drop the subject about sending William to boarding school after the rotten egg fiasco with Herr Mueller. I was certainly not going to mention it.

The next evening as dinner ended, Miss Gordon told William to go upstairs and get ready for his bath, waving her hands wildly as if she were taking a bath and scrubbing herself down. It always amused me to watch her homespun methods of communicating with a deaf child. She did seem to be able to get her point across to William.

Robert watched William head up the stairs, Dog trotting dutifully behind his young master. Then he casually mentioned he had called the Southwestern School for the Deaf and scheduled an appointment for Friday. "I think it would be a good idea to see what the school has to offer."

Miss Gordon and I exchanged a look.

"So the principal is going to give me a tour of the campus and let me see some of the classes," he continued. "And they'll do some testing with William."

I picked up a few dinner plates from the table and went to the sink, stacking plates.

"It's just to check it out. It doesn't mean that I have to make a decision. It's just an informative interview," he added.

I didn't say a word. I just started filling up the sink with warm, soapy water.

"So Louisa, what do you think?" he asked.

Without looking at him, I said, "I think you'll make the best decision."

"I'm asking you what you think," he said, irritation rising in his voice.

I kept my head down. "William is your son. I'm sure you know what's best for him. It's really none of my business."

"None of your business?! None of your business?!" he roared. "Since when have you *ever* minded your own business? From the first day you arrived here, you have been minding *everyone's* business. And now, when I actually ask for your opinion, for the first time, you have none?!"

I stopped washing the dishes and stared at him. "Was ist löst mit dir? Why are you so upset?"

"Blast it, woman! You can really drive a body barmy!" He stomped out of the kitchen, slammed the door shut, and marched off to his office.

I looked at Miss Gordon, who looked back at me, equally wide-eyed. "What was that about?" I plopped down on the chair next to her. "How dare he yell at me! What did I do to deserve that? How many times have I heard the words 'this is not your place, Louisa.' So when I finally know it's not my place to say anything, he gets angry!"

Her brows flickered up. "His point, exactly." She took the dishtowel out of my hand. "Go talk to him. I'll clean up and get William to bed."

"I don't want to talk to him. I'm too angry." I looked directly at her. "What about your opinion? What do you say about William being sent off to boarding school?"

"Well, if you noticed, Robert didn't ask me. He asked you. So, go. Talk to him."

"Wait. What does it mean to drive a body barmy? Did he swear at me?"

"No, no, no. It's a Scottish expression my father used to say. Robert's grandfather. Driving a body barmy is something you do very well. Off with you!" She waved her dishcloth at me as if shooing the butler.

Slowly walking over to the kitchen door, I picked up the car keys that were hanging on the keyboard. I walked over to Robert's office and knocked on the door.

"Come in," Robert said.

I opened the door and barely popped my head in, not quite sure what reaction awaited me.

He looked at me. "Louisa...," he started.

I interrupted him by holding up the car keys. "Can I take you for a drive?"

Slowly, he stood up and walked over to me, taking the keys out of my hand. "I'll go on a drive, but only if I'm the one who's driving. I'm not in the mood to have my life endangered."

We walked over to his beloved Hudson. Robert held the door open for me, then went around to his side. "Where are we headed?" he asked.

I wanted to go back to the place where that awful flight instructor took me. Despite such a disastrous date, the setting was lovely in the day, and I thought it might be even more beautiful in the evening, especially with a full moon overlooking the desert valley as there was tonight.

After I gave him directions, we drove along in silence, the awkwardness of unfinished business lingered between us. When we arrived up on the plateau, I showed him where to park. "Look, isn't it pretty? Those rocks are piled up like tortillas. And look at the valley!" The pale moon cast eerie shadows over the nooks and crevices down below.

Robert craned his neck to look around the parking area. "Is this where that fellow took you? This is where the high school kids come to neck. Look around."

There *were* a number of cars with steamed up windows. "Is necking the same thing as sparking?" I asked.

Once he finished laughing, he looked at me for a long moment, bemused. Then he said, "Louisa, you are a strange combination of the most intelligent and most ingenuous person I have ever met."

Again, a self-conscious silence filled the car, until we both spoke at once. "Wait, Robert. Let me explain something. I wasn't trying to be difficult. I don't have an opinion to give you about sending William to boarding school because I really don't know what the right answer is."

He shifted in his seat to turn toward me. "Neither do I. That's why I wanted to hear what you thought about it. Don't you think I'm worried I could be making a huge mistake? Or that William might feel abandoned again just as he's finally getting over Ruth's desertion? But then again, what if he might be missing something by not being in a school that could help him communicate?"

I sighed and looked straight forward. "I had hoped doing the correspondence classes would be enough for now."

"You started this whole thing."

"I know."

"You said it should be like immersing yourself in a foreign country."

"I remember." *Why* did I ever tell him that? What was I *thinking*? Probably that he didn't really listen to me.

"I can see how quickly he is learning. It makes me think it might be better for him to be at the school, being taught by professionals."

"Oh," I said, trying without much success to hide my disappointment that Robert didn't think I was qualified. I had been working hard to stay ahead of William's rapid progress. "It's just that...I'm concerned you might be making this decision because of pressure from Herr Mueller."

"Apparently, Mueller is trying to concoct misdemeanor charges against William."

So *that's* what started this. "What does that mean?"

"He's trying to build a case to prove William should be in a specialized school or a state institution. Can you imagine anyone pressing charges against a five-year-old boy?" Robert shook his head in disgust. "Still, I can't deny William is unreasonably belligerent with the man."

"But only with Herr Mueller. No one else. Well, he pulls a few boyish pranks at the church, but everyone enjoys him. No one minds his antics. Just Herr Mueller."

He was silent for a moment. Then he looked over at me. "I want you to come with us on Friday."

"Then I'll come." We looked up at the stars for a few minutes, both alone with our thoughts.

Then, Robert surprised me. Shocked me, actually. "Louisa, could we pray about this?" he asked.

Pleased, I smiled and held out my hand.

He took my hand in his and began to pray. "Holy Father, I need your help. I am asking for your guidance over this important decision for William. I need to see the answer clearly."

Then I added, "And, Lord, we want the best for William, but only You know what the best could be for him. Please give us the wisdom to encourage, support him, and understand what he needs. Amen."

Robert didn't release my hand for a moment. "Louisa, I—"

Quickly, I interrupted him and pulled my hand back. "It's all right, Robert. I forgive you for being so abominably rude to me earlier."

He looked at me for a long minute without expression, then turned the keys in the ignition and backed up the Hudson, heading toward home.

It was not lost on me that when I interrupted him, he might have had something else on his mind besides apologizing for saying I could drive a body barmy.

* * *

Friday came too soon—cold and sunny. We left early to arrive in time for our ten o'clock appointment. Miss Gordon stood on the porch, Dog sitting dutifully beside her as sentry guard. She waved good-bye, a mournful look on her face. I felt sad, too, as the car backed out of the driveway.

"Stop looking so woebegone, Louisa. We're just going to check it out. That's all," Robert gently chided.

As we drove along the two-lane highway towards Tucson, I stared at the scenery, lost in reflection about the car ride last February when Robert had picked me up at the train station. I remembered feeling so disappointed with the arid and bone-dry landscape.

On that first car ride, I looked at the harsh rocks and saw only a rusty red color. Now, scarcely ten months later, I could see hues of color and even identify the rock formations. It was as if I put on a pair of new glasses after seeing through an old, outdated pair. The colors were clear and vivid. Shires, buttes, and sheer rock walls shimmered with shades of beige, ocher, salmon and scarlet.

The Southwestern School for the Deaf was situated on a beautiful, expansive campus. We went up to the Administration building and found the principal's office. The receptionist greeted us warmly. "Mr. and Mrs. Gordon, we've been expecting you. And this must be William?" she asked.

Robert and I both interrupted each other, trying to correct the receptionist's impression that we were married.

She didn't bother with us; her eyes were on William. "I'm going to take William for a tour and have him meet a teacher who will do a little testing with him while you and your wife meet with the principal." She spoke slowly and directly to William, asking him if he'd like to go with her. He watched her lips intently and then nodded enthusiastically. Then she led us into the principal's office.

"Mrs. Powell, Mr. and Mrs. Gordon are here to meet you." The receptionist turned and took William by the hand, leading him out the door.

We both watched him leave, feeling protective, but he never even turned back to wave good-bye.

A portly woman stood up to greet us. "You must be Reverend Gordon. We spoke on the phone a few days ago." She shook Robert's hand and then reached out to shake my hand. "And you must be Mrs. Gordon."

"No, no. I'm Louisa Schmetterling. I'm Reverend Gordon's houseguest."

"Oh," she said, flatly, and then asked us to sit down. "Do you know much about this school?"

We shook our heads.

"Well, the school was founded in 1912 when Arizona became a state. Most of our students live close to Tucson and are able to attend the school as a day school. We do have residence halls available for children who don't live nearby."

"Do children as young as William attend the boarding school? He just turned five," I asked, hoping she would say "no."

"Yes, they do. And most of those students go home each weekend."

At least we could see him on weekends.

"Most parents worry that their children will have trouble adjusting to boarding school, but the kids seem to do just fine," she reassured us.

"It's just that...it would be like a candle flame has gone out for us at home," I said.

"Yes. Yes, that's it exactly," Robert added, nodding in agreement.

The principal turned to look at me, thoughtful for a moment. "I'm sorry. Did you say you were just visiting the Gordons?"

I nodded.

"On a vacation?"

"She's our houseguest," Robert explained. "A long-term houseguest."

The principal's eyes shifted from Robert, to me, back to Robert then she got back to the business at hand. She asked us questions about William and was curious to hear about the correspondence course from the John Tracy Clinic.

"How did you find out about the clinic? It just began last year. Hardly anyone knows about it yet, but I've already heard very good things about the coursework."

"My houseguest has an extraordinary talent for researching information," Robert said, arching his eyebrows. Then, he described how we'd been working on oral communication.

"And the whole family is learning, too?" she asked.

"Yes, we're working on it. Louisa has placed paper pictures all over the house to help remind us to practice sound-to-object association with William. Even in the car."

"Excellent! We believe in complete family involvement." She paused and looked straight at Robert. "Reverend Gordon, how fortunate you are to have such a helpful houseguest. My houseguests eat my food and use up my hot water and toilet tissue."

Chin to my chest, I tried to hide a self-satisfied smile.

"May I ask why you've come to us today?" she asked.

I looked at Robert to answer that question. I still wasn't sure why we were here.

"I know there are different schools of thought about how to help a deaf child communicate. I...we have chosen to try oral communication, and we...well, Louisa, actually, has had wonderful results. But we're...I'm...concerned William might be missing something."

"I can appreciate your concern. This school believes in 'total communication.' That means that what you're doing now with William is perfectly appropriate, and when he comes of school age, he can learn sign language. Most of our students come to us without any sign language ability. And most do need to be in a sign language environment to gain fluency. It would be extremely difficult for him to learn it at home, without any fluent signers nearby." She described the academic and life skill goals of the school.

We listened carefully to her, asking questions, finding answers to concerns. An hour flew by. Then the receptionist interrupted us to take us on a tour of the grounds. We were able to see the residence halls, the gymnasium, the cafeteria, and to observe a few classrooms. When we went back to the principal's office, William was seated beside her. She was asking him questions and, with great concentration, he tried to respond to her.

"You're back. So soon!" she said with a smile when she saw us standing there, watching them. "Please sit down. Let's have a little talk before you leave."

We sat down in chairs facing her desk. I thought it was interesting that William stayed seated next to Mrs. Powell rather than coming to sit on Robert's or my lap as I would have expected. He was obviously comfortable here.

"Well, Reverend Gordon, to be perfectly honest, with the enriched home environment William has obviously benefited from, you could wait a few years to enroll him as a boarding student."

"I'm just concerned he might need more professional instruction than we can give to him," Robert said.

"Relax, Reverend Gordon. So far, you're doing a fine job. He is a bright boy. I can imagine you're all barely staying just a step ahead of him. But I understood him when I asked him a question."

I took a sharp breath. "You understood him? You really did?"

"I really did."

I looked over at Robert, who had already pulled out his handkerchief, mopping his eyes.

Mrs. Powell smiled, understanding. "I have an idea. One of our best teachers just retired and moved to Bisbee. Mrs. Violet Morgan. She's trained in speech therapy. What would you think about meeting with her a few times a month just to have a checkpoint? I'm sure she wouldn't mind at all. Trust me, on a teacher's pension, I'm sure she could use the income from tutoring. It might give you peace of mind that you're on the right track or answer any questions you might have."

We took down the Bisbee teacher's name and address and shook the principal's hand as we said goodbye.

"Before you go," she said, "if you have time, we'd like to invite you to eat lunch at the school cafeteria. I think you'll find it to be an interesting experience. Food's not bad, either."

We walked over to the school cafeteria, holding William's hands between us. The principal was right. It was fascinating to watch animated children, eating their lunches, talking to each other in sign language.

William's face was a sight to behold. He couldn't stop watching the children interacting with each other. For one of the first times in his life, around a group of children, I think he felt he belonged. Always before, even in his father's church, he was an outsider.

The car ride back to Copper Springs felt like a gray cloud looming over our heads had dissipated. "William, did you like the school?" I asked.

"Good," he answered, nodding his head. Soon, he leaned against the car door, eyes struggling to stay open, tired after such a full morning.

Thank you, Lord, for answering our prayer so clearly, I prayed as I watched him fall asleep.

When we arrived back in Copper Springs, Dog was sprawled out on the front porch. As soon as Dog saw the Hudson pull into the driveway, he barked and raced out to the car to greet us. William woke up and scrambled out to play with him. As I reached for the door handle, Robert said, "Louisa, wait one moment. I wanted to say..."

"It's all right, Robert."

He sighed. "Do you realize that this is the third time in one week that I have tried to apologize to you and you have interrupted me? Could you please let a man finish a complete sentence?"

I turned toward him, a little surprised by his exasperated tone.

"I wanted to say I'm sorry I doubted your ability to teach William. I'm sorry I let Mueller get under my skin. And I'm very appreciative of the help you've given to my son."

I waited. "Finished?"

"Yes," he said.

"I think you were right."

"Excuse me?" Robert said, stunned.

"I said I think you were right."

"Would you mind repeating that?"

I rolled my eyes.

"So what was I so right about?"

"I actually think it was a good thing for us to go see the school and have confidence that we're doing things correctly for William. Just to be certain. It made me feel better to see it.

It's a good school. A very good school. The children are happy there. But..."

He looked at me.

"There will probably come a day when William should be there."

Turning back to face the dashboard, he said under his breath, "I know." Then he turned back to me. "But not just yet."

Chapter Nine

Later that week, Ernest came over to the house one morning to deliver a telegram. It was from Ada, a cousin of the Gordons', with news that her husband had passed away suddenly and she needed Martha to come to Phoenix immediately. Miss Gordon promptly packed up, Robert took her to meet the afternoon train in Tucson, and instantly, the house's spirits lifted.

For the first time, I was allowed to use the kitchen without asking permission. I cooked my first meal for William and Robert. It was a complete disaster. The meat tasted like cardboard. William spit it out and jumped up to make himself a peanut butter, banana, and potato chip sandwich. Robert was gallant enough to try to eat it, chewed the meat-turned-leather for a few minutes, and finally gave up.

"I'm sorry," I said. "I really don't know how to cook. I never learned. Father and I ate out or took sack lunches because he worked in the evenings." I felt more than a little guilty. Meat was rationed; it felt like a crime to waste it.

Robert only laughed. "Finally! Something you don't excel in." He got up and looked in the cupboard. He pulled out a blue box of Kraft Macaroni and Cheese. It was a fairly new product that made a big hit as a substitute for meat and dairy products. And best of all, two boxes required only one rationing coupon.

Typically, Miss Gordon jumped up as the last bite was eaten and started cleaning up the dishes. In her absence, we lingered at the table. After dinner, Robert played the guitar, and I played the piano. I showed William how to feel the vibration of the strings when I hit a piano key.

I tucked William into bed, turned to say good night, and noticed a framed picture of his mother had been placed on his bureau. Nice touch, Robert, I thought to myself. William pointed to the picture and said, "Girl." It sounded like "grrrr."

"Girl! Yes, William! Girl," I repeated the word very clearly. Then I pointed to him. "Boy," I said, and he repeated a sleepy attempt for "boy." I smiled and kissed him on the forehead.

I turned on the radio while I washed up the dinner dishes. Robert helped me dry and put them away. I was eager for the evening news. The war reports were quite encouraging of late. Tonight, the national news broadcast reported that Hitler's armies were starting to get backed into Germany. The reporter announced that Hitler, knowing he was losing the war, had recently created a new militia, requiring all men aged sixteen to sixty to serve.

Robert took the dish towel out of my hands to hang it on the rack to dry. "Can you imagine, asking a sixty-year-old man to be a soldier? There must not be any men left in Germany," Robert said.

I shrugged my shoulders.

"Doesn't that bother you?"

"No! I pray every day that Germany will lose this war! And soon. Hitler must be stopped!" I said it with such severity that Robert looked taken aback. I turned back to the sink, embarrassed, my face flushed.

He turned off the radio. "Enough news for tonight." He filled up Dog's water bowl and put it by the door before leaving to go to his office. "The end of the war will come, Louisa. Try to be patient."

In the middle of the night, I woke myself up, gasping for air, crying out, trembling in fear.

Robert stood at my door, looking stricken. "Louisa, what is it? What's wrong?"

I was so frightened from my nightmare that I couldn't talk.

He turned on the light next to my bed. "Would it help to tell me about the dream?"

I shook my head.

"Try."

"Der Alptraum. Ebendasselbe!"

"Wait, slow down. English, Louisa. You're speaking in German."

"It's the same nightmare I've had before." My heart raced. I tried to speak between sobs. "I'm in Dachau. In Germany. It's a terrible place. It's a relocation camp for Jews and Gypsies and anyone else the Nazis want to get rid of. It has high fences and barbed wire. And gas chambers. And tall chimney stacks for the crematorium. And the evil there, it's palpable."

I paused to take deep gulps of breaths. "Standing at the fence is my father, my mother, my aunt, and my little cousin, Elisabeth, and Deidre, and Mrs. Steinhart, my other friends, and all of the Bonhoeffers. Everyone I knew and loved in Germany. They're all in the camp, faces pressed against the wire fence, barbed wire above us, and they're reaching their hands out for me. Through the fence, their hands try to grab on to me. Begging me to help them. Asking me for food and water." I gasped for air. "And I just keep walking past."

"It's just a nightmare. It isn't real."

"But it is real! Dachau is real! All of those camps are real!"

"But you're not there. You're here in Copper Springs, Louisa, not in Dachau. You're safe. It was just a bad dream."

"You don't understand. I *should* be there. It isn't right I'm here and they're there."

"No, sweetheart, it isn't right that *they* are there."

William's head poked around my door. The light in my room must have woken him. Seeing his innocent face helped me shake off that feeling of dread from my nightmare. I motioned to have him climb up on the bed. He scrambled up, wiggling under the covers. Calmer now, I asked Robert, "do you mind if he stays?"

"Sure. Will you to be able to sleep?"

I nodded.

Robert turned off the light. "Night," He said before closing the door. I snuggled William close to me. Just as I was drifting back to sleep, my eyes flew open: Robert had called me *sweetheart*.

* * *

My holiday from Miss Gordon only lasted a week. Robert received a telegram from her, telling him she would be returning on Saturday. Miss Gordon wouldn't use the telephone; she didn't trust it. She thought everyone in the county would listen in to her conversation.

Having her away for the week had been such a nice change of routine. William and I galloped our way through correspondence lesson number ten. Robert didn't go out in the evenings as he customarily did. I played the piano whenever I had a whim, which was often. I wondered, a little wistfully, if this was what it would be like to have a family of my own.

Winter, even in a desert, meant the nights grew cold and long as days grew shorter. My garden was winding down. I was outside gathering the last of the broccoli, onions, and carrots into a basket as Rosita and Esmeralda strolled past, Ramon pushing the wheels of his wheelchair beside them.

I had a great admiration for Ramon. I never saw a shred of self-pity. He was proud to have served his country, even if that sacrifice cost him his legs.

"Your Victory Garden looks good, Louisa."

"Thank you!" I replied. "Here, Rosita, take some of my vegetables. I have too many." I put some large onions in her hands and handed Ramon some carrots and broccoli to hold on his lap.

"Louisa, I been thinking. How about you teach my Esmeralda to play on that piano?" Rosita asked.

"Hmmm. I hadn't even considered giving piano lessons. I'll have to ask Miss Gordon when she returns home. She says that a piano sets her teeth on edge."

Rosita laughed. "You think about it and let me know. I think Esmeralda has much talent. I pay you, too."

"No, Rosita, I would teach her as a thank you to you for being such a nice friend to me."

"No deal. Either all business or no deal." Rosita headed back up the street.

Ramon said, "Don't waste your time arguing with Rosita, Louisa. She is like a burro."

I walked over to the church office and asked Robert what he thought about the idea of giving piano lessons. "What do you think your aunt would say?"

He shrugged.

"Then I could help pay for my expenses," I offered.

"Louisa, I didn't give you the piano so you would feel the need to earn an income. If you want to teach lessons and Aunt Martha agrees to it, then the decision is yours. But you keep your money. You more than earn your keep. I just wanted you to be able to play."

"Maybe I could teach on Wednesday nights when she goes to choir practice. I could save the money I earn for my return ticket to Germany after the war is over. It should be over soon, don't you think?"

Robert looked at me with a surprised look on his face. "Well, not in the immediate future. It's going to take patience, Louisa." Then, uncharacteristically abrupt, he said, "If you'll excuse me, I need to finish reading this report from the Presbytery." He went back to studying his paper.

* * *

Anticipating Miss Gordon's critical eye for detail, William and I spent all of Saturday morning cleaning and scrubbing the house while Robert went to the train station in Tucson. When she arrived back home, she looked around and sniffed, "Well, I can see nothing has been done while I've been gone. Someone get me my broom."

After she had re-cleaned the house, I asked her what she thought if I were to give Esmeralda a piano lesson once a week.

Not too surprisingly, she would have none of it. "I need that like a submarine needs a screen door. Besides, a parsonage is not a place for commercial enterprise," she said, effectively closing the subject.

* * *

My first Christmas in America came quietly on a clear, cold day. Robert was busy with the Christmas Eve service, so we opened gifts on Christmas morning. The hit of the morning was a slightly used red bicycle for William from his father, boldly waiting under the tree. Like so many manufactured products, bicycles weren't being made during these war years, so Robert had to hunt to find one. Symbolic, it seemed, of Robert's change in perceiving William as a normal child who was hard-of-hearing rather than as a handicapped child.

I had made a bargain with Miss Bentley for used books from the library's book sale. In exchange, I was the guest reader for the Children's Story Hour for the next three Wednesdays. I'd been eager to get started on teaching William to read, so I was thrilled when I stumbled on a well-loved set of the *McGuffy Readers*.

For Miss Gordon, I chose a slightly used *Good Housekeeping* 1943 cookbook that included a special section for rationed foods. And I found Robert a thick and exhaustive book on the history of copper mining. That book looked new; I doubted it had ever been checked out. A slim audience, I reasoned. Robert was delighted with it.

Then Robert and his aunt surprised me with a radio for my bedroom. "I can't stand listening to any more of those depressing news reports you're so hooked on," she chided.

"But they're not depressing if you hear news reports of Allied victories!" I defended.

Rosita had given me a coupon she had hand-made to be used for a free haircut at her salon. I frowned when I saw it; I knew she was eager to update my hairstyle. I stood up to gather some of the wrappings for Miss Gordon's recycling bin. She was in the kitchen, basting the Christmas turkey, and William was spinning the wheels on his bicycle. The house smelled heavenly.

I sat down again, transfixed, closing my eyes to savor the morning, wanting to cement every detail in my mind. My thoughts drifted back to one year ago today. I was alone on an impersonal cargo ship, tossing about on the freezing winter cold of the Atlantic Ocean, knowing I couldn't go back and unsure of what lay ahead of me. And who knew where I would be this time next year?

Robert interrupted my musings by handing me a brown paper package, wrapped with a piece of twine. I looked up at him, puzzled.

"Open it," he said with a shy grin.

It was a book of compositions by Felix Mendelssohn. I turned over each page, hearing the scores dance in my head. He had remembered Mendelssohn was my favorite composer. I had told him nearly a year ago on that first drive back from Mrs. Drummond's house. I had to blink back tears as I thanked him.

Miss Gordon outdid herself on a delicious Christmas feast and then wouldn't let anyone help her clean the kitchen. "Everyone out! You're all as slow as molasses on a January morning," she said, shooing us out. So I sat by the parlor window, warmed by the afternoon sun, looking more carefully through the book of Mendolssohn compositions, but I kept getting distracted by the sight out the window.

Out on the empty street, Robert patiently taught William how to ride the new red bicycle. Over and over they started. Robert held on to the back of the bicycle seat. As William gained speed, Robert would let go. William would pedal madly until he realized that his father wasn't holding on. Then he would start to weave, his bicycle would lean precariously over, and Robert would catch the back of the bicycle seat to help him regain his balance. And his confidence.

Progress was slow, but the joy on William's face was immeasurable.

Miss Gordon came to see what I was watching. We both watched the hard-at-work pair. Then she remarked, "I don't think I've ever seen them like that."

"Like what?" I asked, eyes fixed on them.

"Happy." With sudden and inexplicable affection, she kissed me on the top of my head and went back into the kitchen.

Not long into the New Year of 1944, Miss Gordon's cousin, Ada, wrote to say she was planning to come for a visit to help her recover from the loss of her husband, Teddy. I relinquished my bedroom and prepared to bunk in William's room on one of the twin beds.

I was expecting a woman much like Miss Gordon, so I cleaned my room inside and out and tried to think up more places for William and me to go, to get out of the house as much as possible. Not for the first time, I grumbled to myself that Copper Springs sorely needed a bus system. Not that I had any place in mind to go, but a bus would have been particularly useful during times of visits from any Gordon relatives.

Robert went to the train station to meet Ada. A few hours later, she burst through the front door without even a knock, as Robert lugged suitcases the size of coffins behind her. "Yoo hoo! Marty Girl! Where are you?!"

Marty Girl? Could she *possibly* be referring to Miss Gordon?

Miss Gordon hurried to the door to greet her. William and I were in the kitchen. I motioned to him to come, and we both went quickly to the parlor to discover the source of this exuberance.

"There's my Marty Girl!" exclaimed our high-spirited guest.

I'd never seen anyone dare to hug Miss Gordon, yet here was a short, generously proportioned woman, head covered with bleached blond curls, pink cheeks, polished crimson fingernails, giving her a bone-crushing hug. Ada's perfume filled the room, a strong rose aroma that latched on and lingered to our clothing.

"And there's my quiet little Billy boy!" Ada smothered William with hugs and kisses, which he wiped off dramatically. "Oh Bobby, he's grown a foot or two since you came to Phoenix last spring to see that doctor. He is adorable. *Just* adorable!"

Then she spotted me. "And you are Louisa. May I call you Lulu? And please call me Ada. No need to stand on formalities with cousin Ada!" She grabbed me so tightly that she lifted me off of my feet, leaving me breathless. And off she went to explore the house, oohing and aahing over every little detail.

I looked at Robert in genuine astonishment. "And she's really, truly a Gordon?" I whispered.

"Yes, of course," he answered, as if anyone could ever doubt the family resemblance. "Well, less so after she married her third husband, a Greek fellow. Teodor Stephanopolos. Teddy, she called him. He was her favorite husband."

Just then, Ada called down to Robert from the top of the stairs. "Bobby, would you be a lamb and bring up my suitcases to this charming little boudoir?"

Robert picked up the suitcases and looked back at me. "Cousin Ada can really kiss the Blarney Stone." He stopped himself. "Sorry. I meant that she can be very persuasive. Just...just be careful," he warned with a smile.

No sooner had he finished that sentence than Dog came charging into the parlor, barking and sniffing, let in the kitchen door by William. He skidded to a halt in front of one of Ada's pieces of baggage: a small crate with a little wire window on one end. From the crate erupted a terrible hissing and clawing sound.

Things were definitely getting interesting in the Gordon household.

Ada talked endlessly about everything and had more enthusiasm for life than anyone I'd ever known. She and her Teddy had traveled the world, in between world wars, and she could wax ecstatic over any country.

"Oh! Africa! The wildlife! The scenery!" Then she would launch into a riveting story about being on safari. "Oh! Egypt! The pyramids! The Sphinx!" And she would regale us with fascinating stories about the pharaohs buried with their riches, still waiting for their heavenly reward.

At least, I thought her tales were fascinating. Miss Gordon, I noticed, seemed less enamored.

When Robert informed Ada that I had studied classical piano, I thought she would nearly faint. She couldn't get enough of my playing. "Oh, Marty Girl, you don't realize what kind of treasure you have, living here with you in Copper Springs." Ada was an enthusiastic patron of the arts. A board member, she often reminded us, of the illustrious Phoenix Symphony.

I don't think Marty Girl had ever given much thought to my piano playing before Ada's visit, other than how the sound annoyed her. Yet, unwittingly influenced by cousin Ada's zeal for music, I even caught Miss Gordon humming a selection I had played. I played more of the piano in that week than I had since Robert had purchased it from Betty Drummond.

"Darling Lulu," Ada would exclaim. "Let's have another concert tonight!" I played as many pieces as I could play from memory: Handel, Haydn, Brahms, Schumann, and Schubert, including all of the compositions from my new Mendolssohn book.

"Any Wagner, dearest?"

"No! Not Wagner," I said. "I refuse to play Richard Wagner's works. Hitler idolized him for his relationship with Nietzsche and for his anti-Semitic beliefs. I *won't* play Wagner."

"Of course. My apologies," quelled Ada. "Well, could you play any Tchaikovsky? I just love Russian composers. Oh, the angst of the Russians!"

"No."

"Italians? Rossini's 'William Tell Overture?' Vivaldi? Scaflatti? Oh, the passion of the Italians!"

I shook my head.

"Any French? Claude Debussy? Chopin?" Her voice trailed off.

"No. Definitely not Chopin. He was Polish. Poland was one of the first countries Hitler took over. Hitler only allowed the study of German composers in University. Well, except for Mozart. He was Austrian, but Hitler quickly adopted Mozart after he invaded Austria in the Anschluss."

"How barbaric! Well my love, we simply must do something about that."

I wasn't quite sure what she meant by that until she started making comments such as: "You know, darling Lulu, Phoenix would be a far more stimulating place for you. Culturally speaking, I mean." Or "Really, Bobby, talent such as Lulu's mustn't be wasted here in Copper Springs. Not that there's anything wrong with such an adorable little village. But I have so many connections in Phoenix!" Or "think of how we could develop her, my sweet Marty Girl!"

The truth was that I had the talent but not the ambition for the concert stage. Not after the war began. The war had changed everything for me.

Ada asked me outright one day if I'd like to come live in Phoenix with her.

"Thank you so much," I declined, "but I am planning to return to Germany quite soon." And I was. I was feeling encouraged about assured Allied victory after Italy's surrender and Mussollini's arrest just a short while ago.

It was apparent Ada was starting to grate on Miss Gordon. I heard her complain to Robert in the morning before Ada woke up, but I had lost my usual eavesdropping capability because Ada had taken over my room and, in it, my radiator pipe.

As I came downstairs one morning, I overheard Miss Gordon grumbling, "and in her book, there's nothing right about Copper Springs. It's Phoenix this or Phoenix that." Then she must have heard my footsteps coming down the stairs, and the subject was promptly dropped.

Another time, I was even more astounded as I listened, furtively, to her rant and rave to Robert. "And so poor Dog has been stuck outside all week just so that vicious little cat can have the run of the place and ruin the furniture!"

Since when had Miss Gordon felt any concern for Dog's feelings?

I was starting to see a new side of Miss Gordon, one that gave me the slightest trace of tenderness toward her. I could see how she had grown up in the shadow of Ada, always being outdone by her flamboyance, her social status, her matrimonial state.

Ada was larger than life. And now, for the first time, I think Martha Gordon had something or someone in her life that cousin Ada envied. And wanted. *Me.*

I spent the rest of Ada's visit basking in my new status as favorite houseguest. Thanks to Ada, I had been elevated from a mere annoyance to an annoyance with some potential. I was sorry to see the week come to an end. Until, that is, the very last night. After that, I was more than ready to say goodbye to Ada. In fact, I would've carried her all the way to Phoenix myself, given the opportunity.

Miss Gordon had gone to bed, as had William, and Robert had left for a meeting with the church elders. I was getting ready to go upstairs myself when Ada called to me from the kitchen, "Lulu, darling, come join me for a little entertainment. Let's have a little card game before I leave town tomorrow."

I sat down at the table with her. Next to her was a tall bottle of clear liquid and two small jelly glasses. "I've never played cards before, Ada."

"Never played cards?! Oh Lulu, darling, we have some catching up to do. Don't you worry. I've always wanted a protégé. I'm going to teach you an easy little game called Blackjack."

We played a few hands as I caught on to the concept.

"Sharp as a tack, that's my Lulu girl!" she enthused. "Let's make it a little more fun. My Teddy loved this game." She poured the glasses with an inch of the clear liquid from the bottle. "So whenever we reach twenty-one, we drink!"

As soon as her cards added up to twenty-one, she yelled, "down the hatch!" and swallowed her drink in one gulp.

I followed her example. As the clear liquid reached the back of my throat, the stinging began. It felt as if I had bees in my throat. "What is this?" I asked, coughing violently.

"Ouzo! It's Greek. One of the last bottles of Teddy's special collection before he died." She brushed away a tear from the corner of her eye. "He would've been crazy for you, Lulu. You're the daughter we've always wanted. And you would've loved my Teddy, too. The Greeks know how to enjoy life like no one else."

I didn't want to be rude but this Ouzo tasted like petrol. She didn't seem to notice my grimacing face as she refilled the glasses. Just one more hand of cards, I warned myself. I didn't want to hurt Ada's feelings, especially as she was so fond of me, but I had no intention to drink petrol all night. Another hand of cards went quickly, and Ada bellowed "Bottoms up!" and gulped down her Ouzo.

Again, I followed her example to be polite and looked for an opportunity to excuse myself and go to bed. Ada had other ideas. No sooner was my glass back on the table, but it was re-filled. I was starting to get warm. Hot, actually.

"Lulu, sweetness, I would love it if you would come to Phoenix this summer and play the piano for my bridge parties."

What did she just say? My thoughts felt fuzzy. Did she say something about bridges?

"So what would you say if we put a little wager on the next game? If I win, you come and play for my bridge parties this summer. If you lose, you come and play for my bridge parties."

"Pardon, Ada? Would you mind repeating that?"

"If I win, you come and play for my bridge parties this summer. If you lose, then you come and play for my bridge parties," she patiently repeated. I nodded, not really concentrating, distracted by the queasy pit in my stomach from the Ouzo.

I wasn't sure how much time passed before Robert came in through the kitchen door. For an eternity, he just stared at us, eyes wide open, jaw dropped in horror. "Oh, cousin Ada! *No!* You *didn't!* You *couldn't* have! Louisa, how much have you had?" He picked up at the half-empty bottle of Ouzo and glowered at Ada.

I stood up. The room started spinning. "It's not her fault, Robert," I tried to say, but suddenly I had to run upstairs to the bathroom. *Fast.*

The next morning, I woke up after hearing a persistent knocking at the door. Robert came in, holding a glass that looked like tomato juice in it. "William came downstairs and told me you're dead." He handed me the drink. "I said I would come up to check and see if you're a goner."

"Close," I said feebly, "but not quite."

"Drink this," he said. "And take these." He handed me two aspirin.

"Oh no, Robert, I can't possibly drink that. Or anything else. Ever again."

"Trust me. It will make you feel better."

I took a sip, nearly gagging. My tongue felt thick.

"Keep drinking."

I took a few more sips and grimaced. "What is this?"

"You don't want to know. But I promise you'll feel better if you can drink the entire thing."

"I recall your cousin telling me the same thing last night." I dropped my head back on the pillow.

He laughed. "How much did she take you for?"

I opened one eye. "What do you mean?"

"Blackjack. What did she make you bet?"

I cringed. "Robert, please stop shouting at me." I tried to sit up in bed, hands holding my throbbing head. "She said something about playing the piano on bridges." I tried to get up, but if I moved, my head pounded like someone was beating it with a drum.

"Louisa, you've been had by a card shark."

"What does that mean?"

"Ada cornered you into playing the piano at her bridge parties. It's a card game for the socialite set."

"You could have warned me. She seemed like such a nice lady."

"I did! The day she first arrived I said to be careful of her."

"But you didn't say what to be careful of. You never said anything about Blackjack and Ouzo. I'm not blaming you. Good heavens, I'm a grown woman. I'm a Resistance Worker. I have no one to blame but myself." I was thoroughly disgusted with myself.

"She's pretty smooth. I've been a victim of her charms myself." He went over to open the curtain, letting the merciless sunshine in, piercing my eyes with pain.

Wincing, I asked, "What did she get out of you?"

"Preaching. Two sermons a day for a week at her church's revival meeting. Under a tent. In Phoenix. In August. No air conditioning." He shuddered at the memory. "Drink up. She's almost ready to leave so you'll need to come downstairs as soon as you can."

I scowled at him which only got him laughing. His face was annoyingly bright with good humor. "Hurry up, she's waiting for you," he said. He stopped when he got to the door and turned toward me with a wicked grin. "Such a pity. Who would've thought? A Resistance Worker, succumbing to the oldest trick in the book. You're losing your edge, Lulu."

My sentiments precisely.

I took a shower, dressing slowly so that my head wouldn't explode, and then went downstairs. Robert's concoction, whatever it was, did help settle my stomach. A little, anyway. As I stepped into the kitchen, Ada rushed over to me with open arms. "There's my darling Lulu!" She was apparently unfazed by the Ouzo.

Miss Gordon's eyes swept over me. "What's wrong with you? You look like death warmed over."

"She's got a touch of the flu," Robert offered quickly.

Miss Gordon eyed him carefully then whipped around to look over at the kitchen sink. There lay a broken egg shell, a can of tomato juice, vegetable oil, and some hot pepper sauce. She spun on her heels to Ada. "A touch of the flu, my foot! Ada! What did you do to that girl?"

"Nothing, Marty Girl. Nothing at all!" Ada smiled the sweetest smile, gave everyone enormous hugs that left us reeking of heavy rose perfume, and swept out to the Hudson. Dragging her heavy suitcases, Robert followed behind to take her back to the train station in Tucson.

Miss Gordon watched Robert load up the car with Ada's behemoth suitcases. There wasn't even room for William to tag along. "I'd like to give that woman a dressing down," she muttered under her breath. Then she turned to me, with ever so slight a hint of sympathy in her voice. "Louisa, I blame myself. I should've warned you. That woman can't be trusted. Given a bottle of Ouzo, she could charm the spots off a leopard."

That remark got me wondering if, like Robert, she had once been the unfortunate victim of Ada's gambling savvy, but I doubted I would ever be privy to that story. I looked out the kitchen window as I saw the Hudson pull out of the driveway, Ada chattering away to her captive chauffeur. Dog followed the car down the street, barking angrily, grievously insulted, anxious to get the last word in at Ada's visiting feline.

"Louisa, I've been thinking. Since you've got your heart set on it, I suppose you could teach piano an afternoon or two here at the house."

I turned around and looked back at her, astonished.

"Well, Mrs. Wondolowski has been badgering me to have you teach her son, Arthur. I suppose it wouldn't really hurt the church's image to have the parsonage be used for a commercial enterprise," she grudgingly conceded.

I smiled, feeling cheered, and went over and gave her a big hug, not caring if she liked it or not.

Chapter Ten

With the blessing of Miss Gordon, my piano teaching career began. Two afternoons a week, I taught a few neighborhood children the fundamentals of piano.

And in the nightstand next to my bed was a drawer, my version of a bank account, collecting money for my return trip to Germany. Miss Gordon called it a "saving my bacon" drawer. I suppose I could've opened a bank account at Mueller's bank, but I wanted no interest from Herr Mueller, financially or otherwise.

"Can you imagine?" I said to Robert one morning at breakfast, pointing to the front page of the newspaper. After a three year blockade, the Russian city of Leningrad was finally freed from the Germans. "Nine hundred days under siege! The Germans couldn't overtake them because their resistance was so strong. It says that the Russian people carried on with their life, attended school, and took exams, even though they experienced daily bombings. The death toll had reached over 600,000 people...starved or killed. So immeasurably sad. But they did it! They beat back the Nazis."

I inhaled a deep sigh of satisfaction, assured that Allied victory was just around the corner.

* * *

Long after midnight one night came a knock at the door. I heard Robert go downstairs to answer it so I rolled over to fall back to sleep. A minute or so later, he rapped on my door and opened it. "Louisa, come downstairs. There's someone here for you."

I threw on my bathrobe and went down to the parlor. There on the davenport sat a woeful young woman, bruised and bleeding, eyes cast downward.

"Glenda?" I asked. "What's happened to you?" I rushed to her side and pushed her hair back from her face to examine her bruises. "Robert, please get me some hot water and clean cloths. Bandages and peroxide, too." I turned back to Glenda. "Do you need a doctor?"

She shook her head. "No, don't call no doctor. I just can't go back there no more."

Robert brought me the supplies to clean her up.

I looked at him and said, "You can go back to bed. I'll explain more to you in the morning."

"Sure you don't need help?" he asked, concerned.

"No, thank you."

As he headed back up the stairs, Miss Gordon stood at the top, arms crossed like a general facing battle. Robert cut her off before she started on a tirade. "Tomorrow. We'll talk about it tomorrow. Go back to bed, Aunt Martha."

She turned and firmly shut her bedroom door.

I bathed Glenda's bruises and cuts, swabbed peroxide onto the swelling lesions, bandaged her as best I could, and gave her some aspirin for the pain. "You're safe here," I said, as I settled her in for the night in my bedroom.

In the morning, I woke to hear a loud whisper in the kitchen. It sounded like the buzzing of an angry bee. Still sleepy, I walked into the kitchen and saw Robert and a dour looking Miss Gordon. Conversation ceased as I walked in. I filled up a coffee cup, sipped it, and braced myself for Miss Gordon. As if on cue, she launched a verbal blitz.

"Was that you sleeping out there on that sofa? I thought it was that girl. Do you mean to tell me that you gave up your bed for a common harlot?"

"She needed to rest. She's badly hurt. I knew you and Robert would be up early. I didn't want you to awaken her."

"Louisa, where did you meet her?" Robert asked.

I took a sip of coffee. "In the library. When William and I would be in the children's department, I often saw her over in a corner. Her name is Glenda. She's been trying to teach herself to read. That's how we became acquainted. I've been helping her learn."

"And you haven't said a word? How long has this been going on?" asked Miss Gordon.

"A few months."

"You've exposed William to that girl!" she accused.

"But it's not like *that*. She's trying hard to make a change. Sometimes people end up in circumstances that they'd never dream they'd be in. I'm only trying to help her." I put down my coffee cup on the counter.

"There's not a circumstance sorry enough on this earth to make someone become a prostitute," she said with a scornful air. "A girl goes that way because she's a bad apple to start with. And now you've sullied the Gordon name by bringing her into this house! A minister's home! Of *all* places."

She narrowed her eyes and began her final attack. "Louisa, you are the very soul of aggravation! I have put up with a dog, and I have put up with notes stuck all over this house, and I have put up with a permanent houseguest, but this is the last straw. Either that girl goes or I go. Today!" Her nostrils flared in outrage.

I took a deep breath. *Lord, give me patience!* "I'm sorry. I'll make other arrangements for Glenda. Today." I slipped out the backdoor.

Robert followed behind me, carrying my coffee cup. "Wait, Louisa! Where are you going?"

"Just to take a walk. Please leave me be." I kept walking.

"I really wouldn't do that if I were you," he called out with authority.

I stopped and turned slightly. "And why not?" I snapped, not interested in hearing *another* Gordon opinion.

"Because you're wearing your bathrobe. And you're barefoot."

I slumped my shoulders and turned back to go to the house.

"Come sit down on the steps with me for a minute."

He handed me the coffee cup as I sat down next to him. The contrast of its warmth felt soothing in my hands as the crisp morning air surrounded us.

"You didn't do anything wrong, Louisa. Just the opposite. You saw a woman trying to better herself, and you've tried to help her."

"I never dreamed she would come here in the night, Robert."

"She must trust you. She probably doesn't have anyone else she can count on."

"I'm sorry about your aunt." I rolled my eyes.

"Well, we could have guessed her reaction."

"That's why I never mentioned Glenda! I knew she would chew my head off."

"Bite your head off," he corrected, trying to hold back a grin. "And she sure did."

I frowned at him. That's *exactly* why I didn't adopt American expressions. I always got them wrong. "Glenda is going to need someone to take care of her for a while. Someone treated her terribly."

"Mick," he guessed, frowning. Mick Hills ran the Tavern where Glenda worked. "He's got a reputation for a fiery temper."

I looked into my coffee cup and said, more to myself than to Robert, "What am I going to do with her?"

"We'll figure something out," he said. He jumped up and looked down at me. "You know, I just might have an idea. When Glenda wakes up, have her try to eat something, and clean her up as best as you can. Loan her some fresh clothes. I might have just a place for her."

"Why? What are you thinking?"

He wouldn't answer. He took my coffee cup and finished off the last few sips, handed it back to me, smiled, told me not to worry, jumped into the Hudson and backed out of the driveway.

After watching him drive down the street, I slowly turned to go back to the kitchen, steeling myself for another encounter with Miss Gordon.

She was so disgusted with having a girl like Glenda in the house that she woke William up and took him on errands, just so he wouldn't be "further corrupted by Glenda's influence." Amazingly, she even took Dog with her, to keep Dog uncorrupted, as well, I suppose.

I did exactly as Robert asked and helped get Glenda dressed in one of my skirts and blouses. Her eyes looked so beaten down. She did everything I asked, just like a little child.

An hour or so later, Robert pulled into the driveway. He popped into the kitchen and asked if Glenda was ready to go.

"You'd better come, too, Louisa." We put Glenda in the backseat. As we drove down the street, we passed Herr Mueller standing in front of his bank. He stopped and stared at us as we drove past him. His stare made me shudder. Robert would say I was just being paranoid, but Herr Mueller always seemed to be watching me.

"Glenda, we're taking you to a woman named Betty Drummond. She lives alone on a little farm, way out of town. Her grandmother died recently, and Betty's been lonesome. She's good at nursing, too. Nursed her grandmother for years. I went to talk to her this morning, and she agreed to take care of you, at least until you're back on your feet. Does that sound fine to you?"

Glenda nodded. "But I ain't ever goin' back to Mick's. I'm done."

"I'm glad to hear you say that," Robert said. "We'll help you figure out what to do when you're mended."

When we reached Betty's home, she had already made up the guestroom for Glenda and put flowers from the garden by the bedside. "Nobody's done such nice things for me before. I thank you," she said, climbing into bed.

"You're safe now, Glenda. No one can hurt you out here," Robert said. "If you don't mind, I'd like to say a prayer before we go."

Glenda looked away. I put a hand on her shoulder as Robert bowed his head, not waiting for her answer. "Lord, please heal Glenda's body and her spirit. We ask you to bless Betty, too, for being so gracious as to take care of Glenda. We know you love Glenda, Lord, for you brought friends to her to take care of her. We pray for your protection over her, and for justice to be delivered to the person who harmed her. Amen."

Then he added, "Glenda, Louisa and I will come out now and then to check on you."

One little teardrop escaped and rolled down her cheek before she wiped it away.

Downstairs, I handed Betty a bag. "I brought some books for Glenda. She's just learning to read. She's smart, too. She's already on first grade readers. I thought you might be able to help her, if you have a free minute."

From the look on Betty's face, I wasn't sure who was going to benefit more—Glenda from Betty's care or Betty, from having someone to fuss over.

On the car ride home I looked over at Robert and smiled at him. "Nice work, Reverend."

He glanced back at me with a shy grin. "Well, Betty could use a little extra cash right now. The church has a budget to pay for emergencies like this."

I knew the church didn't have any such emergency fund. I knew Robert would be paying Betty out of his own modest salary.

After dinner that evening, Mick Hills came to our door. Miss Gordon opened it and nearly suffered heart failure. She sent Mick over to Robert's office. Back she marched into the kitchen, grumbling loudly with a resentful toss of her head in my direction, "twice in one day. I start the day with a prostitute and end the day with a panderer. That's a fine kettle of fish."

I darted out of the kitchen, hoping to avoid hearing another diatribe about how I had further sullied the fine Gordon name.

A while later, I heard Robert come in through the kitchen door. I ran downstairs to meet him. "What did he want? Why did he come to see you?"

"Where's Aunt Martha?" he asked, glancing around for her.

"She went up to bed with a headache."

Robert sat down at the kitchen table and pulled a seat out for me. "He said Glenda has talked about you at the tavern. He took a guess that she came here."

"He doesn't know where she is now, though, does he?"

He shook his head. "No idea. He didn't even seem to care about that. He just wanted me to know that he wasn't the one who hurt Glenda. And he gave me this for her." He pulled out a crisp new one hundred dollar bill. "He said it was her back wages."

"Who did harm her?"

"He refused to say. All that he said is that it won't happen again."

I turned over the hundred dollar bill. "Do you think this money is to keep Glenda silent?" I asked.

"I hadn't thought of that." He scratched his chin. "Do you think she might confide in you about who did this to her?"

"I don't know." I tilted my head. "Are you convinced Mick was telling you the truth?"

"I can't be positive, but I didn't get the impression that he was lying." He looked straight at me. "Why? What are you thinking? That someone wants to keep Mick quiet, too?"

That's *exactly* what I was thinking. And I had a sneaking suspicion who that someone might be. There only one man in this town with money to throw around. But to Robert, I only shrugged. He often told me that my imagination worked overtime and probably would've dismissed my concerns as being ridiculously suspicious. I needed proof.

And, this morning, I might have found it.

* * *

A few weeks went by before Robert and I went out to check on Glenda and Betty. Glenda's bruises were healing well, and she was thriving under Betty's motherly care. As Betty went to the kitchen to prepare a pot of tea for us, Robert gave Glenda the hundred dollar bill from Mick, explaining that it was back wages. A shadow passed over Glenda's face as she accepted the cash, almost reluctantly.

"How is your reading coming along?" I asked her, trying to change the subject.

She brightened immediately and told me there was a book on her nightstand that she was almost able to read completely.

"Let me go get it and hear you read aloud." I ran upstairs and then, quietly, closed Glenda's bedroom door. I felt a pang of guilt as I snooped around but not enough to stop me. There was something in this room that I needed to find.

I opened up the drawer to her nightstand but it wasn't there. I hunted in her closet and found the sweater she had been wearing that night she came to the parsonage, bruised and bleeding. I checked the pockets. And there it was: a man's large ruby ring.

When I had given Glenda my clothes to wear, I had picked up her sweater and the ring dropped out of the pocket, rolling on the floor. She had been in the room with me at the time and snatched the ring off the floor, hiding it in her hand.

Today, I slipped the ring into my skirt pocket, picked up the book, and hurried downstairs.

Glenda read the book aloud. I asked her to read it again, just for practice. "Even better! Glenda, you're doing very well."

After tea, Robert and I said goodbye to the two women. We both felt much better than we had the last time we'd left them as we drove down the highway.

Suddenly, reddish-brown walls of dust covered the Hudson. Robert pulled off to the side of the road as far as possible and set the emergency brake. "We need to wait this out," he said. Dust storms usually only lasted a few minutes, but they could strike without warning in the desert and make driving conditions very hazardous. "Roll your window up tightly."

I used the lull to tell Robert my suspicion that Herr Mueller was the one responsible for hurting Glenda. I told him all about her nephew, Tommy, and that I thought Herr Mueller might be deceiving Glenda about Tommy's whereabouts.

His skeptical response was just what I had anticipated. "Louisa, I realize you don't like the man, but you can't just leap to the assumption that he would be visiting a brothel, beating up a girl and kidnapping a child."

"Why are you so certain it couldn't be Herr Mueller?"

"Because he's a married man. He attends church. He's a leader in the community. Those aren't the kind of men who visit brothels."

And he called *me* naïve. "What if I could prove it to you?"

"How? Glenda and Mick won't say who is responsible."

"Do you ever remember noticing a large ring on Herr Mueller's hand? It was big and flashy with a bright red ruby in the center."

"I never noticed."

I took the ring out of my pocket and held it out in my hand.

He picked it up and examined it. "Where did you get this?"

I explained how I had found the ring in her sweater a few weeks ago.

"Louisa, I don't want you to do anything about this right now."

"Why not? I have proof! I just need to convince Glenda to talk. I think she took this ring as insurance."

"What do you mean?"

"I just have a feeling she knows she might have trouble getting her nephew back. I think she took the ring to be able to force Herr Mueller's hand."

He was thoughtful for a moment. "I still don't want you to do anything about this right now."

"But why not now? Glenda is doing much better. You saw that for yourself."

"Because I'm going out of town for a while and I don't want to have to worry about this while I'm gone."

What? Robert was leaving? "When? Where are you going?"

"I'm going to North Carolina for a General Assembly meeting for the Presbyterian Church. I'm leaving at the end of next week."

"How long will you be gone?"

"A week or two."

I was quiet after that.

"Louisa, for now, Glenda is mending. She needs peace and quiet. Leave it alone until I get back."

Just then the dust cloud lifted, and he started up the Hudson, heading home. But as it lifted and the air cleared, I was left feeling completely churned up inside.

* * *

The evening before he left, Robert went up to his room to pack. I brought up fresh laundry Miss Gordon had ironed for his trip. With my arms full of laundry, I knocked on his door and waited until he opened it.

"If I was learning English all over again, I would skip learning grammar and take a class that just taught common expressions. It seems as if that is the true spoken language of all Americans," I decided as I handed him one stack of shirts.

He put the laundry on his bed. "Especially true in Copper Springs," he said. "It's a fascinating language of word pictures." He pulled his suitcase down from his closet shelf. "Why? What did Aunt Martha say?" His eyes were smiling.

"She wondered if the cat's got my tongue."

He laughed as if that was a very funny remark. He was feeling quite cheerful about this trip.

I wasn't.

"Why is that so funny? I know the words, but I just can't understand what they mean. I just hate feeling...not smart."

"Exactly why it is amusing!"

I raised an eyebrow at him, irritated.

"It's a saying used when someone seems unusually quiet. It comes from an old punishment when the tongues were cut out of prisoners' mouths and fed to the cats."

I looked at him in horror which only got him laughing again. I shuddered in disgust and handed him the other armful of laundry.

"Thank you. I'll need these." He put the pile down next to his suitcase and started to pack. He glanced up at me. "You do seem a little out of sorts lately."

I ignored that remark. "When are you coming back again?"

"I've told you three or four times. A few weeks. Why do you keep asking me?"

"Because it's always changing." It was always getting longer.

"Well, I've heard Dr. Peter Marshall might attend."

"Who is Peter Marshall?"

"He's a Scottish minister with an excellent preaching reputation. He pastors the church where Abraham Lincoln used to worship, right in Washington D.C. Called New York Avenue Presbyterian Church."

"A Presbyterian *and* a Scotsman. No wonder you want to meet him."

"Aye, lass. A winning combination," he said, feigning a Scottish accent.

I threw a ball of socks at him from the pile of laundry on his bed. He caught it and tossed it into his suitcase, an uncontrollable grin spreading across his face. I sat down on the bed across from the suitcase. "And you have a ride to the train station?"

"Yes. Judge Pryor said he could take me. We're leaving at dawn. He has some law business to do in Tucson and then I can leave the Hudson for you and Aunt Martha. You're going to start taking William to that Bisbee tutor, right?" He glanced up at me as he was putting clothes into his suitcase.

I nodded. "First meeting is scheduled for next week."

"I might talk to Judge Pryor about Mueller and the ring, Louisa. I just want you to promise to leave it alone until I get back."

"I promise. I told you that," I said, sounding a little more annoyed than I intended to sound.

He stopped packing and looked right at me. "Are you all right?"

"I'm fine."

"Have you heard some news about Dietrich?"

"No. Still no trial. He is getting some letters smuggled out. The warders and the guards are helping him, amazingly

185

enough. They let him have visitors. But that's all that I've heard."

"Are you worried about him?"

"Of course."

"Is that why you seem so quiet lately?"

"I told you. I'm fine."

"Not worried about Glenda?"

I shook my head.

"Or Mueller?" He eyed me with suspicion. "You're not cooking up another crazy evil scheme that he's up to, are you?"

I frowned at him and stood up to leave. I was not interested in being preached a sermon about the pitfalls of an overactive imagination. I put one hand on the doorknob and turned back to him. "I heard on the news this morning the Germans are withdrawing in Italy. And that's after surrendering in Crimea just a few days ago. Hitler is starting to get backed into Germany. Things are looking good for the war to end soon, don't you think?"

"It's certainly looking better. In Europe, anyway. We're still in for a long fight on the Pacific front, though."

"You'll be back in two weeks?"

"Probably three. Maybe four."

I shut the door behind me, holding on to the doorknob for a moment.

During the night, I woke up and couldn't get back to sleep, so I went downstairs to get one of Robert's thick theology books to read. That always did the trick to help me fall back asleep. He was in the parlor, sitting on the davenport, staring at the fire. I didn't expect him to be downstairs; I thought he had gone to bed hours ago.

"What are you doing up? I thought you were leaving early." I curled up on the opposite end of the davenport.

"Same as you. Couldn't sleep," he answered.

The fire crackled, warming the room with its dancing light.

"So...you're looking forward to this General Assembly meeting?" I asked.

"Yes. I really am. They're creating an important report on a theology called dispensationalism."

"Are you for or against it?"

"It's a little more complicated than that," he said in that condescending tone I knew so well.

"I know, Robert. I've read about it. Dispensationalism believes in a literal interpretation of the Bible and makes careful distinctions between different periods of God's dealings with man." I looked over at him. "Does that cover it?"

Surprised, he answered, "impressive scholarship, Miss Schmetterling."

"Do you think I just borrow your big books to use as a doorstop?" I said, smiling, and turned back to watch the flickering flames of the fire. For a long stretch of minutes, we continued to sit without talking.

Then, without thinking first, I blurted out, "it just won't seem the same while you're away."

He reached over and took my left hand in his, weaving his fingers with mine. "Louisa, I..."

"Don't," I whispered. "Robert, please don't say it." I rose to my feet. "Have a safe trip. Godspeed. And please hurry back." I kissed the top of his head and quickly went up the stairs to my room. I just couldn't bear to see the look in his eyes.

* * *

I thought the first few days after Robert left would be the hardest, but I was mistaken. Each day grew longer, and rather than feel as if it brought his return closer, it only seemed to extend it further.

Throughout each day, I would think of something I wanted to talk to him about, or share a sentence from a wonderful book I was reading, or have William show off his newest words, only to remember that he was gone and it would be weeks before he returned.

To add to that, I worried about the way we left things between us. I knew I had to stop him that night before he said another word. I hoped that by stopping him, things wouldn't change between us. Our friendship could remain just as it was.

Miss Gordon, William, and I went to church on Sunday. In Robert's pulpit stood a minister called a 'supply pastor.' Retired ministers filled in for the active ministers while they were away or on vacation. Reverend Hubbell, an elderly minister recruited from nearby Douglas, a border town to Mexico, agreed to deliver the Sunday sermons for Robert until he returned.

He looked shockingly frail, his skin papery thin, and he had a raspy, feeble voice, not unlike how I imagined Noah's voice would have sounded after climbing a set of stairs in the Ark. Yet when he stood up at that pulpit, out thundered a booming voice.

The text he chose was Ecclesiastes 5:1-7. "When we come to worship before the Lord," he bellowed, "come quietly! Be prepared to listen more than you talk. God is communicating. God is speaking! Listen to the wisdom of King Solomon: 'Keep thy foot when thou goest to the house of God, and be more ready to hear, than to give the sacrifice of fools: for they consider not that they do evil. Be not rash with thy mouth, and let not thine heart be hasty to utter any thing before God: for God is in heaven, and thou upon earth: therefore let thy words be few. For a dream cometh through the multitude of business; and a fool's voice is known by multitude of words. For in the multitude of dreams and many words there are also divers vanities: but fear thou God'."

A nagging thought kept popping up but I squelched it. Was I listening to God about my future? Of course I was! I assured myself. I was convinced God would want me to return to Germany as soon as the war was over.

Reverend Hubbell came over after the service for a light supper of soup and sandwiches before driving back to Douglas. After the blessing, we passed around dishes, and I waited for an opportunity to ask him something that had been needling me.

"Reverend Hubbell," I asked, "do you know a minister in Douglas named Sid Carter?"

"Sid Carter?" he wheezed. "No, can't say that I do."

"Are there many ministers in Douglas?"

"Oh, goodness, no. Just a handful. I know just about everyone in that town. Never heard of a Sid Carter."

I *knew* it. I just *knew* it.

After he left, William and I spent the afternoon at loose ends. Finally Miss Gordon spoke up. "What is the matter with the two of you? You'd think someone had died. For the love of heaven, he'll be back before you know it."

I laughed and turned to say to William, "Do you miss your Dad? You look sad." I made a greatly exaggerated sad face.

"Dad home?" he asked.

"He will come home in three weeks. Twenty-one days," I answered, pointing to the calendar on the wall and counting off the days to underscore what I was saying.

William sighed.

Miss Gordon was right. We needed to get our minds on other things. When she went upstairs to take a nap, I took William out for a bicycle ride. I ran alongside him, up and down the street, Dog galloping along beside us. William didn't really need me trailing him, so I sat down on the grass with Dog and watched him ride. "Not far," I said, using my hands to gesture that he should stay close.

"Okay," he yelled as he pedaled madly down the street toward town.

Rosita came outside and sat down with me. "Louisa, did William just say 'okay'?"

"Yes! That is one word that he can say clearly. Isn't it amazing?"

She smiled, eyes locked on William. "Father Gordon must be so happy."

"He is." I had stopped correcting her title for Robert long ago.

"Seems empty here with him gone."

"He'll be back soon enough," I said, trying to keep my voice light.

"Louisa?" she asked with a shy grin. "I have some happy news. You are the first to know. Ramon and I, we are expecting a baby!"

I hugged her. "Oh, Rosita! That is wonderful news! That is the best news I have heard in a long while."

She chattered away about the baby as I watched her, soaking up her happiness.

Suddenly, I remembered William. I hadn't seen him bicycle back toward me in the last few minutes. Any time he had a little taste of freedom, it meant we ended up with a visit from Herr Mueller. An irate and apoplectic Herr Mueller.

I excused myself from Rosita and went down the street to look for his red bicycle. I found it leaning against the Muellers' fence. Herr Mueller's car was parked on the street. I looked around for William but couldn't find him. Then I saw him scurry around to one of Herr Mueller's car tires, preparing to let the air out of the tire. Quickly, I rushed to him. "William," I said with a stern look of warning. "No!"

He looked back at me with complete innocence written on his face. He grinned and ran to get his bike. He pedaled home as I followed behind him.

What I didn't realize was that he had already flattened one tire by the time I interrupted him. Nor did I notice the baked potato from last night's dinner stuffed into Herr Mueller's car tailpipe. Herr Mueller informed us of those indiscretions later that day in another angry outburst that left Miss Gordon nursing a violent headache.

On Wednesday morning, Miss Gordon and I took William to Bisbee to meet Mrs. Morgan. Violet, she told us to call her. Her personality was just like the flower. Soft and warm like a spring day. She wanted some time alone to evaluate William, so I took Miss Gordon over to the Prospector's Diner. Wilma winked at me when we sat down. "Hi, Wilma," I said, greeting her like an old friend.

"Hey ya, dollface. When are ya coming to work for me?"

"The diner is just a little too far from where I am living, but I thank you for the offer."

"Whatcha gonna have?"

"I'd like boiled leaves. What would you like, Miss Gordon?"

"Actually, I'll have a cup of joe and a life preserver," she answered.

"You got it, dollface," Wilma said, working the gum in her mouth over to one cheek.

"Miss Gordon, you never cease to amaze me!" I said, laughing.

She tried not to look pleased, but smiling eyes betrayed her. Wilma brought her back a cup of coffee with a doughnut and a cup of tea for me. We sat in the quiet, enjoying the atmosphere of the diner. I hesitated to disturb the pleasantness of the moment, but I had been longing to ask her something. I had learned, through experience, it was always best to wait until she was in a good mood. The timing seemed right so I plunged ahead. "What was she like?"

"Who?" She looked at me as if I had lost my mind.

"Ruth."

Miss Gordon stiffened her shoulders, reminding me of Robert. It was the first mannerism I'd ever observed that they shared. "You should ask Robert," she said in a clipped tone.

"I have. He has told me a little about her. I just wondered what your impressions were of her."

She sighed and looked out the window for a long moment before answering. "Well, she was beautiful. Like a movie star."

I hoped she would elaborate. The Gordons could never be accused of sharing more information than was absolutely necessary.

"Did you like her?"

"Like her? At first, I suppose. She could be charming when she wanted to. She and Robert were sweethearts in high school. They seemed like a perfect couple. He so handsome and she so pretty." Her face softened, as if lost in a sweet memory. Then it hardened again. "She was determined to have him, that's for sure." She stopped and sipped her coffee, dipping her doughnut in the steaming brew, slowly chewing. Maddeningly slow.

"So she changed after they married?" I prompted.

She breathed in and out. "Before, I think. They were engaged while he was in seminary and then when his folks died, he decided to come back to Copper Springs." She took a long sip of coffee.

I knew I had to wait patiently for more details.

"She was furious with him for not being willing to leave Copper Springs." She folded the napkin on the booth. "I'm not sure she ever stopped being angry."

"But they married despite that?"

"Robert had promised to marry her. He's a man of his word."

That was certainly true. That's why I was here in his home. He had kept his promise to Dietrich, too.

"I guess she figured she could persuade him to go back to New York after they married. But he wouldn't budge." Then, resuming her businesslike manner, she asked, "why are you asking me about her?"

"It's just so hard to imagine a woman who could leave her own child, much less a husband."

"Robert certainly deserved far better. He deserves far better."

I nodded.

She put her coffee cup down and peered at me with those arched eyebrows. "I wouldn't want to see him hurt again. Nor William."

Her comment caught me off guard, partly because I had not considered Miss Gordon to be overburdened with perception and partly because I shared her concern. My eyes welled up with tears. I looked down at the now tepid tea cup in my hands. "I never meant for this to happen," I whispered.

"Love doesn't come with a warning," she said in a brisk tone, but there was tenderness in her eyes.

"That's not it..." I started. "I belong back in Germany."

"Seems to me everyone you knew in Germany is either dead or arrested," was her dry response. "Seems to me you were rescued from a doomed life." She glanced at the clock on the wall. "Now, let's be off. It's time to get William." She slid out of the booth and went to pay Wilma.

I just sat there for a while, holding my tea cup, stunned by her harsh closing words. Kindness was fleeting with Miss Gordon.

When we arrived back at Violet Morgan's house, we found the pair still hard-at-work. Violet was complimentary about William's progress but gave us specific assignments to improve his enunciation.

I had an ulterior motive of my own in wanting William to be able to express his thoughts. I wanted to get to the bottom of why William always targeted Herr Mueller for pranks. So far, all I'd been able to get from him was "Man bad."

That much I knew.

Once, as we watched Herr Mueller from the broken window in the library, William said to me, "Man bad. Girl go. Man take Girl." It made me wonder if William had ever seen Herr Mueller with Glenda when we'd been in the library.

"You can't rush this, Louisa. It's best to keep building the foundation of vocabulary," advised Mrs. Morgen, without even knowing there was something I was trying to understand from William.

Patience, I sighed—a quality I had always had in short supply.

As we left her house, I noticed a little "room for let" sign by the door. Tuck that away for later, I thought to myself, as an idea started to blossom.

Chapter Eleven

I jumped out of bed one night to run downstairs and find Robert. I had been reading information about schools for the deaf. Gallaudet University in Washington D.C., founded by Thomas Hopkins Gallaudet as a school for deaf students, had a football team.

Back in 1894, the team's star quarterback invented the concept of the football huddle. The quarterback worried that other teams—deaf *and* hearing—were stealing his hand signals at the line of scrimmage. He gathered his players in a huddle to keep his sign language private. Other teams borrowed the idea; soon the huddle became as much a part of the game as helmets and pads.

Robert would love to hear this story. He enjoyed football and had taken William and me to the local high school's games last fall, even though the Copper Springs Coyotes hadn't won a game since he had graduated over fifteen years ago.

"It doesn't matter if they win or lose, Louisa, we need to support our team," he would say, loyal to the end.

I almost got down to the last step before I remembered he wasn't home. He was still in North Carolina.

The next two weeks inched along. I kept fighting off a strange feeling of anxiety, like something terrible was coming. The last time I had that persistent dread was just before I left Germany, when I first realized that the Gestapo was watching me.

For a week, a grim looking man followed me from place to place. He didn't try to keep himself hidden; he was purposely trying to intimidate me. As I thought back to that Gestapo agent, I realized why Herr Mueller's presence made me so edgy. Herr Mueller had the same disconcerting manner of appearing out of nowhere, watching me, unconcerned if I noticed.

We finally received a postcard from Robert, addressed to William with a message added for Miss Gordon, but nothing written to me.

A significant omission.

I woke up one night from another bad dream, turned on my light, and picked up my Bible, opening it up to Psalm 68. "God setteth the solitary in families," wrote the Psalmist.

That couldn't be meant for me, Lord. I'm not lonely. I'm fine on my own. I just want to make a difference. I'll do that if you will just get me back to Germany.

I didn't feel the peace that I usually found in prayer. Why did God seem so distant? Why didn't He respond like He usually did?

Reverend Hubbell had added a remark at the end of last Sunday's sermon that kept gnawing at me. "When you're churning," he roared out in his pulpit voice, "God's truth can't find an anchor."

The next afternoon, I drove the Hudson, quite skillfully I felt, to visit Glenda and Betty. I scarcely recognized Glenda. Her eyes had a lightness of spirit I'd never seen before in her. We sat down to have tea under the shady porch.

When Betty went inside to make another pot of tea, I unveiled my plan. "There's a room to rent over in Bisbee in a woman's house. Her name is Mrs. Morgan. She's a retired schoolteacher from the Southwestern School for the Deaf, and she is tutoring William a few times a month. And Glenda, that's not even the best part! I can help you get a job at a diner near Bisbee!"

I expected Glenda to look delighted, but she looked indifferent. I felt terribly disappointed. "What's wrong? I thought you might like this idea."

"Miss Louisa, I appreciate what you're trying to do for me. I really do." She gazed at me. "But I just ain't ready."

"But you're healed now! And this plan would help you get Tommy back. Don't you want to get him back as soon as possible?"

"Yes, ma'am. Yes, I do. And I got something that'll help me get him back." She looked directly at me, an unusual thing for Glenda. "But not 'til I'm ready."

The "something" she referred to must be the ring. Did she know I had taken it? I would've loved to question her about it, to confess I had removed it from the sweater in her closet, to ask if Herr Mueller had been the one who hurt her and ask why she took the ring in the first place.

For a moment, I felt we were dancing around the subject. But I said nothing. I had made a promise to Robert to leave it alone. And a promise is a promise.

Glenda interrupted my thoughts. "I do thank you for your trouble, Miss Louisa, but I just ain't ready," she repeated.

Not ready? Not *ready?* What was the *matter* with people in this town? No one seemed to be ready for change. When I first arrived in Copper Springs, Robert didn't want William to be taught how to communicate because he didn't think William was ready. He was *wrong.* Glenda had been beaten up at the tavern where she worked but wasn't ready to make a change. And here I had a job and a place to stay for her!

Lord, give me patience! I silently demanded.

"Miss Louisa, the thing is that Miss Betty's been teachin' me a lot about the Bible, and I just ain't ready to leave it yet. I spent a life without it and got myself into a heap of trouble. It just seems as if it wouldn't hurt me none if I took a little more time to get acquainted with it before I get on my way."

Just then, Betty came outside with the teapot and poured us each a fresh cup.

"The truth is, Miss Louisa, I just never figured God thought much of me," added Glenda.

"And He sure does," reassured Betty. "One of the great mysteries of all time is that God cares about each and every last one of us. Says so in the Good Book. Am I right, Louisa?" she asked, looking to the pastor's houseguest for official confirmation of theology.

My heart sank; it felt as heavy as a brick. "Yes, Betty," I said. "Yes, you're right." *Oh Lord, what was the matter with me? What was happening to me that I thought I had the right answer for everybody? About everything?*

I felt a sting as I thought of that verse Reverend Hubbell pointed out at church, when I could have sworn he looked straight at me as he spoke: "A fool's voice is known by a multitude of words."

Chagrined, I stood up to leave and reached over to hug Glenda. "Of course I understand, Glenda. I'm sorry if I pressured you. I just want to help. I'm much too eager. It's one of my worst faults."

* * *

The following day, William and I were returning back from the library when we spotted Robert standing on the front porch, home from his trip, talking to Miss Gordon.

William galloped to greet him, and Robert scooped him up for a hug. But as soon as I reached him, I could tell things had changed. Or rather he had changed toward me. He greeted me almost like a stranger.

"How was the meeting?" I asked with interest.

"Good. It was excellent. Well worth the trip," he answered without elaborating.

"Did they thoroughly cover dispensationalism?" I asked.

"Thorough is just the right word for it."

"And Peter Marshall? Did you get to meet him?"

"Yes. Yes, I did." Then he turned to his aunt. "Aunt Martha, Dr. Marshall had the thickest Scottish burr I've ever heard. Just like Grandfather Gordon's." And with that, they went into the house, as Robert continued his stories from his trip.

As I remained alone on the front porch, it struck me that just a few weeks ago, he would have wanted to share these stories with me.

The next week reminded me of when I first arrived in Copper Springs. Robert stayed away from the house, insisting he needed to catch up on work. There was probably some truth to that, but I knew there was more to it. He was avoiding me. I had hurt him, and I didn't know how to get things back where they used to be.

One morning, as I was getting dressed for breakfast, I could hear Robert's and Miss Gordon's voices downstairs in the kitchen. It caught my attention because Robert didn't like to talk at breakfast. He liked to read the morning paper in the peace and quiet of a new day, he often said.

Do not eavesdrop, Louisa. Do not eavesdrop, I told myself over and over, as I inched closer to the radiator. But then I heard someone mention my name. I carefully unscrewed the cap of the radiator and leaned my ear against it.

"Robert, put down that paper and listen to me," I heard Miss Gordon order. "I said that Cousin Ada wrote to ask if Louisa could come and stay with her this summer. She says she's been pining for company since her Teddy died last winter. I thought I should write her back today but I don't know what excuse I should give her to say that Louisa can't come. You know how insistent Ada can be when she gets something in her head."

I heard the rustle of the newspaper as Robert put it down on the table. "Maybe it's not such a bad idea."

"What? Why would you say that? You know how devoted William is to her."

"Exactly because of that. William needs to realize that Louisa is not planning to stay in Copper Springs. It might be good if he sees her come and go; he'll get used to the idea. That way, when she leaves for good, it will be less of a blow to him."

"Are we talking about William here?" she asked. "Or you?"

Then there was silence.

I could just envision Robert's back stiffening as it so often did when I asked him a question that was too personal, too pointed.

"I'm going to take my coffee and paper into my office," Robert answered, his voice bristling. I heard the kitchen door close behind him.

I screwed the cap back on the radiator and sat down on my bed. After overhearing that conversation, I realized I *couldn't* get things back the way they were. The connection between Robert and me had been broken.

The sad, apparent truth was that the time had come for me to leave the Gordon home. What made me sadder still was that I agreed with Robert. It *would* be better for William to realize that I would be leaving soon. With Mrs. Morgan available to help, it seemed like a good time to prepare him for that eventuality.

Since Glenda wasn't ready for my wonderful plan for her new life, I thought it would be wise if someone could use it. So that someone would be *me*. And, I reasoned, I'd rather work as a waitress, earning money for my return ticket to Germany, than to go sit in Phoenix and play the piano for Ada's bridge parties. I still couldn't think of her without feeling queasy.

By remaining close by but not actually in Copper Springs, I could continue to see William as often as possible. For as attached as that little boy was to me, I felt the same attachment to him. And I couldn't deny it would be wise to separate myself from Robert, too.

My feelings about his absence during that trip to the General Assembly Meeting caught me by surprise; I realized I was getting perilously dependent on him. I nearly slipped up, too, that last night before he left.

I knew the crucial importance of remaining detached. I was even a little ashamed of myself, but I had a renewed resolve. My back-up plan was in place. Maybe this was all a blessing in disguise, I decided. Maybe God was helping me to prepare to return to Germany, by providing a way for me to separate from those relationships in America that might make it complicated for me to leave.

That evening, after Miss Gordon went up to her room to listen to her soap opera and William was tucked into bed, I went over and knocked on Robert's office door.

"Come in," he said. He barely glanced up at me from his desk.

"I just wanted to tell you something." I leaned against the door. "While you were away, we took William to Bisbee to see the tutor. During the hour William studied with Mrs. Morgan, your aunt and I went over to have coffee at the Prospector's Diner. Do you remember that waitress, Wilma? The one who said I fell off the turnip truck? And then she offered me a job?"

He nodded, showing no expression.

"Well, she offered me a job again. She really meant it. So I've been thinking it over. The war should be over soon, and I really should earn some more money to return to Germany. And then I noticed that William's tutor is renting a room out in her house. So, you see, the two opportunities presented themselves on the same day."

He leaned back in his chair. Now I had his attention.

"I thought it was very timely. Providential, actually. I'm going to accept Wilma's job offer and move to Bisbee. That way, I could still see William fairly often, and we could keep up with the correspondence lessons. Mrs. Morgan is an excellent tutor; I think she will be able to help you and your aunt carry on with William's language skills. It won't be quite the same, but at least I could continue to see him. At least until I return to Berlin."

His facial expression didn't change. With a level gaze, he finally said, "so you've worked this all out."

"Yes. It's all settled. I'll leave next week when William has his session with Mrs. Morgan. Your aunt could drive us over and then I'll just remain."

"So that's what you want to do." He rubbed his chin.

"Yes. It's all decided," I said, looking down.

"And you've prayed about this?"

I glanced up at him. The *nerve* of that remark. How *pious!* How *patronizing!* I wanted to shout. Instead, I said as coolly as I could, "Please don't use your pulpit voice with me." The truth was that I hadn't yet prayed about this decision. I'd done everything but pray.

"Just out of curiosity, does Wilma know your only job qualifications are playing the piano and spy work?"

My eyes grew wide; I felt as if he had just slapped me. I turned to leave. Then I stopped, hand on the door, and turned my head to look back at him. "I never used to think you and your aunt had any similarities, but lately, I'm seeing quite a family resemblance." I slammed the door behind me.

Back in my room, I tried to read but had trouble concentrating.

After an hour or so I heard Robert come into the house, climb the stairs, and stop at my door. He gave a gentle knock, waited to hear my voice, then opened the door and poked his head in, a trace of apology in his eyes. "I'm sorry. I'm sure you'll make a fine waitress." He closed the door but then opened it again. "Just stay out of the kitchen," he added. And then he shut the door and went to his room.

If the book I was reading wasn't so heavy, I would have thrown it at the door behind him.

Robert must have told his aunt that I was leaving by the time I came downstairs for breakfast. Her face looked like she had eaten a persimmon. She poured my coffee wordlessly.

The four of us ate breakfast just like when I first arrived in Copper Springs. The only difference was William's animation. He threw words out in a steady stream and kept us all distracted from other underlying issues. I had planned to wait until later in the week to tell him that I would be leaving. I dreaded that conversation.

The week reminded me of how time ground to a halt when I first arrived at the Gordon household and tried to keep out of Miss Gordon's way. Robert and I were polite to each other, a guard against unpleasantness. Mostly, we avoided each other.

It wasn't very hard. I stayed in my room until I heard him leave in the morning. He returned to his office right after dinner each evening. And from the sixth of June on, I had one ear glued to my Christmas radio, listening to incoming reports about D-Day.

Thousands of Allied troops had landed on beaches in Normandy, France in a surprise attack so that the march to Germany, to *victory*, could begin.

But no sooner had that news hit than the Germans retaliated by launching the first V-1 rocket at Britain. The 'V' came from the German word 'Vergeltungswaffen,' meaning weapons of reprisal. Weapons of revenge. Up to 100 V-1 rockets fell every hour, around the clock, mostly targeting London, indiscriminately injuring and killing thousands.

Listening to the news made me feel reassured that moving to Bisbee was a wise decision. As tragic as the reports about the V-1 rockets were, I knew more than most that the Nazis retaliated when they felt threatened. To me, it was another clear indication they were losing the war. Surely, the war would be over soon.

The night before I was planning to leave, I stayed up in my room and packed. It didn't take long; I didn't come with much nor was I leaving with much. I looked around the room to see if I'd forgotten anything. There were a few theology books I had borrowed from the downstairs bookshelves that needed to be returned. Books in arms, I went down to the darkened parlor and straight to the bookshelves, looking for the places on the shelves where they belonged.

"So that's where my *Scofield Reference Bible* went," a voice said.

I jumped; I hadn't realized Robert was sitting by the fireplace. "Lieber Gott! Robert, I didn't know you were there." I looked down at the books in my arms. "Yes, I'm sorry. I didn't know you had been looking for it."

"All packed up?"

"Yes." I turned back to the bookshelves and slid the books back in their place.

"Probably helps that you never really unpacked to begin with."

I spun around on my heels. That *did* it. "I *always* told you I was planning to return to Germany. From the very first day, I have never wavered from that. It's *always* been my plan to return after the war is over. *Always*."

"That's true. I can't disagree with that. That's been your plan," he said with sarcasm.

"Then why do you sound as if that's not the right thing to do? Didn't you agree to let me live here with the understanding that I would be returning after the war?"

"Yes. Yes, I did." He jumped to his feet. "But things change, Louisa. Circumstances change. People change. Life doesn't always work out the way you've planned. And for someone who has been pushing me to accept change from the day you arrived here, you're not even willing to consider it for yourself."

I looked at him for a long moment. Then I went to sit on the davenport. I asked, "Is that why you're so angry with me?"

The question seemed to hang in the air for a while. He turned toward the fireplace, lost in reflection. Finally, he spoke. "I'm not angry with you. I'm angry with myself."

"Whatever for?"

He walked over to the fireplace, placing one hand on the mantel. "Because I didn't learn from my mistake."

"What do you mean?"

"When I was away at the meeting in North Carolina, I thought about this a great deal, Louisa. It suddenly became so clear to me. I realized I had allowed myself to get emotionally involved with the same kind of woman as Ruth." There was cold anger in his voice.

I gasped audibly. "I am *not* like her," I said, now seething. "I am nothing like her. I can *not* believe you said that."

He didn't answer me. Nor did he look at me.

"I *never* made a promise to you like she did. I am *not* abandoning you or William like she did."

He glanced at me. "You're both ambitious women."

"How so? I've never asked you for anything."

Now he looked straight at me. "You both want something badly enough that you'll leave people who love you for it. She wanted a fine life: fortune and status; you're after more noble things. You want to ride back on your gleaming white horse and save Germany, single-handedly."

Those words cut me to the quick. I glared at him through a blur of hot tears as a maelstrom of fury welled up within me. "How *dare* you trivialize how I feel about Germany! You make it sound foolish and silly. You don't have *any* idea what it is like to lose your country. You sit here in the desert and think you're helping to fight a war by collecting tin cans and eating oleo on your bread. You have *no idea* what war is like! You have *no idea* how dark this evil is! *Hitler's evil.* And yet you say that I am the naïve one!"

I tried to calm down before repeating, insistently, "Robert, I am *nothing* like her."

A long stretch of minutes passed. He watched the fireplace while I watched him.

Then the real issue that had been avoiding so carefully spilled forth. Still looking at the fireplace, he said, "Louisa, is there something so wrong about me that you...and Ruth...couldn't love me?"

My heart nearly melted. "Wrong? Something so wrong about you? Oh, Robert, no. Just the opposite. There's something so *right* about you."

The way he looked at me then, so unguarded, I knew I had to get upstairs fast, or I would never be able to leave tomorrow.

* * *

The next morning, I waited until I heard Robert leave for his office before going downstairs. Miss Gordon wouldn't even look at me. She went outside to hang wet laundry on the clothesline as soon as I walked into the kitchen. I still hadn't told William I was moving out. My plan was to have Mrs. Morgan help me tell him this afternoon, at his tutoring session.

I ate a silent, lonely breakfast, gathering my courage to go let Rosita cut my long dark hair into the fashionable bob she was so eager for. I knew how much this meant to her; I tried not to envision myself as a lamb being led to the slaughter.

I went into Rosita's beauty salon holding my Christmas coupon. She knew it was my last day. She led me to her chair, wrapping a big apron around me. "At last, Louisa! We are going to make you into a Hollywood movie star. No more looking like you came from the Old World."

After she finished, I looked in the mirror and had to bite my lip to keep from weeping.

"Bonita! Sì, amiga?" she asked. Rosita had the biggest heart in town but very possibly could be the worst haircutter in the state of Arizona. One side was longer than the other side. And the bottom edge was cut in a zig-zag.

Oh, well, I thought, trying to console myself. Hair grows back.

Ramon wheeled his chair over and looked aghast at my hair. "Rosita, would you mind going to Ibsen's store and buying some of that #10 hair dye for Mrs. Wondolowski? She has an appointment this morning."

"But Ramon, I am just about done with Louisa's bob. Un momento?"

"No, bambina. I need that dye right now. Before she comes in. Louisa understands. ¿Sì? ¿Comprendes?"

I nodded. I comprehended completely.

"Oh, Louisa, I come back soon to finish up." And off she hurried to Ibsen's store.

As Ramon watched her disappear, he whipped out his scissors to straighten my cut. "I'm sorry, Louisa. She means well, but I have got to get the scissors away from her."

"Maybe she'll stay home when the baby comes."

"She says she wants to bring the baby to work!" he rued.

"Ramon, have you ever thought of having her open a restaurant? Copper Springs doesn't really have a decent place to eat."

"That could be an interesting idea," he said, frowning, as he examined the back of my head.

By the time Rosita returned from the store with hair dye #10, my new hairstyle was greatly improved, and my countenance brightened considerably.

"Oh, see, I told you that it would be perfect!" she said, not realizing that her husband repaired her damage.

I jumped up when I saw her pick up a pair of scissors, eyeing my edges. "It's wonderful, Rosita! I think it's fine just the way it is." I hugged her goodbye and promised to keep in touch and that I would be back to see her new baby. Then, feeling quivery, I left before I started to cry.

Not today, I told myself. I needed to keep my feelings under control today.

I walked up to the parsonage and stopped at my Victory Garden. Even though it was too hot to grow much of anything now, it still showed signs of glory. The second year in a garden was always better than the first. I hoped Miss Gordon would try and care for it, but I doubted it. Her artistic sense was not noticeably developed. She was in the backyard unclipping the laundry she had earlier hung to dry, so I went over to help her finish.

"I see Rosita finally had her way with your hair." She eyed my new haircut with disapproval.

"Should I get William down from the tree house so he can eat his lunch? We need to be at Mrs. Morgan's before too long," I said.

"There's time enough."

As the last towel went into the basket, I said, "Miss Gordon, I want you to know how grateful I am for the hospitality you've given me for the last year and a half."

She didn't respond. We walked into the kitchen for relief from the glaring sun. She put the basket on the floor and inhaled deeply. "Answer me one thing, Louisa."

I looked at her, curious. I think it might be the first question she had ever asked me.

"Why are you so all fired sure you need to go back to Germany?"

That wasn't hard to answer. "Because I believe God wants me to return."

"Seems to me there's some other reason."

Puzzled, I tilted my head at her. "What do you mean?"

"Seems to me you feel as if you owe God something for saving your own backside and getting you out of there."

I looked down at the laundry. "Would that be so wrong? To feel an obligation to God?"

"Not if it's for the right reasons. I'm just not so sure about yours'."

"It's just that...it's just that...I do owe God something." I went to the kitchen window and looked outside. "I have to prove it to Him."

"Prove what?" asked Robert, hurrying down the stairs into the kitchen. I had noticed the Hudson parked in the driveway but assumed Robert was in his office. "Louisa, *what* do you have to prove to God?"

"Prove that...," I turned and looked at him. "I have to prove He didn't make a mistake."

"What mistake?" he persisted. "What kind of mistake could God have made that you feel you need to prove something to Him?"

I couldn't get the words out. From deep inside of me came a profound emotion, something I had buried long ago from the daylight and only seemed to rise up when I had a nightmare. It felt like a dam had broken and emotion poured forth. I couldn't hold it back any longer. "Saving me," I choked.

"Why should I have been allowed to survive when so many people have lost their lives? It isn't right! It isn't fair! Miss Gordon, that day in the diner, you said everyone I knew was dead or arrested! You were right! Everyone! *Every* family member. *Every* friend. *Every* neighbor. They're gone! Gone! Can you imagine? If the entire town of Copper Springs, all of the people you've known and cared about your entire life, if they were suddenly gone, arrested or killed by a mad man?"

I sat down at the kitchen table and put my head in my hands. "Don't you understand?" I cried out in frustration. "I never should have left Germany! I should be dead or arrested just like the others. Like Dietrich. He is the one who should be here. Not *me*. Don't you see? He's the one with so much to give to the world. And there are so many others just like him. I have to go back and prove to God He didn't make a mistake. I have to go back and make my life count for something!"

Then I buried my head down on my crossed arms, too deeply into crying to stop. I don't remember crying so long or so hard in my life since my father's death. The kitchen table had probably never witnessed such a torrent of unrestrained emotion before, certainly not in the Gordon household.

Miss Gordon slipped upstairs, no doubt grateful to get away from my dramatic outpouring of sentiment. Her feelings were just like the bun in her hair—tightly wrapped up and pinned into place.

Robert sat down next to me, waiting, stroking my hair a few times. Then, after I had no more tears to shed, all he said was, "God has His reasons, Louisa. There are many things we'll never understand this side of eternity."

I looked at him through a blur of tears. "That's just too simple an answer."

He went over to a kitchen cupboard and pulled out Miss Gordon's Bible, opening it to the sixteenth chapter of the book of Proverbs as he sat back down next to me. "The Lord hath made all things for himself, yea, even the wicked for the day of evil." Then, he said, "Even the day of evil, Louisa. Even that is under His control."

He took a handkerchief out of his pocket and wiped my tear-stained face. "There's something I want you to think about. I don't even want an answer right now. Just think about it. Pray about it."

I looked up at him, wondering what he was going to say.

He cupped my face in his hands, looked me right in the eyes and asked in a voice of great tenderness, "what makes you so sure your life doesn't count right here?" Then he left the kitchen.

I stayed at the table for a while longer, completely spent. Finally, I stood up and gazed out the kitchen door window at the church. I felt a pull toward the church from deep inside. I knew the sanctuary would be empty.

I loved to be in a church—any church—when it was empty. It felt sacred, and even though I knew it didn't matter where I prayed, somehow I felt as if I had God's ear when I knelt in prayer in church. I walked over to it, opened the door, and sank into a pew.

I didn't know how much time had passed when someone put a hand on my shoulder; I flinched in surprise. I had been so lost in my misery I hadn't heard anyone come in. It was Herr Mueller.

"May I join you, Fräulein?" he asked, blocking the pew.

"I was just leaving."

"Nonsense. You just arrived."

How long had he been watching me?

"A moment of your time, bitte. I have just learned something quite interesting. There was a young woman who disappeared in Berlin a while ago. Just like that. Vanished." He snapped his fingers. "Just a few weeks before you arrived in Copper Springs."

He sat down next to me. "The German government would like to talk to this woman. It turns out she had a very influential circle of friends. Dietrich Bonhoeffer, for example. Hans von Dohnanyi, for another. You might not be aware of this unfortunate turn of events, but both of these men have been arrested under suspicion of conspiring to assassinate der Führer."

"I don't know what you're talking about." I felt the pounding of my portending heart. I stood up to leave. He grabbed my arm with his hand, forcing me to sit back down. He handed me a large envelope.

In it were pictures of Dietrich, Hans and I, in Berlin. One was at a street corner, another in a car, another coming out of a building. I remembered each of those meetings; they occurred during that one week when the Gestapo agent was following me. That week before I left Germany.

"Your secret is safe with me, Fräulein. I believe we can find an arrangement that will satisfy everyone. No one needs to know you are not Louisa Schmetterling, and I, in turn, will be able to help your friends."

"What do you mean?" My voice was shaky; I felt as if this were a nightmare I couldn't wake from.

He moved in closer to me so that I could feel his hot sour breath on my neck. "I would like to have more private discussions with you each Wednesday night while my wife is at choir practice. Come to my house at seven o'clock sharp."

"I'm leaving today to go live in Bisbee, Herr Mueller."

"Even better! Bisbee is not so far, Fraulein. It has a wonderful hotel—the Copper Queen. We'll meet there."

I narrowed my eyes and snapped, "so you can do to me what you did to her?"

His mouth gaped like a hooked fish. Finally, he spat out, "she came to me of her own free will."

Seeing him caught off guard gave me needed courage. With my free arm, I slapped his face as hard as I could. His hand went up to his cheek, and a drip of blood trickled from the corner of his mouth. He took out a handkerchief and wiped away the blood. In a tone of chilling anger he warned, "you do not want to make me an enemy, Fraulein. Your friends in Germany depend on you."

Suddenly, a door clicked open. "Louisa?" Robert's voice filled the church from the narthex.

Herr Mueller grabbed the envelope from me and slipped it inside of his coat jacket just as Robert entered the sanctuary and walked up to us, a concerned look on his face. "Mr. Mueller? What's going on?"

"Ah, good day, Reverend. The Fräulein and I were just chatting." Like a chameleon, Herr Mueller's voice and countenance resumed calm. All that betrayed him was my handprint, still red, on his cheek. "Well, I must be off. Bis später, Fräulein." He got up and walked out of the church.

"What happened?" Robert asked. Impatience rose in his voice. "Louisa, what just happened?"

I remained in the pew, chin quivering, trying not to cry.

He sat down next to me. "I came to tell you it's time to take William to Mrs. Morgan's. What did Mueller say to you? You're as white as Aunt Martha's sheets." Then he leaned back against the pew. "Oh, no. Was it something about William? Did William do anything to Mueller while I was away?"

"No, no. It's nothing like that."

"Oh, Louisa, you didn't tell him about the ring."

"No! I promised you I wouldn't and I *didn't*. Please, it was nothing. Let's go. We need to get William to Mrs. Morgan's on-time." I stood up and started to walk past him, but he extended his arm to block me. Without looking at him, I said, "Robert, I can handle this myself."

"Why are you so determined to be the Lone Ranger?" he said with exasperation.

I gave him an equally exasperated look.

He shook his head. "Sorry. A radio program. What I meant to say is what is so wrong about asking for help?" He stood up, took my shoulders, and turned me to face him. "Louisa, I want to help. Tell me what Mueller said to upset you."

I was quiet for a moment. "He knows," I said. "He knows everything. He knows I'm an illegal immigrant. He knows all about Dietrich and Hans. He even had photographs. He wants to use that information against them. Against me. "

Robert's face revealed disbelief. "*What*? How? *How* could he have possibly found out?"

I explained what he said and the Wednesday night "arrangement" he had suggested. Robert's face changed from disbelief to anger. He clenched his jaw, and his hands tightened into fists. "I want to get the police involved," he finally said.

"And what would you tell them? That I have a false passport? Or that an upstanding church member made a proposition to me? No, Robert. There's nothing to be gained."

"What do you suggest then? We can't let him get away with trying to blackmail you. And you're certainly not going near him."

"Let that be the least of your concerns," I said with a weak smile.

"Louisa, don't joke about this. This is serious business."

"I'm only half-joking. But I know Nazis. I've seen their tactics. Herr Mueller is just using information as leverage; he has no intention to help anyone. Other than himself."

He looked as worried as I felt.

"Do you remember I told you I recognized his surname? There is a Nazi in Berlin with the same name as Herr Mueller. I can almost guarantee they are related. They even look alike. And they certainly act alike."

"What are you thinking? That Mueller is a Nazi sympathizer? Living here in Copper Springs? Louisa, that seems outlandish."

"Outlandish? Outlandish?!" A flash of anger surged within me. "Robert, this is why I haven't told you my doubts about Herr Mueller! You say I'm too suspicious or that I'm acting as if I'm still doing Resistance Work. From the first moment I met Herr Mueller, I felt full of doubts about him. When Glenda was harmed, it only confirmed my suspicions."

Robert crossed his arms and paced back and forth a few steps. "Look, Louisa, stay here. At least for a few more days. I'll call Mrs. Morgan and the diner and let them know not to expect you just now. I want to make sure Mueller isn't up to something."

I nodded, relieved. Herr Mueller's threat was not to be taken lightly. We were both pensive as we walked home.

After dinner that night, I tucked William into bed and then went to get a book in my room. I could hear Robert and Miss Gordon talking downstairs. I went over to the radiator, reprimanding myself for listening to their conversation as I unscrewed the cap.

"Oh, no!" I heard her say in a worried voice. "Robert, I think I told him. It was right after you had lunch at his house. He asked me where you had met Louisa, and I told you had met a friend of hers while in seminary. He asked me all about your friend. It seemed a little odd, but I thought it was common knowledge. You've spoken of Dietrich Bonhoeffer often. You've even quoted him in your sermons. I just thought everyone knew."

Robert was silent.

I went down the stairs and walked into the kitchen. "Tante Marta, you meant no harm." I went over and hugged her. We had come a long way.

"Louisa?" asked Robert, noticing for the first time. "What in the *world* happened to your hair?"

Chapter Twelve

I tried to put the conversation with Herr Mueller out of my mind, but I kept coming back to a single desperate conclusion. A feeling of nervous dread kept rising in my stomach; I knew in my heart Herr Mueller was planning something.

Robert wanted to do something, but we didn't know what to do next, or who to talk to, because we couldn't prove anything. So we ended up waiting. And waiting. For what, we didn't know. Miss Gordon called it "waiting for an axe to fall."

Just that morning, as I read from the Bible, I came across a verse in the Psalms: "Rescue me, O Lord, from evil men, protect me from men of violence, who devise evil plans in their hearts and stir up war every day."

Lord, rescue me from Herr Mueller, I prayed constantly. Wednesday night came and went, like any other night, except Robert stayed close to the house. When he didn't think I noticed, he watched me with worried eyes.

By Friday, the answer arrived in the form of a serious looking man dressed in a plain dark suit standing on our doorstep. Miss Gordon hurried to get Robert from his office.

"Aunt Martha, would you mind taking William upstairs while Louisa and I talk to this gentleman?" Robert sounded calm but looked troubled.

The man looked straight at me. "Are you Louisa Schmetterling?"

I nodded.

"Do-you-understand-English?" he asked, as if I had a hearing problem.

"Yes," I answered. My mouth felt dry.

"I'm a field officer for the INS."

I glanced at Robert, puzzled.

"Immigration and Naturalization Services," he explained.

The officer pulled out some papers from his briefcase. "Ma'am, it has been brought to our attention that you might be in this country under false pretenses. You have until Monday morning to prove that you are here legally. There's a hearing scheduled on Monday for your internment at Crystal City, Texas. We will return for you at 10 a.m. on Monday for the hearing."

He handed me the papers. "And I'm compelled to warn you that if you flee, you will be classified as a fugitive and arrested when found. Also, the Reverend will be considered an accomplice and charged accordingly. Do you understand what we're telling you?"

I was stunned. Robert reached over and took my hand.

"What kind of proof do you need?" asked Robert.

"Legal documentation," he answered.

Of which I had none.

The officer saw the panic in my eyes. "Don't you fret, Ma'am. Crystal City isn't a bad place. Think of it as a vacation paid for by the U.S. Government. It's just until this war ends. That'll be soon. It's just government policy to not take any chances with possible domestic disloyalty."

"Why Texas? Why not the internment camp in Phoenix? Pagogo Park?" Robert asked.

"Pagogo Park is only for male POWs. Crystal City has families living there. She'll make lots of new friends," he added.

The absurdity of that comment gave me a moment to pull myself together. Robert walked the officer to the door. Then he returned and stood next to me. Still stunned, we watched his car disappear through the parlor window.

Finally, Robert turned to me. "Mueller did this. I still can't understand how he knew who you were, that your passport was false." Then his eyes lit up. "Unless...unless he got into my lock box at the bank! Louisa, what time is it?"

I thought back to the clock in the kitchen. I had looked at it, nervously, when I heard the officer knock on the door. "Around half past three."

"I'm going to run to the bank and check the contents of my lock box. I'll be back as soon as I can, but I have to wait until Mueller is out of the bank. I don't want to make him suspicious. Louisa, please try not to worry." He brushed my cheek with his hand.

Miss Gordon, who had been listening all along, raced out of the front door onto the porch as Robert bolted down the steps. "Robert! Do something! We can't let her go."

Robert didn't return for hours. I tried to not worry; I tried to pray until I could find peace. I prayed about it, left the matter entirely in God's hand, trusted Him to control the outcome, then I grabbed it back to worry all over again. I felt the same fear that a siren elicits at night—a fear I had hoped to leave behind in Germany.

It wasn't that being interned troubled me. On my long and lonely train ride, zigzagging from New York to Arizona, I had passed internment camps of Japanese Americans in some of the western mountain states and asked the train conductor about them.

He explained that President Roosevelt had signed Executive Order 9066, ordering all Japanese Americans, who had been living on the west or east coast, to relocate to these camps. It was obvious the conductor was pleased with the President's decision.

As I passed the camps, I didn't think the camps looked very threatening. Still, it gave me a chill to see them. I knew they weren't like prisons. Workers came and went through the day; the camps offered schools and activities. But I worried about Herr Mueller's connections. I had met many Muellers in my Resistance Work. Upstanding citizens with a secret, evil life.

I wondered what lay ahead of me. I felt desperate for a specific message from God as I thumbed through my Bible. "Whither shall I go from thy spirit? or whither shall I flee from thy presence? If I ascend up into heaven, thou art there: if I make my bed in hell, behold, thou art there. If I take the wings of the morning, and dwell in the uttermost parts of the sea; even there shall thy hand lead me, and thy right hand shall hold me." Reminded of those ancient words of King David from the book of Psalms gave me some consolation.

Finally, Robert came in through the front door after Miss Gordon had gone upstairs to give William a bath. I was grateful for the timing; it gave us the opportunity to talk alone. "Your passport is gone. So is Ruth's ring and some stock certificates. Mueller has emptied out my box." He sank down on the davenport and motioned for me to sit down next to him.

"I went to see Judge Pryor. I showed him the internment orders. He said they're legitimate. He said we can appeal the papers, but it would take a long time. He said you could also seek political asylum, but again, in both cases, you would have to go to the internment camp and start the proceedings there."

I took a deep breath. I had expected something like that. Herr Mueller exacted reparation for rebuffing him. "I'm not afraid of going to the camp. It's all right, Robert. I'm ready.

Dietrich often said that being safe and being at peace is not the same thing."

"Wait, Louisa. You need to hear this. Judge Pryor called his nephew in Washington. The one that works for the federal government."

I nodded.

"Well, apparently, Crystal City is not just an internment camp. It's a camp run by the Justice Department. It's used for hostage exchange. With Germany. The United States agrees to exchange valuable individuals for American citizens held in Germany. If you're right about Mueller, then it's likely the German government will want you back. Probably to be used as evidence against Dietrich. And who knows what they'll do with you when they're done."

He paused. "Even the judge's nephew couldn't help us. He told the judge that when the Justice Department is involved with hostage exchange, there aren't many loopholes."

Those icy fingers of fear reached into my heart again. Ironic that I should leave Germany to be safe, only to land in a town with an individual who had the power and connections to send me back. I knew Herr Mueller was shrewd, but I hadn't anticipated such a clever trap.

An entirely legal one.

Robert stood up and walked to the fireplace. He took a deep breath, and turned to face me. "But there is one loophole. The judge told me there is still one ironclad way to keep you here. He called it the 'old fashioned way'."

I looked up at him, not understanding.

When our eyes met, he took another deep breath. "Marry me. Tonight. You could become an automatic citizen with proper documentation."

For a moment, I was speechless. I covered my cheeks with my hands. Recovering my powers of speech with difficulty, I finally sputtered out, "I can't. I can't do that to you. I can't! No, Robert, the war will be over soon."

He shook his head. "Louisa, listen to me. And don't interrupt me. For once in your life, woman, do not interrupt me." He came over and sat down on the davenport beside me. He was quiet for a moment, his hands clasped together, gathering his words.

Then he said, "Louisa, when I was in seminary with Dietrich and Frank, I knew that they had a passion and a conviction that I lacked. I've always been keeping something back. From Ruth, even from God. I think God has given me a second chance, to give myself to Him wholly, without reservation."

He raked a hand nervously through his hair. "When I married Ruth, I never even asked God for His opinion. Look at how that turned out. But for this, for you, I have asked God what is the right thing to do. That's why I took such a long time getting back tonight. I was praying. Louisa, I believe that He is blessing this decision. I really do. Please say yes, for me as well as for you."

"But what about William? What will he think of marriage? As a joke? As a legal agreement for convenience? The last thing I want to do is to turn his world upside down again. And then, after the war, you end up as a twice-divorced minister. No, Robert. I will *not* damage your lives like that. Like *Ruth* did."

"Then don't. I mean, don't leave. Stay here with us. You belong here with us. We need you, Louisa. I need you. William needs you. Even Aunt Martha needs you."

Miss Gordon? That, I doubted.

Robert quickly read the look on my face. "Well, maybe not quite like William and I need you."

Then he gave me that straight-in-the-eyes look of his that always made my stomach flip-flop. "Louisa, I love you. I don't want you to go. Please. Give us a chance."

I searched his eyes as I did that first night I arrived when I told him about my involvement with Resistance Work and asked him if I should stay or go. Tonight they were warm. Trusting. I couldn't believe this was the same man who had met me at the depot station. Then, he was a man who looked beaten down from life. Burdened. But now, his eyes had life and strength inside of them, such resolve.

I turned away from Robert and went to look out the big picture window. I crossed my arms tightly against my stomach. I breathed in and breathed out, trying to find peace. I had learned long ago to read God's answers to any troubling decision by looking at my heart, my spirit, for a prompting of His peace, but for this issue—remaining in America—I knew I had closed my mind to God's leading.

Tell me what to do and I will do it, Lord!

I thought of Rosita's comment, that maybe God needed me here in Copper Springs, more than he needed me in Germany. Robert's voice echoed in my mind: "What makes you so sure your life can't count here?" I gazed out the window at the quirky town, at the odd, sharply angled, red rocky hills behind it, at Robert's church with the peeling paint.

Again, I lifted a silent prayer. *Just tell me what to do, and I will do it, Lord. I'm ready to listen. I'm finally ready to listen.*

At that precise moment, I knew that, somehow, I did belong here. I no longer had any doubts that God had plucked me out of Berlin and dropped me here in Copper Springs for

His purposes. But it wasn't just about Robert and William needing me. I needed them. They had become my family.

That verse in the Scriptures I had stumbled upon, "God setteth the solitary in families," that verse was God's message to *me*. I'm not sure I would ever be able to fathom why God had spared my life and not others—others in Germany far more deserving than I, but I knew He had blessed me by bringing me here. And He wanted me to accept his blessing. For the first time in a very long time, I knew, without any doubt, that I was right where I was meant to be. Finally, lightness lifted my soul. All of the tension I had carried for months now, maybe even for years, seeped away.

I turned back to Robert and said, "I would be honored to be your wife."

* * *

The ceremony was brief and uneventful. We stood in the judge's living room. The judge's wife, for whom I had made a choir robe in an extra-extra large size, acted as our witness. After a few words, the judge pronounced us husband and wife.

Then came an awkward pause. "Well, Robert, if you're too timid to kiss your bride, then I will." He reached out for me, but Robert, thankfully, stopped him. The judge was a kind and wonderful man, avuncular almost, but I did not intend to let him kiss me.

Robert laughed. "Thank you, Judge, but I think I can manage." He turned to me and gently cupped my face in his hands, as he did a few days ago in the kitchen, but this time it wasn't to wipe away tears. He kissed me first on each cheek, then, tenderly, on my lips. It might have been all of the excitement of the day, but my knees felt as quivery as Miss Gordon's green gelatin dessert.

* * *

At breakfast the next morning we told Miss Gordon and William we had been married by Judge Pryor. I wasn't quite sure how she would react to this "solution" to my immigration problem.

To my surprise-and delight-she began to dab at her eyes with that dishtowel she always had tucked in her apron. "Well, it's about time *somebody* did *something* around here," she said, peering straight at Robert.

Ah relief! Emboldened, I decided I would just start calling her Aunt Martha. I doubted she would ever volunteer such familiarity.

About William's response, I had no doubt. He stood up on his chair and clapped and yelled so loudly I feared he might rouse Chief Cochise from his grave. For a child who had just learned how to communicate, he was making up for lost time in leaps and bounds. Even Dog started jumping and barking in the excitement.

Aunt Martha threw up her dishtowel in mock despair. "Oh, for the love of heaven," she muttered, as she swept out the door to get away from the happy chaos.

I grabbed William, hugged him, and gave him kisses all over his face. I couldn't love a child more. From the corner of my eye, I saw Robert watching us, cup of coffee in his hand, one hip leaning against the counter, his serious grey eyes brimming with tears.

The next morning was Sunday. At church, I gazed around at faces now familiar to me. At the end of the service, Robert surprised me by asking me to stand up and come up to join him. I walked up to him, a little puzzled. He smiled at me, his eyes reassuring, and took my hand.

Then he turned to the congregation and announced, "I would like to introduce to you my wife, Louisa Gordon."

Like the last time, I wished he had given me notice he was going to introduce me. All eyes turned to me, my cheeks burned, but this time, the elderly man who whistled throughout the hymns started to clap. Then another joined him and another, until the entire congregation stood up and clapped.

I quickly realized there was a reason behind Robert's announcement. He kept his eyes locked on Herr Mueller's face to see him react to the news. As the church ladies crowded around to congratulate me, Herr Mueller grabbed Ernest and slipped out. I watched Robert and saw him give a nod to Judge Pryor, who followed Herr Mueller out.

After a while, Robert came over to me. "Louisa, we need to go. Please excuse us, ladies."

The judge met us at the house with a grave look on his face. "Robert, you were right. Mueller went straight to the telegraph office and made Ernest open up on a Sunday morning. I waited until after Mueller left the telegraph office and then I went in. Ernest didn't want to talk much, being that he takes that blasted oath of office so seriously, but you can kind of work your way around things and Ernest will let loose. He admitted Mueller had to send a telegram to his ailing father. He wrote it out in German, and Ernest had to send it out in Morse code. Here, Louisa, I wrote it down to see if you could figure anything out."

I read the little piece of paper he held out to me: "Heinrich Mueller." My mind started racing. I looked up at Robert. "I *told* you. There are too many coincidences."

Judge Pryor looked back and forth between us. "What? What does that mean?"

"The head of the Geheime Staatspolizei is a man named Heinrich Mueller," I explained.

"I'm still not following," he said.

"Geheime Staatspolizei. Gestapo. The secret police."

The judge's eyes went wide with shock.

"If Mueller got into my lock box, don't you think he could have gotten into others?" asked Robert. "And if so, what has he done with the valuables? Could he be sending this town's money and valuables back to Berlin?"

He was thoughtful for a moment. "Judge, do you think you could get into your safety deposit box tomorrow morning? You'd have to wait until Mueller is away from the bank." He rubbed his chin. "Who else could we ask, without stirring up notice? We don't want to tip our hands to Mueller, or create hysteria in the town."

"I think I can get Ernest in on this," said the judge. "I need to question him about other wirings that Mueller might have done, anyway. If he's upset that his safety deposit box is empty, which I have a hunch it will be, he'll start talking."

He stood up to leave.

"Thank you, Judge Pryor, for everything you've done for us," Robert said.

"Robert, if you and Louisa are on to something, then it is this town that will be thanking you."

* * *

The next morning, Monday, Robert asked Aunt Martha to take William out so that he wouldn't be home for the INS field officer's appointment with me.

Soon after they left, Judge Pryor knocked on the kitchen door. "I thought you might need a little extra clout."

The sight of that kind face gave me needed courage. I poured him a cup of coffee, hoping he wouldn't notice my trembling hands. The same serious looking man drove up to the parsonage at 10 a.m. sharp. Robert and the judge met with him in the parlor. I stayed in the kitchen. For the first time in my entire life, I was not tempted to eavesdrop. It felt like an eternity, but it really only lasted a few minutes.

"Louisa, please come in," Robert finally called out to me. I walked into the room, and nodded to the officer.

"Ma'am, I just wanted to give you my heartfelt congratulations," said the officer. "My brother married a war bride; she's done him proud. Five kids already and one on the way! Two sets of twins."

I froze. In the turmoil of the last few days, I realized there was a rather sizable topic I had not considered.

The judge walked the officer out to his car, then hurried back inside. "Your guess was spot-on, Robert. I checked this morning before I came over here. My box was empty. Everything's gone. Ernest's box was empty, too. He's adding up the amount of cash Mueller has wired to a specific location. Soon as I get that information, I'll get a warrant written up to search Mueller's office at the bank."

Robert turned to me. "Louisa, go get the ring."

"Good thinking. We can add the charge of battery to the list," said the judge.

"I do think Glenda would be more willing to make charges against Herr Mueller if she thought he was going to be arrested," I said.

"I wonder how long this has been going on," the judge thought aloud.

"It can't be too long," answered Robert. "I put Louisa's passport in my safety deposit box just over a year ago. Nothing was missing."

"This is more than missing assets in the bank," I said. "I suspect Mueller is becoming more daring as Germany is losing the war. My guess is he's getting pressured to send more money." Then I added what I'd been thinking about for a while now. "I think the real reason he came to Copper Springs in the first place, years ago, was to buy the mines and send copper to Germany through Mexico. His wife told me he travels to Mexico every week." I reminded Robert about the convoy of trucks we had seen.

"So you think stealing from the bank has been an afterthought?" Robert asked.

"I do."

Robert and Judge Pryor exchanged looks.

"You're probably right," Robert sighed. He looked at the judge. "She's always right."

I leaned back on the davenport. It made me heartsick to think Herr Mueller was aiding the Nazis, sending valuable minerals from America's land, her heart, right back to the enemy she was fighting. I put my hand to my forehead and closed my eyes. "I am so sorry."

"Don't you be sorry, Louisa. Mueller's been stopped. That's all that's important. He might have continued this thievery for years; we were certainly fools enough to let him." Judge Pryor shook his head in disgust and left to go to the telegraph office.

I ran upstairs to get Herr Mueller's ring and put it in my pocket.

When Robert and I arrived at the telegraph office, we found Ernest and the judge pouring over the ledger. The judge looked up and saw Robert. "Mueller wires money regularly to a bank account in Switzerland. He's been doing it for years."

"Judge, he told me he had a sick father who needed the support," Ernest rushed to say. "I never thought another thing about it. It's not my job to get into people's business. You know that, Judge. I took an oath of office."

"I know, I know all about your oath, Ernest. Now keep adding up those figures."

"Let's see. Here's one from last summer. He wired $1,325."

One thousand dollars, three hundred, and twenty-five dollars. Mrs. Drummond's money. Sent covertly to the Nazis. I felt as if I might be ill. I sat down in a chair and put my head in my hands. Thankfully, no one noticed; they were leaning over the counter, examining the ledger, trying to connect all of the dots of Herr Mueller's operation. I went outside to get fresh air, leaning against the building and breathing deeply.

Down the street, I spied Robert's church. I knew I had to get inside and soak up the quiet. I didn't even know how to pray about all of this. My thoughts were so jumbled; so much had happened in scarcely a few days' time.

I went into Robert's office to find his Bible, turned on the desk light, and sat at his desk. His Bible was right on top. I picked it up, anxiously thumbing through it, looking for something to help console me, landing on Proverbs 3:25, 26: "Be not afraid of sudden fear, neither of the desolation of the wicked, when it cometh. For the Lord shall be thy confidence, and shall keep thy foot from being taken."

Comforted, I smiled. *The Lord shall be my confidence.* I took a deep breath and started to feel calmer.

I heard a door open to the sanctuary. "Robert? I'm in here," I called out.

But there was no answer.

A chill went up my spine. Intuitively, I sensed who was in the church. I took the chunky ring from my pocket and placed it in Robert's Bible, closed it and put it on his chair just as Herr Mueller walked into the office. He locked the door leading to the sanctuary behind him. I stood behind the desk, ready to face him, as boldness from some deep place welled up within me.

"Frau Gordon. May I congratulate you on your nuptials? What a clever trick. I wouldn't have thought it possible for the pious Reverend to lie in a vow before God."

"You sent that INS officer, didn't you, Herr Mueller? And you've been sending money from the people in this town to Berlin to support the Nazis, haven't you?"

A shadow crossed his face. Encouraged, I decided to take the offensive and keep going. "Robert and Judge Pryor are over at the telegraph office right now, adding up the money you've wired to a bank in Switzerland. Money that belongs to the people in this town. You've been found out. It's over, Herr Mueller." Slowly, I started moving toward the door.

"Oh, no, it isn't, Fräulein." His face twisted into a wicked grin. "You are my most valuable commodity now. You're coming with me." He came around the desk to grab me as I turned and kicked him hard in the shin. He leaned over in pain as I tried to slip past him. He was doubled over, clutching his shin. I reached a hand out to the door that led outside, only to feel a sharp blow strike the back of my head.

I had the strangest thought before everything went dark: Ruth left her wedding ring on Robert's pillow so he would know she left. I left Herr Mueller's ring for him so that he would know to find me.

Chapter Thirteen

I had no idea how much time elapsed between the confrontation with Herr Mueller in the church and the point when I regained consciousness. The back of my head had a swelling knot; blood trickled down my neck. My hands and my feet were bound with rope.

Where *was* I? In the back of a filthy truck. Gingerly, I sat up. There were boxes and sacks scattered everywhere. I wiggled over to the back opening of the truck. I peeked out the opening and saw Herr Mueller, at the front of a mine, talking to a miner, his arms waving and pointing as if giving directions.

I noticed a boy trudging out of the mines. I only spotted him because he had a shock of bright red hair. The miner called the boy over and pointed to another truck. Wearily, the boy climbed onto the back of the truck and waited, legs swinging back and forth like a pendulum.

I tried to get the ropes off of my hands; I was going to have to work quickly to escape out the back of the truck while Herr Mueller was preoccupied. Just then I heard Herr Mueller's voice yell out as he walked back to the truck. "Carter! I want that ore delivered today! No excuses!"

I whipped my head around and looked at the man Herr Mueller called Carter and then at that forlorn boy. Curly red hair like that wasn't very common. It was as loud as a trumpet. *Glenda's nephew!* I was sure of it.

Herr Mueller walked to the truck. I wiggled to where I had been laying so he wouldn't think I had regained consciousness. He glanced quickly at me in the back of the truck, then walked around to the driver's seat and climbed in.

He started the truck, backed it up, and headed down the bumpy, dirt road leading from the mine to the highway.

I wondered which way he would drive when he hit the highway. I hoped it might be north to Copper Springs, but I doubted it would be so. He turned south, just like that convoy I had seen one night when I first arrived in Copper Springs, when Robert and I returned from visiting Mrs. Drummond. Toward Mexico.

Think, Louisa, think.

I knew my chance for escape was better now than it would be in Mexico. Copper Springs was only a few miles from the border town of Naco in the Mexican state of Sonora. I hoped to get the attention of the border guards when we stopped, but Herr Mueller either knew them well or had paid them off. Or both. He didn't even stop the truck; the border guards waved him through. Herr Mueller sped through the border so quickly that I didn't have any opportunity to be seen. My heart sank as I watched the United States recede from the bumpy view out the back of the truck.

I settled back, leaning against the truck's side, resigning myself to the realization that I was going to be stuck for a while. I weighed my options and tried to review the skills I'd been taught in the Resistance.

Rule number one: Try to escape. Herr Mueller was driving so fast I dare not try to jump out the back; I doubted I would survive the fall on such steeply curving, rocky roads. My best chance for escape was to get the ropes untied, so I concentrated on trying to loosen them. They were so tight they were making rope burns on my wrists as I wiggled my fingers.

My feet felt numb. I tried to wiggle over to one of the sacks to see what was inside. It took a few minutes, but finally

I was able to open one up. Inside the sack were money, papers, valuable coins, jewelry, and countless other personal treasures.

With my hands tied together, I pulled out one of the papers. It was a stock certificate for a company called International Business Machines made out to Edward and Isabel Pryor. Judge Pryor!

I looked through more sacks. They were filled with assets stolen from the bank's safety deposit boxes. Besides stock certificates, war bonds, and cash, there were marriage and birth certificates, charm bracelets, rings, gold coins, Confederate money, even baby teeth. Treasures of the town. The sacks were so hastily bundled together that I deduced Mueller must have just recently started looting the bank. But that also meant he wasn't planning to return to Copper Springs.

Just then, one of the sacks moved.

I froze.

A little sandy haired boy popped his head out of the sack and grinned sheepishly at me. *William!* I almost said his name but quickly caught myself. I showed my bound hands to him, and he scrambled out of the sack to help me untie the ropes. As soon as my hands were freed, I worked on my feet. After a quick hug, I pulled away to look at him carefully. "How did you find me?"

"See Bad Man. See you. Go find Girl."

William must have seen Herr Mueller put me in the back of his truck and somehow climbed in, unnoticed.

I still had to reduce what I wanted to tell William to the bare essentials. I tried not to show it, but I was terribly worried to see him. I knew Robert would be frantic. I needed to warn William.

"Hide from Bad Man. Stay in truck," I said to him. What I wanted to tell him was: "William, I don't know where we're going. I don't want Herr Mueller to see you. He may try to hurt you. Stay in the truck as long as you can and try to find me. We're going to escape when we get a chance." I wasn't sure how long I could keep William safe, but seeing him only resolved my determination: I was *not* going to let Herr Mueller win this battle.

Herr Mueller careened off the bumpy main road and on to a single lane dirt road. Another worry. How could Robert find us if we were heading into a remote area?

Think fast, Louisa.

I looked at the sacks and grabbed one. If I could leave a paper trail, perhaps it might alert someone to Herr Mueller's hideaway. I tried to get only identifying papers, not cash or coins. I leaned out of the truck and dropped the papers low toward the road, so they wouldn't fly up and broadcast to Herr Mueller what I was doing. Herr Mueller was speeding so quickly that I had to use one hand to hang on to the truck's side, leaning over the back.

In scarcely a few hours' time, we arrived at what seemed to be an oasis in the midst of a desert. A Mexican guard stopped the truck, apparently not accustomed to seeing Herr Mueller drive a truck. Herr Mueller barked at him, and the guard bowed respectfully and let him drive up the long driveway, lined with palm trees, to a palatial Spanish house.

I quickly motioned to William to get back in the sack, and I re-tied my hands and feet. Herr Mueller stopped the truck at the top of the hill crowned by a large gurgling fountain in front of the house. Deep fuchsia-colored bougainvillea climbed the walls of the grand house's stucco exterior.

Just as I had often wondered in Copper Springs, how did Herr Mueller seem to have an abundance of water available to him in a desert land?

A Mexican man quickly ran out to open his truck door. Herr Mueller spoke to the man in Spanish, walked to the back of the truck, and opened the hatch door. "Well, look who has woken up. Hello, Fräulein, welcome to my home-away-from-home. Mi casa es su casa."

He pulled me to the edge of the truck and untied my feet so that I could walk. He grabbed my arm roughly and walked with me to the front door. I glanced at the truck as the man drove it back down the hill, and begged God to protect William and keep him out of sight.

An older Mexican woman opened the door just as Herr Mueller and I approached the entryway. She curtsied to him, noticed the ropes around my hands, but avoided my eyes.

"Maria will take you to the guest room. Fräulein, I trust you will be quite comfortable in my home. Later, there is someone whom you will be most interested in meeting."

I wasn't interested in meeting *any* of his acquaintances. "Herr Mueller—how long am I going to be here? What are you planning to do with me?"

He laughed a throaty laugh. "You want to leave so soon? You don't like my hospitality? Not to worry, Fräulein. You won't be here long. But first, I have a few loose ends to tie up here." His eyes narrowed to slits, warning darkly, "and don't try anything stupid."

Herr Mueller turned and walked away from us, down a hallway of terra cotta tiles. Just as I thought about trying to get past Maria to the door, she clapped her hands, and another servant stepped out from behind the wall partition, carrying a fierce looking rifle.

Maria motioned for me to follow her as the guard followed behind me. She led me down a separate hallway, past many doors, and finally opened a door to a bedroom. The room was beautifully decorated in Spanish décor, including a large bed, nightstand, desk and chair, with a small private bathroom. I had a grudging admiration for Herr Mueller's taste for fine living until it occurred to me that the townspeople of Copper Springs were, unwittingly, financing his luxurious quarters.

"¿Està bien?" Maria asked.

No, Maria, being kept as a prisoner was not good for me, even if the accommodations were luxurious. But I only nodded.

"Traerè la cena pronto."

Pronto? I remembered Rosita calling out to Esmeralda to be "pronto." I think it meant quick or fast. "¿Cena? ¿Comida?" I asked Maria, hoping she was telling me she would bring food soon. I might have just been kidnapped, but it hadn't diminished my appetite.

"Sì, sì. Traerè la cena pronto." Maria untied the ropes on my hands and backed cautiously out of the room. I heard her lock the door from the outside, give orders to the guard in Spanish, and then shuffle back down the hallway. Then I heard the guard scrape a chair along the tiled floor before sitting down on it.

I rubbed my sore wrists and went over to the window to look outside. Decorative wrought iron bars prevented the obvious escape. I examined the bars more closely. They were impossible to bend or break, but...a small five-year-old boy just might be able to squeeze through the narrow railings. I looked below the window and saw bushes.

There was only a three-foot climb from the house's foundation up to my window. Where could William be? How could I let him know where I was? I kept rubbing my wrists and went into the bathroom to wash off the dried blood from Herr Mueller's blow to my head.

In the bathroom mirror, I studied my reflection. The blouse I was wearing nearly shouted right back at me. It was a bright red plaid top that Rosita had given to me recently as a hand-me-down. Rosita was so well endowed that I had ample fabric to spare. I had planned to tailor it but hadn't had a chance yet. I pulled it up out of my skirt and bit through the bottom edge, tearing a few inches along the entire hem.

I returned to the window and scanned for the truck where William was hiding. A guard looked over at the house, stared at my window, and lazily started strolling around. I craned my neck as far as I could and saw the very back edge of the truck, parked close to the house. I kept looking at the truck, hoping to see William.

Once, I could have sworn I saw his head pop out, but then he was gone again. I wondered if he might be safer if he stayed in the truck, but I wasn't sure how long Herr Mueller planned to keep me here. I tied my homemade flag onto the bars of the window. I prayed the guards wouldn't notice, but that William, somehow, would.

Lord, how can a child understand how serious this situation is? And you know William, Lord. You know how audacious he can be around Herr Mueller. Please send angels to protect him.

I tucked my shirt back in and stayed posted by the window, hoping to catch sight of William before the guards did. I was concentrating so intently that my heart skipped a few beats, so startled was I when Maria unlocked the door to bring a tray of food.

"¿Todo está bien?" she asked.

I nodded, not really sure what to think about her. Could she be an ally? How devoted was she to Herr Mueller? She set the tray on the desk and left. At least I couldn't complain about the food. It looked and smelled delicious. I recognized some of the dishes from Rosita's cooking. Thankfully, there were generous portions. Before I ate, I wrapped up food into the flour tortillas, trying to save as much food as I could for William. I put the food in a towel and hid it in the bathroom. I wasn't sure if or when Maria would return for the dishes.

Too soon, Maria shuffled back down the hallway and unlocked the door. She seemed to be a little less suspicious of me, perhaps assuming, erroneously, that I wasn't going to try and escape. She left the door open while she came for the tray. I saw the guard sound asleep in his chair, snoring loudly. Just as I was about to slip out the door and past the guard, from the corner of my eye, I saw the top of William's head jump up and down, like a kangaroo, trying to peek in my window.

I tried to distract Maria so she wouldn't notice him. "Maria, are you the cook, too? ¿La cocinera? The dinner was so good! Comida es muy bueno!" I walked over to the open door and leaned against it so that she had to turn away from the window. *It worked.*

Maria picked up the tray, shook her head to say "no" and left, locking the door behind her. I heard her kick the guard's chair, giving him a tongue lashing in Spanish for sleeping on the job.

William popped his head back up from the bushes under my window. I ran to the window and looked for the guards, signaling to William to crouch down behind the bushes. As soon as the guard turned and walked around the corner of the house, I reached down and pulled William up by the hands, carefully helping him squeeze through the bars. "William! You are so smart! How did you find me?"

He pulled at my sleeve and pointed to the window, indicating that he saw my flag made from my blouse. I quickly took the flag down and turned back to hug him. Then I jumped up and ran to the bathroom to get the food I had hidden for him. He, too, was famished and gratefully ate.

As he ate, I looked around the room to see if there was a place I could hide him if someone came to my room. Under the bed seemed to be the most logical spot. I said to William, "Girl comes. Brings food. Hide under bed. Wait."

"Girl?" William asked eagerly. "See Girl?"

"Yes. Girl comes. Brings food. Hide!" I answered.

I hardly slept, as exhausted as I was. I kept waking up, convinced I heard footsteps coming down the hall, but it was only the window-rattling snore of the guard posted at my door.

I worried about Robert and Aunt Martha. I could only imagine the anxiety they must be experiencing. What were they thinking had happened to us? Had Robert found the ring? Did he realize it was a clue? Close to dawn, I fell into a troubled sleep.

When I woke up, William was nowhere to be found. Panicking, I looked under the bed, in the bathroom, and the closet. The door was still locked. He must have sneaked out through the window while I was asleep. I shouldn't have been surprised. That boy was fearless. Just then, I heard Maria's shuffling footsteps, probably bringing breakfast to me. As soon as she came and went, I peered out the windows.

Not long afterward, I heard Herr Mueller's footsteps come down the hall. He spoke to the guard and knocked on my door. My heart was pounding. I still had not caught sight of William. Where could he have gone? I was terribly frightened Herr Mueller might spot him.

"Well, Guten Morgen, Fräulein. How are you enjoying your accommodations?"

I tried to sound braver than I felt. I didn't want to let Herr Mueller think he could intimidate me, but my throat felt tight and raw. "Actually, Herr Mueller, I find them to be a bit confining."

"Yes. Yes, I see your point." He glanced at the window's iron bars. "Normally, I would apologize for keeping you so...shall we say...limited in your surroundings...but I just don't quite believe you can be trusted. Have patience, Fräulein, it won't be much longer. Soon we will be on our way back to our homeland!" He smiled broadly.

So *that* was the plan. Herr Mueller was going to return me to Germany. First, he tried legal means within the United States, by tipping off the INS. When that plan was thwarted, he decided to deliver me there himself.

"Herr Mueller, I think I have guessed your strategy. A clever one, too. I think you bought up the copper mines while they were devalued during the Depression. You knew Germany would need the copper for its inevitable war. You take the copper from those mines and ship it all of the way back to Germany. Am I close to the truth?" I asked, trying to flatter him into revealing more.

He looked pleased. "You underestimate me. I have a far more extensive network than merely shipping copper to Germany." He pulled out a cigar and puffed on it until the smoke made me cough.

With a pang, I noticed it was a Wolf cigar from Hamburg. Dietrich's favorite.

"Do you know much about copper, Fräulein?"

I nodded, reminded of Robert's lengthy discourses on copper production.

"Let me enlighten you even further. I sell my low grade copper ore, the ore from the open pits, to the United States Government for a very substantial profit. The lower grade ore takes a long time to process, and little good is derived from it. A pity for America, but she is happy to pay me for my ore, and is grateful for any help for their futile war effort."

He sat in the desk chair and put his feet up on the bed where I was sitting. I stood up and walked over to the window.

"The high grade copper ore from my mines is sent across the border to Mexico," he continued. "Labor is cheap, the high grade copper is easily processed, and the pure copper is shipped to Germany, where I am immensely benefiting der Führer."

He jumped to his feet and clapped his hands in delight. "It gets even better, Fräulein. Then, I take the leftover minerals from the high grade copper: sulfur dioxide, slag, and even better, Fräulein"—now he was getting animated—"the impurities from the copper metal are gold, silver, nickel, and platinum, and I sell it a second time at the going market rate to the United States. The beauty of it is that they pay more for those leftovers than they paid for the ore in the first place!" He laughed with delight. "Some call it a 'double dip.' Brilliant, yes?"

Diabolically brilliant. "So those leftover minerals, those would be the copper tailings?"

"Excellent!" he said with great satisfaction. "I am glad you can appreciate my genius."

This man's inflated ego could fill a copper pit. "It would appear you don't need me, Herr Mueller. Why not just let me go?"

"I don't *need* you. Not in *any* capacity," he sneered, looking me up and down with repugnance on his face. "But my cousin, Heinrich, is very interested in having a little chat with you. Perhaps you've heard of my dear cousin? He is a very important man in Germany."

The very Heinrich Mueller I had feared when I first met Herr Mueller.

"Heinrich thinks you might be able to enlighten him about Dietrich Bonhoeffer's treasonous activities. So, for now, Fräulein, I hope you will relax and enjoy your accommodations, confining though they may be."

I thought back to that lunch at Herr Mueller's house when I first arrived in Copper Springs, naïvely telling him I was convinced Hitler was losing the war. I remembered that picnic in Robert's office when I openly shared details about Dietrich's involvements in those plots.

I was right; so was Dog; there was someone listening to us. *Herr Mueller.* How naïve could I have been? I never dreamed that sharing information with Robert could have such disastrous consequences. And now William's life was at risk, too. Even more haunting, it was possible I had made things worse for Dietrich and Hans.

"One more question, Herr Mueller. Is child labor part of your scheme?"

He turned back toward me, eyes narrowed. "Insinuating what?"

"Glenda's nephew, Tommy. I saw him at your mine. How could you do it? How could you make a ten-year-old boy work in a dangerous mine?"

He threw his head back and laughed. "Oh, you don't miss much, do you?! A boy that age is just the right size to be lowered into our mines and carry out some tasks in the deep crevices that only small hands could do. Explosives in small crevices, for example."

A child's life, dismissed with a shrug. Was there any evil this man wouldn't commit? Was nothing too low for him? He was utterly devoid of a conscience.

He sat back down and crossed his legs. "I've had great success using children. Only trouble is that little boys grow up. Fortunately, there always seems to be a child here or there who isn't really looked after. I had thought that the Reverend's brat might be a candidate for the job, though, I'm not sure he has enough brains to complete a task. It would've been nice for that boy to have something to do other than to torment people."

He slapped his hands on his knees and stood up to leave. "Too bad, Fräulein, that we did not meet under other circumstances. I must say that you are not the naïf I had expected you to be." And he started chuckling to himself all over again. After he left, the aroma of his putrid cigar smoke lingered in the room behind him.

Rather fitting.

As soon as I heard Herr Mueller walk down the hall, I ran back to the window. This time, I caught sight of William's blond head behind the truck the servants were packing. He was letting the air out of each truck tire. I held my breath as I saw a guard walk back toward the truck. *O Lord, protect him!* Suddenly, the guard spun on his heels and went back toward the house, as if he'd forgotten something.

William finished the last tire and then peeked around the truck, looking for guards, and ran under my window. I pulled him up and through the bars. "What were you doing?" I asked.

"Look Girl. No see Girl. See Bad Man." He shook his head with grave disappointment.

What was he talking about? Why was he looking for a girl? Who was he looking for? "Who, William, who?"

"Girl!" he said again, getting frustrated with me. "Look. No see Girl!"

"What girl?" I said, equally frustrated.

"Girl!" He responded, exasperated with my obtuseness.

I put my hands up to cover my face. This line of questioning wasn't getting us anywhere. I asked him if he saw many men guarding the house.

He shook his head and held up the number four. Four guards. That was better news than I had expected. I was still determined to find a way to escape, and William's espionage work was proving to be helpful.

Just then, I heard a guard shout out. He had just discovered four flat tires on his truck. Soon I heard other guards loudly complain. Herr Mueller came outside and waved his arms up and down in anger. I could only understand a little bit of the Spanish/English/German ranting and ravings, but apparently someone had put soap in the fountain by the magnificent front entry, and bubbles were pouring forth.

I went into the bathroom. Just as I suspected, the big bar of soap that had been there when I arrived yesterday was missing.

Chapter Fourteen

All day long, I watched the guards hurriedly pack the trucks with more boxes, furniture from the house, and paintings packed in wooden crates. William remained glued to the window. He kept saying he was looking for "girl."

I kept a close eye on him in case he had any other capers up his sleeve. I had to admit he would have been a wonderful worker in the Resistance; he did excellent reconnaissance work. And better still, one of the cardinal rules of Resistance Work was to confound the enemy by creating chaos and confusion with whatever weapons or supplies we could get our hands on. William had a genius' flair for getting Herr Mueller wildly upset.

Sometime in the late afternoon, I heard high heels clicks down the hall, accompanying Maria's now familiar shuffling. I quickly got William under the bed, motioning for him to wait quietly. The key turned at my bedroom door lock. A tall, slender woman came through the door behind Maria, who was holding my dinner tray. Maria put the tray down on the desk.

"Gracias, Maria," the woman said dismissively.

Maria shuffled away. The woman was dressed in a pale blue silk blouse and skirt, matching high heels; her sandy blonde hair was held back in an elegant French twist. She fixed her eyes on me; it was evident some kind of calculation was being made. Her steady gaze made me feel uncomfortable.

Then my heart skipped a beat. Nearly stopped, actually. I recognized this woman. I knew her from the picture on William's bureau.

This woman was Ruth.

"So. You are Louisa," she said. "I can see you know who I am."

She seemed to enjoy the shock on my face. I was at a rare loss for words, stunned by her sudden appearance. The pictures I had seen in the shed and in the tree house barely conveyed her beauty.

She was breathtaking, with alabaster skin and delicate features, like fine Dresden china. Her face was so lovely it almost hurt to look at her, the same way it hurt to listen to beautiful music. I think she was even more beautiful than when she was younger. Except...except for her eyes.

I remembered that first picture I had seen of her, where I thought her eyes showed mystery. Not so now. They glittered coldly.

"Friedrich has told me all about you." She walked over to the window. "But you're probably wondering why I'm here."

Afraid to trust my voice, I only nodded. I shot up a silent prayer. *Lord, please keep William under the bed. Lord, keep him hidden!* I wasn't sure what worried me more: Ruth spotting William or William seeing Ruth.

I cleared my throat. "Shall we sit down?" I asked her. Intentionally, I sat on the desk chair that William and I had positioned by the window to keep a lookout, and Ruth leaned against the bed, facing me. William was only inches away from her.

She took a silver box of cigarettes and a lighter out of her skirt pocket and lit it. "You don't mind if I smoke?" She didn't wait for an answer.

Why did everyone feel an inclination to smoke in this hot, stuffy little room?

"Interesting, isn't it? That you and I are from such different worlds, and yet seem to share a similar taste in men?"

No doubt, my face betrayed my disgust. "I despise Herr Mueller."

Ruth's lips tightened.

"Ruth, Herr Mueller doesn't love you. He doesn't love anyone but himself, with the possible exception of Adolf Hitler. I don't know what he's promised you, I can only imagine, but in the end, he will destroy you."

"Actually," she said haughtily, "I was referring to Robert."

That comment caught me off guard. I didn't know how to respond, so I pressed on about Herr Mueller. "I lived in Germany under the Nazis. I know what these men are capable of doing. They're merciless."

"You'll soon find out even more about them. Because, darling, you're on a one-way ticket right back to Berlin," she said, smiling coldly.

A chill ran down my spine. This woman was heartless. "Ruth, *how* could you leave?"

She narrowed her eyes. "Don't you dare judge me. You of all people! We're not so very different, you and I. We both know how to use men to get what we want. After all, you just married Robert to avoid deportation."

Without thinking, I blurted out, "I am *not* using Robert! I love him!" That pronouncement surprised even me. I was not even aware of when I had come to that realization.

She smirked, as if I had just made a joke, and walked over to the window. She inhaled her cigarette and slowly blew the smoke upward, just like Aunt Martha's movie starlets.

"I am *not* like you," I said, struggling to compose myself. "What I meant was *how* could a mother leave her own child?"

Eyes fixed out the window, she said, "It was better that I left. I never wanted a baby. Robert did. He wanted a houseful. Not me. I never had the feelings for the boy that a mother should have. And then he wasn't right. Something was never right about him. He cried and cried and cried. He was *always* crying. Robert was better with him."

She threw the cigarette down on the tiled floor and twisted her shoe on it to extinguish it. "It's better for him to be with Robert," she repeated, though her voice lacked conviction.

I couldn't quite decide if she was trying to convince herself of that or excuse herself. She walked over to the door, apparently finished with our conversation.

Just as she reached her hand for the doorknob, I asked, "Wait! Aren't you at all curious about William?"

She paused.

Finally. A crack in her armor.

"He's a wonderful boy, Ruth. He looks like you. He keeps a picture of you by his bedside." I could tell I had found a hook; her shoulders softened, ever so slightly.

She kept her head down. "Did Robert ever find out what's wrong with him?"

I rose to my feet and went closer to her, hoping to detain her a little. "Yes. William is deaf. But he's learning how to communicate. He's learning to lip read and to speak. To talk, Ruth! And be understood. He's *extremely* intelligent."

I stopped for a moment to let her take that in. "The only thing wrong with William is that he has a damaged nerve in his ear. He can't hear. That's *all*. But if he were to have been born in Nazi Germany, he would have been sent to a concentration camp and *eliminated*. That's the word the Nazis use for killing innocent people. Innocent children. Disposed of, like rubbish. William wouldn't have been permitted to live, because he wasn't perfect. That's the Germany that Herr Mueller loves. That's the Germany he wants to take you to."

She whipped around. "I know all about Germany. I've already been, two years ago when I first left Copper Springs. Friedrich has taken me all over the world on his business trips. Rome, Buenos Aires, Rio de Janeiro. Trust me, Louisa, I know *exactly* what I'm doing. I couldn't be happier."

Just then, we heard a pitiful sound—a wail or a moan—it sounded like an animal caught in a trap. It came from William. He had poked his head out from under the bed and recognized his mother. His eyes were wide with shock.

Ruth stepped back, clearly stunned. Then she opened the door and rushed out, slamming it shut behind her. I heard her walk, almost run, down the hall, her stiletto high heels echoing their staccato notes.

It suddenly occurred to me that she hadn't locked the door in her haste, but then I heard the guard walk over, lock it, and go back to his chair.

I went over and hugged William. He buried his face in my shoulder. I didn't know what else I could do or say. I just held him and rocked him in my arms. He didn't cry. He just seemed to go deep within himself.

My mind whirred with worries. What if Ruth told Mueller that he was here? I couldn't come up with any reasonable plan of escape; I was guarded too carefully. Nor could I jeopardize William's safety by trying to escape, either. Again, our only option was to wait.

I just kept sensing that word from God. *Wait.* But for *what?*

Obviously, Mueller was preparing to leave this villa, and it looked as if he didn't intend to return. From what I could see at the window, he was emptying the house of all valuable assets. All afternoon, the servants hurriedly carried out cardboard boxes, oil paintings, in large gilded frames, and wooden crates to the truck. How much of it was stolen? I wondered, fairly certain of the answer.

Later, when Maria came in to bring dinner, I watched her carefully but didn't notice any sign of a change towards me. Could Ruth have some tiny flicker of maternal instinct left in her and not have told Herr Mueller that William was here, hidden in my room?

I *hoped* so. I *prayed* so.

I wondered if I was taken along with Herr Mueller, if Ruth would somehow get William back to Robert. But judging from her reaction when she saw him, I didn't hold much confidence in that plan.

In broken Spanish coupled with gestures, I tried to ask Maria when Herr Mueller planned to leave.

"Mañana."

Tomorrow. Not much time left to hope for a rescue. I pondered uneasily what to do next. I wondered if Robert could find my paper trail. I decided Maria might be a better risk to hope for help than Ruth.

I tried to prepare William for what I thought might happen, but I didn't want to frighten him. I told him if I was taken away, he was to wait until he knew the trucks were gone, and knew for sure that Herr Mueller was gone, and then to find Maria. I was determined not to let Herr Mueller get near William. I found paper and a pencil and wrote Robert's name, address and phone number on it. With a prayer, I put it in William's pocket.

He was troubling me; I couldn't read his expression. He looked far away.

It was a terrible feeling to have to entrust a little boy into the hands of Herr Mueller's servants, but I had no other choice.

That night, again, I barely slept. Random thoughts bounced around in my head. Puzzles pieces started falling into place.

Just last week, in the church, when Herr Mueller tried to blackmail me into being his mistress, I accused him of "wanting to do to me what he did to her." I had meant Glenda. I now realized that by his answer, "she came to me of her own free will," he thought I meant Ruth.

Then my thoughts bounced to William, sleeping fitfully next to me. Spitting on Herr Mueller's shoes, throwing rotten eggs at him. Could William have seen Herr Mueller visit Ruth at their house? Is that why he hated Herr Mueller so much? Somehow, he must have known Ruth left Copper Springs with Herr Mueller but was unable, or too young, or both, to communicate that piece of information. Could he have been looking for her this morning when he slipped out through the window?

Then the last piece of this puzzle fell into place and I sat straight up in bed, heart hammering.

To William, *girl* meant Ruth! I had never taught William a name to call his mother. Neither had Robert. Since she was never spoken of in the Gordon home, she was never even given a name. Not Ruth, not Mother, not Mommy. When he had pointed to her picture by his bedside and said "girl," I had thought he meant "female." Ignorantly, I chided myself, I then taught him the word for "boy." He was asking me for her name. That's why he said, "Bad man, Girl go."

How could I have been so blind? He had been trying to tell us all along Herr Mueller was involved with Ruth. His tricks on Herr Mueller, and now his limited words, were all such obvious signs that William knew. He knew his mother had left with Herr Mueller. He *knew*.

I shuddered. What if Herr Mueller were to know William was here with me? What would he do?

I thought back to Ruth asking me if I loved Robert. I answered her without thinking. My answer came from deep inside, yet I knew it to be true. How close I felt to him—how much a part of the fabric of the Gordon family. With an ache in my throat, I realized I might not see him again.

In the middle of the night, I was startled awake from a restless sleep by a key turning in my door. I sat up, trying to hide William. My heart pounded so fast I thought it might explode. Please don't be Herr Mueller, I prayed. Don't be Herr Mueller.

Ruth tiptoed in. "Louisa! Get up and get William. Now! *Hurry!* I'm getting you out of here."

She didn't need to say another word; we sprang into action. We crept out of the room where we had been kept as prisoners for the last few days, past that blessedly useless guard who was sound asleep, snoring loudly. We moved quickly, obediently, behind her. She led us down the hall and out a back door. A car was waiting. She handed me the keys. "Drive as fast as you can! Don't stop!"

As we scrambled into the car, William stopped, turned and said something to her.

"What did he say?" she asked me, her eyes glued to him.

"He wants you to come home."

A shadow crossed her face.

"Ruth," I whispered, "come with us."

Her eyes hardened, and she glared at me. "You just don't understand, do you?" she whispered in an angry tone. "Robert never understood, either. Friedrich has promised me the world. Copper Springs holds *nothing* for me."

Oh Ruth, you're so wrong. It held everything for you.

I helped William into the car, got into the driver's seat, and looked back at her one more time before starting the engine. She was already gone.

I turned the key and pressed the gas pedal like I'd never done with Aunt Martha in the car, gunning the motor. The car roared down the steep driveway, past another sleeping guard. I glanced in the rear view mirror and saw him jump up, then stumble around in a state of complete confusion.

When I came to the end of Herr Mueller's long road, I felt a rising panic, unsure of which way to turn. I looked left and right but still had no idea which way to go. I knew the next few minutes were critical for our getaway.

Oh Lord, please help! Which way? I looked up through the bug-splotched windshield, scanning the inky black sky, and there it was, shimmering, a beacon. The copper star! I pressed the gas pedal to the floor and turned right. William looked over at me, eyes wide, clinging to the door handle so that he wouldn't slide around on the seat as I veered around sharp curves.

As the sun started to rise, I saw a sign for the border at Naco. I drove so fast the car practically flew through the custom gates. I wasn't going to stop until I was on United States' soil. Border patrolmen surrounded the car in alarm as I poured out the story of our kidnapping. It didn't take much to convince them; they had already been notified by the FBI to be on the look out for Friedrich Mueller and two kidnapped victims.

William and I were taken into the U.S. Customs Office. One agent offered, "Ma'am, would you like to call your husband and let him know you're both safe?"

My *husband?* The sound of that word amazed me. As I dialed Robert's office, an odd thought burst unbidden into my mind. It was the very first phone call I had made in America since the calls I used to make back in Germany, delivering messages of the Resistance. Not so very different.

Aunt Martha answered the phone. She began to get choked up when she heard my voice and realized we were both safe and unharmed. She said Robert had been out looking for us at Herr Mueller's mines with a group of men from the town and that there was a prayer vigil going on at the church. She said she would get word to Robert right away and let him know where to find us.

Finally, I started to relax. We were safe.

The Customs Agent pummeled me with questions before alerting the FBI, the FBI attaché in Mexico City and the Mexican Police. I tried to give every possible detail that could help them locate Herr Mueller. I tried to give them directions to the villa, tried to recall every detail I could remember about the trip: old signs, odd landmarks, unusual trees. I knew Herr Mueller was slippery enough to get away; every passing minute was crucial right now.

Someone was kind enough to get me a cup of coffee and a glass of milk with cookies for William, who finally fell asleep in my arms. A good sign, I hoped, but I had a nagging worry about how seeing his mother again had affected him.

At last, Robert appeared at the door. When I woke William, he saw his father's face and ran straight into his arms. Robert scooped him up and held him tightly, tears flowing freely. I held back, not wanting to intrude on this private moment, but Robert kept his eyes locked on me, holding one arm out to gather me in. William and I fit perfectly in the circle of his arms.

Chapter Fifteen

There have been a few times in my life when a hot shower was worth a king's ransom. That's how it felt when I took a shower back at the parsonage in Copper Springs, washing off the gritty dirt of Mexico, the dried blood in my hair from the blow on the head from Herr Mueller's gun, and the anxiety of the last few days. Afterwards, Aunt Martha gently put some ointment on my raw, blistered wrists and ankles.

"More battle scars," I said, trying to keep my voice light.

Aunt Martha wiped the corner of her eye as a tear leaked out. Her tenderness always took me by surprise. It made such brief, infrequent appearances.

She had even made a temporary truce with Dog, letting him sleep in her room at night during our absence. "Well, what was I supposed to do? He was just so pathetic, missing William, hanging around me with that sad look on his face," she said in her defense. She made us a dinner of William's favorite food, hot dogs and baked beans, and graciously ignored Dog as William fed him scraps right from the table.

"Louisa!" Robert practically bolted out of his chair. "In all of the excitement, I nearly forgot to tell you! The last place anyone had seen Mueller was up at one of his mines. A group of us spent the last few days combing through it. We didn't find a trace of you or William, but you'll *never* guess who we did find."

"Glenda's nephew?"

His shoulders slumped in abject disappointment. "How on *earth* did you guess that?"

I explained how I had seen a boy there when we stopped at the mines.

"Curly bright red hair?"

I nodded.

"Hard to miss. Anyway, he's back with Glenda now, over at Betty's." He scrunched up his face. "I don't know *how* you know so much."

"Nice work, Reverend." I smiled at him, but when our eyes met, my cheeks started burning. How ridiculous! I've been eating across the table from this man for over a year now. Why was I suddenly self-conscious? What had changed?

Everything.

Hoping Aunt Martha wouldn't notice my silly schoolgirl blush, I quickly reached over to pick up William's napkin off the floor before Dog scooped it up. Tucking it under his chin, my concern over him grew. True, we were both weary past endurance, but it was more than that. The sadness he had shed had returned.

I knew why. Seeing his mother brought his grief right up to the surface again.

I dreaded one final thing left to do. I hadn't told Robert about Ruth yet; I was waiting until we might have a moment alone. I thought William might bring her up at dinner, but since he hadn't, I didn't either. Truth to be told, I was postponing the conversation until it was inevitable.

That moment arrived too soon. A knock came at the door, and Robert answered it as I was upstairs tucking William into bed. He fell asleep quickly; I, too, couldn't wait to get to bed.

Robert met me on the stairs as I was coming down to say goodnight. "Louisa, there's someone here to see you." I followed him into the parlor. "This is Agent Gullberg with the FBI. He has some news."

"Ma'am, how are you?" The agent looked at me with concern in his eyes.

"Better now. Thank you," I answered.

"We need to talk to you tomorrow, but tonight I just wanted you to know that we found Mueller's house. Your directions were good, ma'am. Your paper trail tipped us off. That was right smart thinking."

I gasped. "Did you capture Herr Mueller?"

He shook his head in disappointment. "No, I'm sorry to say we didn't. He had cleared out a few hours earlier, and the house was near emptied. Quite a place, too. A regular Caesar's Palace. There wasn't a single living soul in that house. Looked like everyone scattered: servants, guards, everyone. All of the border patrols have been notified. Don't you worry, ma'am. We'll catch him."

I frowned. "I don't think he could cross on land. I think he would try to leave by ship. I thought I heard one of the servants mention the Mar de Cortes." The Gulf of California. Then something the agent said triggered a horrible thought. "Did you say there wasn't a single living person in the house?"

"Yes, ma'am. I did. There was just one dead body. A woman. She had been shot straight through the heart. One clean shot. We still haven't identified her, but we're pretty sure she's an American. That's the reason I came by tonight. I wondered if you might have any idea who she was."

Instantly, I knew.

I was sure the body belonged to Ruth. She had betrayed Herr Mueller by letting us escape, He had found out and killed her for it.

I looked over at Robert. I realized the gravity of the significance that this information, once revealed, would hold for him. And the fresh pain it would bring. But I had no choice.

"Please excuse me for a moment." I went upstairs to William's room, tiptoed in, and listened to the steady breathing of his deep sleep. I took the picture of Ruth that was by his bedside and tiptoed back out. I went downstairs, back to the parlor. I took a deep breath, pulled the picture frame out from behind my back, and showed it to the agent. "Could this be her?"

Recognition dawned on his face. "Yes! Yes, that's her! Who is she?"

I looked over at Robert. I felt such sorrow for him. What was his expression? Confusion? Anguish? Pain? His jaw was clenched, letting the shock sink in.

I turned to the agent. "Her name is Ruth Gordon. She used to live in Copper Springs. She had run off with Herr Mueller almost two years ago and had been living at his villa in Mexico." I glanced at Robert. "She came to the room where Herr Mueller had kept me hostage. She said she wanted to meet me. William was hiding under the bed, but as Ruth and I talked, he poked his head out and saw her."

I paused and flashed a worried look at Robert before continuing. All color had drained from his face. "Later that same night, she came back and helped us escape. She had a car waiting for me and handed me the keys. I am quite sure that Herr Mueller found out what she had done and killed her for it." There. It was said. Almost all of it.

"Mind if I take this picture for now? To identify the body?" the agent asked.

I nodded.

He looked at Robert and then back at me. He lowered his voice and said, "So if her last name was Gordon, was she somehow related to the Reverend?"

"Yes. She was his wife and the mother of the little boy who was with me."

He scratched his head. "But I thought you were his wife."

"Well, yes, well, it's a long story," I answered, hoping he wouldn't ask any more questions.

Robert just sat on the davenport, his head bowed down, chin on his chest. The only sign of the impact of what he had just heard was how he was gripped his hands tightly together, as if they kept him in one piece.

After saying goodbye to the agent, I closed the door behind him and saw Aunt Martha had been listening from the kitchen. She looked at me, shook her head in sadness and disbelief, and walked up the stairs like an old woman.

I sat down beside Robert. "I was planning to tell you about Ruth tomorrow," I started. "I'm sorry." I waited a moment and softly said, "Is there anything you want to know?"

Robert shook his head as if he didn't want to hear anything more. I just sat there next to him, not saying a word.

Finally, he glanced at me sideways, his pain stark and raw, and asked in a low and gravelly voice, "is there anything more I should know?"

I told him everything. He leaned over, holding his head in his hands. I told him about the conversation Ruth and I had in my room. I felt I needed to tell him every ounce of truth, even the part I dreaded the most: As we were leaving, William had asked Ruth to come home. I told him that I asked her to return with us and that she had refused.

Then Robert stood up and glared at me, eyes blazing. "How could you even ask her that? How dare you! You had no right!"

"She saved our lives, Robert. She saved us because of William. And that choice cost her dearly. She lost her life because of helping us to escape. I'm sure of that."

The truth was I don't really know why I asked her to return with us. It was almost as if the Holy Spirit said it through me. Only God could be so willing to offer Ruth one more chance to make things right, one more opportunity to make a fresh start. I knew it wasn't from me.

Abruptly, Robert walked to the door. "I need to be alone for a while." His face held such anguish; I felt as if I had just poked a raw wound.

I watched him back the car out of the driveway and drive down the street. Then the frantic anxiety of the last few days started to seep away, leaving me with a deep physical exhaustion.

* * *

Aunt Martha let me sleep late the next day. When I woke, I went downstairs and found a kitchen table laden with food. Cookies and pies, cakes, and jars of homemade jam and preserves.

"What's all this?" I asked her.

"Folks have been bringing food by all morning long. They've been worried about you and William. About Robert, too."

So was I. "Did he come home at all last night?" I glanced out the kitchen window to see if the Hudson was in the driveway. It wasn't.

She shook her head. She looked terribly tired.

"Please don't worry, Aunt Martha. He'll be all right. He just needs a little time." I tried to sound convincing.

I looked for William but found Dog, sitting patiently, below the tree house. I even think he was worried, if dogs did worry. I climbed up into the tree house and spotted William, playing with his toy trucks. "Want to work on a lesson?" I asked him.

He shook his head.

"Want to play catch with Dog?"

Again, he shook his head. He just kept moving his toy trucks around, re-organizing them, checking over their wheels.

Oh Lord, please help this fragile home.

Dog and I walked over to the church office, but there was no sign of Robert.

After lunch, Judge Pryor stopped by the house to see me. "Well, Louisa, looks as if you and Robert stumbled onto something mighty big. This is going to put Copper Springs on the map."

"Do you have any idea yet how much money Herr Mueller stole?" I asked.

He stalled.

"Oh no. Is it worse than we thought?"

"We're just starting to find out," he answered. "There are more FBI agents coming to town, all the way from Los Angeles. It looks as if he has cleaned everyone out. Looted all of our assets. Most folks don't even know how much they've lost yet."

After filling him in on Ruth's involvement with Herr Mueller, I confided, "Robert left yesterday and hasn't been back yet."

"Don't you worry, sugar. He'll be back when he's ready. He's just needs to sort it all out. He knows what he has waiting for him here."

I hoped he was right.

Agent Gullberg came back in the afternoon; we went over every detail I could remember so that he could fill out more reports. At the end of the interview, he handed me back William's picture frame of Ruth and asked me what should be done with her body.

"Pardon? I don't quite understand what you mean."

"We need a place to send it for burial."

I looked back at Aunt Martha who was listening to us from the kitchen. She shrugged, as if she didn't know what to do, either. So I made a decision. "We should bury her here, then, in Copper Springs."

"Fine. I'll have someone get back in touch with you when the body is ready to be delivered. Thank you, ma'am."

I wasn't sure Robert would approve of that decision, but he wasn't around when it had to be made. No matter what, that woman was William's mother.

Aunt Martha and I tried to keep up light chitchat, talking about the different foods people had brought by. We had an early supper. William's eyes stayed glued to his plate. It made me understand why the doctor thought he might be retarded; his sadness covered him like a blanket.

Suddenly, I realized one other place where Robert might have gone. *Of course!* "Aunt Martha, I know where Robert is! Do you think Rosita would let me borrow her truck?"

Her eyes grew large. That thought seemed to alarm her. "I suppose so," she said, apprehension in her voice. I kissed William on the top of his head and ran down the street to Rosita's house to ask her for the truck keys. She looked reluctant, mortified almost, until I explained where I was going and why.

She handed the keys to me. "Be careful, Louisa! The gears are sticky!"

I thanked her, jumped in the old Ford, and rumbled off down the street before she could change her mind. It was more than a little annoying to me that everyone considered me to be an inept driver. I had just driven, successfully, through half of Mexico. In the rearview mirror, I saw Rosita making the sign of the cross on her chest as I turned the corner and sped out of town. I knew the prayer was for her Ford.

I arrived at the yawning copper pit and found Robert's car. I walked around the crater, searching for him. I thought there would be workers there today but it was deserted. I was starting to get worried and fought back a frightening thought. But then I saw him.

He was sitting on a ledge, head in his hands. I wondered if he had been at this pit all night and all day. He looked, to borrow one of Aunt Martha's phrases, like something the cat dragged in. Scruffy with dark whiskers shadowing his cheeks and chin. Dark circles under distant gray eyes. Dried tear marks traced his cheeks. He wasn't even wearing his trademark tie. And his suffering was palpable.

He didn't look up when I reached him. I sat down beside him and quietly said, "Robert, please come home."

He gave me a stranger's glance. "I need to be alone," he said, in a tone that made it clear he wished I hadn't come after him.

I sighed. "Please don't do this."

He stood up and walked away from me.

I followed him, knowing he didn't want me to. "Don't do what you're doing now. Shutting yourself away. It's just like it was when I first got here, when you spent your time away from the house, and William spent his time up in the tree house, and no one in the parsonage talked to each other."

He stopped abruptly. "You could not *possibly* fathom what I am experiencing."

"Then tell me! Tell me how you feel!" I could tell by the look on his face I had pushed him too far. He was angry with me. And I was glad. At least it was *some* emotion. I wanted him to fume; it was better than this paralyzing sadness. "Go ahead! Get mad! Robert, you have every reason to be angry!"

It worked. The simmering volcano erupted. "Do you have any idea how it feels to know that *my wife* ran off with Mueller? And that she was living just a few *hours* away in Mexico? Or to realize what a *fool* I've been—working with Mueller on church business and banking business-while he was having an *affair* with my wife? You and I had lunch at his house not so long ago! Lunch!" He kicked a stone as hard as he could in complete disgust. "What's the word for me...a first class cuckold? How do I even dare stand in a pulpit to my congregation after this?"

Now the volcano was spewing.

"Not to mention what Ruth did to William, not once when she left, but twice? He asked her to come back with him, and she, essentially, abandoned him again! I'm glad she's dead. I really am. But I still have to keep living and try to repair the damage she's done. Once again."

He practically spat the words, then turned and walked away.

I trotted behind, trying to keep up with him. "Robert, there's not a person in this town who wasn't fooled by Herr Mueller. Everyone! He stole from and lied to the entire town." In my mind popped the filled sacks of treasured possessions, even some beloved child's cast off baby teeth, in the back of the truck. Probably on their way to Germany by now.

He spun on his heels to face me. "No, Louisa, *not* everyone! You knew right when you met him. And William knew."

"But that's only because I had come from a country that was filled with Herr Mueller types. And William knew because he had seen them together." I told him about misunderstanding William's meaning of "girl."

I paused before saying what I had really come to the pit to say. "Robert, there is another way of looking at this."

"And what way is that?" he said, arms crossed in defiance.

"Do you remember telling me you believed God was giving you a second chance to give yourself to Him?"

"Of course, I remember. That was just a few days ago," he said, irritation rising in his voice.

Could it have only been a few days ago? So much had happened to us; it felt like months had passed. "You said God wanted all of you. I think you're right, Robert. I think God is asking more of you."

Bitterly, he answered, "then it's more than I am able to give."

"Wait. Listen to me for a moment. I think God gave you a gift in this encounter William and I had with Ruth. You have your answers about her. She can't hurt you or William any more. You know why she left and with whom. And you know that nothing could change her mind; she would leave again. The choices that she made, all of them, were hers to make. And hers to die for. But now it's over, Robert. And I truly believe God wants you to move forward with your life."

His arms dropped to his side. He shook his head and looked at the sky as his gray eyes filled with tears. "Was she evil like Mueller?"

I didn't answer him right away though I had given that question some thought. Herr Mueller had sold his soul to the devil long ago. But Ruth? "I think she might have been so selfish that she couldn't truly love anyone but herself. But whatever horrible choices she made in her life, she did help William and me to escape. She did one thing right. Try and remember that."

He turned and kicked at the mounded earth, looking remarkably like his five-year-old son.

"There is one person who has shared your experience, Robert. William. Ruth treated him the same way she treated you. This time, share your grief with him. Heal together, not separately. William needs you in a way that only you can help him. Only you can understand how he feels."

I stopped for a moment to let that sink in. "You're needed at home. Your son needs you. I need you. Please come home."

There. I was finally finished. I said everything I had come to say.

He covered his face with his hands for a moment. Then he exhaled heavily, as if the fight had finally left him. "Who's the minister now, Louisa?" he asked, a sad sweetness in his voice. He took my hand and looked right at me with the look that I had come to expect from him. A look that I had come to want from him.

"Actually," I said as I took his other hand, "I'm the lucky one. I got the package. You and William." I swallowed and hastened to add, "and Aunt Martha."

Then we walked, hand in hand, back to the automobiles. "I'll follow you home," he said, holding the door for me as I climbed up into Rosita's truck.

It might have just been my imagination, but I could have sworn I saw a trace of amusement light his eyes as he watched me back Rosita's truck up and shift from reverse to first gear, making a horrible sound as I ground the gears.

Home, I repeated to myself. I was going home.

Chapter Sixteen

The Mexican Police sent Ruth's body back to Copper Springs for burial. We had a small service for her, just the four of us, headstone and all, and put her in her final resting place in the cemetery next to the church. It seemed a touch of irony that she had tried to get away from Copper Springs most of her life, yet here she was, back to stay.

We had struggled to find the right epitaph to be inscribed on her headstone, finally settling on: "We hope she found the peace she was looking for."

After William solemnly laid a long-stemmed white rose on the grave, Aunt Martha took him home. Robert and I stood at the gravesite a few minutes longer, both of us lost in our thoughts about this woman who lay before us, far below in the ground.

Finally, I broke the silence. "I think you were right."

"What could I possibly have been right about?" he said, still looking down at the fresh grave. "I'm shocked to hear those words from you." He glanced at me with a puzzled look on his face.

"Ruth and I are a little bit alike."

He groaned. "Oh Louisa, I never should have said that. Please forget it."

"She even said so herself. But I disagreed with her reason," I admitted. "Anyway, just a little bit alike. We both are, were, no, I mean, are stubborn women."

"Pushy, too," Robert added.

I raised an eyebrow at him.

"And you both think you're right about everything and everybody."

I frowned at him.

"But there's a big difference between you. Ruth wanted everything her way. You're willing to wrestle with God to make it His way. The difference is...well...quite literally, it's a difference between life and death." He looked back down at Ruth's grave.

"Now there's an interesting sermon topic," I said with a half-smile.

Robert turned to me. "You know, for one brief moment, that day you disappeared, before I realized that William was gone, too, before I realized Mueller had taken you, before I found the ring, I thought that maybe you...," his voice trailed off.

It slowly dawned on me what he was trying to say. I turned to face him. "But you knew, didn't you? Robert, you knew I wouldn't have left. You knew that, didn't you?" I searched his eyes for my answer.

It was important to me he knew he could trust my promise, even if it was made hastily before a judge to ensure my citizenry. I might share stubbornness and pushiness and self-righteousness with Ruth, but that was where the similarities ended. I kept my promises. I was *not* like her.

He looked at me and smiled. "I knew."

I stepped a little closer to him and slipped my hands into his. "There is just one other thing more I haven't told you. Something I did tell to Ruth."

He took a step closer to me.

"I told her I loved you."

Then he kissed me, gently at first, then with deep feeling, not even caring we were right in front of Ruth's grave. Rather symbolic, I felt. Ruth's hold was finally broken.

Epilogue

Not long afterwards, Robert and I had an official church ceremony to, what Robert called, really 'seal the deal.' Reverend Hubbell, the retired supply minister from Douglas, was kind enough to do the honors. The judge's wife banged out her rendition of Mendelssohn's *Wedding March* on the organ, a special request by Robert as a surprise for me. The musicianship might not have been stellar, but I suspect Felix Mendelssohn would have been delighted to know his music was being played and appreciated in Copper Springs, Arizona.

Our courtship began on our wedding day. We started our life together with a renewed optimism, as the war in Europe slowly drew to conclusion.

The world of the Allies rejoiced, on April 30th, 1945, when Adolf Hitler committed suicide by shooting himself in the mouth after poisoning his mistress.

Hitler's Thousand Year Reich had crumbled within a decade.

One week later, Germany surrendered unconditionally. Hitler's henchmen scattered like rats to a sewer system. Some were found in the days and months and even years following the war, but Heinrich Mueller, head of the German Gestapo, has not been found. Nor has his cousin, Friedrich Mueller of Copper Springs, Arizona. Fortunate fools. But one day, I take comfort in the fact they will stand to be reckoned with before the Almighty Lord.

Hearing of Hitler's death made us eagerly expect to learn of Dietrich's release from prison. We were anxious to tell him our story and the role he played in bringing us together. He was never to learn of it. To our great sorrow, we heard that Dietrich's trial had finally happened, after two years in horrible prisons with appalling, inhumane conditions, just three weeks before Hitler died.

In the kangaroo court of Nazi Germany, Dietrich and his brother-in-law Hans had been found guilty of treason and were hanged on April 9th, just one week before the Allies reached the camp where he had been held in Flossenberg. No one was notified of their death, not even Dietrich's parents. They finally heard of their son's death on a radio broadcast from the BBC.

When the news finally reached us, and we heard of the gruesome details of his execution, we both wept for our beloved friend. Heaven's gain was earth's loss.

* * *

The townsfolk of Copper Springs survived. Perhaps because no one went unscathed, it was easier for the town to help each other get through Herr Mueller's devastating deception. Even his own wife, Hilda Mueller, was left penniless and homeless. Amazingly, she knew nothing of her husband's secret life.

In a remarkable show of charity, the town embraced her. She started working part-time as a receptionist at Ramon's Barber Shop and part-time as a hostess at Rosita's Cocina, a little Mexican restaurant the Gonzalves' opened up not long after their baby boy was born.

Herr Mueller's house, which had been heavily mortgaged so that he could free up the cash to take with him, was auctioned off for a penance to the bankrupt town and has become the new Copper Springs library and town offices.

And an interesting development happened in the local churches. They started filling up. Emptied bank accounts made for full churches.

Ruth's death ended up being a blessing, easier to handle than her abandonment, for her death brought closure. William and Robert healed together, and this time, their wounds healed strong.

William's language skills and speech have continued to develop so clearly he is now understood by many people in Copper Springs. He is starting to read and write and can lip read so well Robert and I can no longer have a conversation without his input.

Once a month, we take him to Violet Morgan, the retired teacher in Bisbee, for tutoring, and we always stop by the Prospector's Diner to visit Wilma and check on her newest waitress, Glenda. In a fitting touch of irony, Glenda sold Mueller's ring at our repeated insistence and used the proceeds to make a down payment on a little home for her and her red-haired nephew, Tommy.

All too soon, we are going to have to seriously consider letting William attend the Southwestern School for the Deaf. But I have another idea I've been mulling over, in which William might be allowed to go to the local public school. I'm still working on a strategy to persuade Robert.

There's something else I need to tell him, first. William is going to have a new role soon, as a big brother. For a month or so now, I've been feeling suspiciously similar to how I felt after Ada's visit. I've already chosen the baby's names. If a girl, she'll be Marta. If this baby is a boy, his name will be Dietrich.

Aunt Martha has let me start to teach her to play the piano though we've been on the same beginner's piece for three months now. One thing I've learned about Aunt Martha, if I accept her where she is and give her time, she can surprise me.

A book I had once read described good and evil as equal and opposing forces: the yin and the yang. Natives in Southeast Asia wore fabric skirts made of a large black and white checked pattern, like a checkerboard, to symbolize the balance of good and evil.

I think they're wrong. I have seen, with my own eyes, how good is greater than evil, God is greater than Satan, and God's good ultimately triumphs. The scales of light weigh heavier than the scales of darkness. And as dark as the night can get, and it can get very dark, indeed, the sun will rise and expose the day.

Reading Guide for Copper Star

What were Louisa's redeeming qualities? What was the least likeable aspect of her personality? In what ways did we see Louisa's character change? In what ways did her character remain constant? Have you had a "Louisa" in your life?

What did you think, at first, about William? What compelled William to play tricks on Herr Mueller? What was he trying to prove?

How was the attachment that William and Louisa felt for each other, from the very first, believable? What did they contribute to each other?

Let's talk about Robert. Louisa described him as "a man typical of his generation: He guarded his emotions and kept his opinions to himself, veiled by a gentleman's exterior." Do you think Robert's attitude was typical for that time period? Is there any merit to being that kind of person?

What kind of a minister do you think Robert was? Did you admire his fortitude or did it frustrate you? Was it right or wrong for him to go into the ministry, knowing he didn't feel called to it?

The Gordon household was an orderly home. "Even Aunt Martha's hair was pinned neatly into place, just like her emotions." Louisa arrived and turned the household topsy-turvy. She liked to face things head-on, whereas Robert and Aunt Martha kept their feelings private. How does this relate to your life? Whom are you more like?

How did you feel when Aunt Martha said she didn't want a choir robe made by a German or a Jew? Why did she seem so reluctant to accept Louisa? What did you think of the way that Louisa handled the choir robes?

Louisa and Aunt Martha had a love-hate relationship. When did it shift to a bond between them? What caused the change? Have you ever had a relationship that changed from one of antagonism to one of loyalty? Was the change permanent?

Playing the piano helped Louisa escape into a world without troubles. What helps you to escape your world?

Why is the title, *Copper Star*, a metaphor suitable for the book?

How did you feel when you learned that there were hostage exchange camps within the United States? Do you think it was right or wrong? Did your feelings change after knowing Louisa could have been a hostage exchange?

What compelled Louisa to want to return to Germany? Was it an appropriate motivation? What do you feel your primary motivation is in life? Have you ever felt "not good" enough?

Faith in God is clearly a significant part of Louisa's life. What role does prayer play in her life?

In *Copper Star*, where was God's grace most evident?

Did you know anything about Dietrich Bonhoeffer before you read *Copper Star*? If so, did you learn anything new about him?

Did he seem like a real person to you? If you'd like to learn more about Dietrich Bonhoeffer, read *Letters and Papers from Prison*. It's a collection of letters smuggled out by sympathetic guards during the twenty months Bonhoeffer spent, under suspicion but without charges, in Berlin's Tegel prison.

About the author

Suzanne Woods Fisher writes books and publishes articles from her home in the San Francisco Bay Area. She shares a busy home with her husband, four kids, and a steady stream of puppies she raises for Guide Dogs for the Blind.

Find her on-line at: www.suzannewoodsfisher.com

Acknowledgements

A longing fulfilled is sweet to the soul. (Proverbs 13:19, NIV)

With all my heart I thank God for giving me the passion to write and the encouragement to persevere.

A special thanks to the How girls, Lisa Marquardt, Deb Coty and Linda Danis, my first draft readers. I owe you!

Grateful thanks to my editor, Dawn Carrington, for her commitment to excellence.

I especially want to express gratitude to my husband, Steve, and to my wonderful children, Lindsey, Gary, Meredith and Tad, who gave me the time, space and freedom to write.

A special thank you to the John Tracy Clinic of Los Angeles for checking the manuscript for accuracy, sharing information about Spencer and Louise Tracy and their son, John, in the early days of the Clinic, and for enthusiastically supporting this project.

The author gratefully acknowledges the following trademarks:

Good Housekeeping magazine and cookbooks: Hearst Communications, Inc. CORPORATION DELAWARE 959 Eighth Avenue New York NEW YORK 10019

Cheerioats (now called Cheerios): GENERAL MILLS, INC. CORPORATION DELAWARE Number One General Mills Boulevard Minneapolis MINNESOTA 55426

Kraft Macaroni & Cheese: Kraft Foods Holdings, Inc. CORPORATION DELAWARE Three Lakes Drive Northfield ILLINOIS 600932753

Zenith Radionic A2A Vacuum Hearing Aid: Zenith Electronics Corporation (formerly Zenith Radio Corporation) 2000 Millbrook Drive, Lincolnshire, Ill. 60069

LONE RANGER, INC., THE CORPORATION MICHIGAN 17TH FLOOR-STROH BLDG. DETROIT MICHIGAN

International Business Machines Corporation CORPORATION NEW YORK New Orchard Road Armonk NEW YORK 10504

BBC: The British Broadcasting Corporation Broadcasting House Portland Place; London W1A 1AA UNITED KINGDOM

Crayola Crayons (current owner) Binney & Smith Properties, Inc. CORPORATION DELAWARE 2035 Edgewood Avenue Easton PENNSYLVANIA 18045

The text of the 1917 Scofield Reference Bible is now in the public domain. Oxford University Press published a copyrighted revision of the Scofield Bible in 1967 with a slightly modernized KJV text. The Press continues to issue editions under the title *Oxford Scofield Study Bible*, which it offers with other translations. Oxford University Press, Great Clarendon Street, Oxford OX2 6DP

Ford Motor Company, Dearborn, Michigan 48126

Enjoy this excerpt from Goldeneyes
© 2007 Delia Latham
Coming 2008 from Vintage Romance Publishing

In the darkness of a Depression-era night, a man addicted to alcohol commits a heinous crime that impacts the lives of two entire families, and over two decades will pass before the horrible wrong begins to be made right.

He thought she was not going to answer the door.

No one responded to his first two knocks. He heard no stirrings from within the house and decided it was possible she wasn't home. His gut feeling, though, was that the woman was there, ignoring his persistent tapping at the door.

"Mrs. Kelly? Mrs. Kelly, are you there?" He landed three more solid raps against the splintered wooden door and turned to go, disappointed. He would have to try again later.

Behind him, the door creaked open. He turned and saw Annie Kelly for the first time. She was the most beautiful mess Clarence Camden had ever laid eyes on.

Her silver-gold hair – not silver as in gray, but a beautiful silvery gold – had obviously not been brushed that day, or possibly the day before. Her face was colorless in the dimly lit room, the cornflower blue eyes stark against the paleness of her skin. She wore a spotted and wrinkled gingham housecoat with all the buttons in the wrong holes.

She looked half dead, and he wanted nothing more than to pull her into his arms and make everything better. He couldn't find his voice.

Finally the woman spoke, so softly he had to strain to hear. "Yes? I'm Mrs. Kelly."

Again he opened his mouth, and for a moment, feared he would never again be able to speak. He desperately cleared his throat and found his elusive voice.

"I'm sorry to disturb you. I know you've been through a difficult time, and I apologize for dropping by like this."

She just stood there, her eyes lifeless and dull, obviously waiting for him to state his business and leave. He shifted his weight from one foot to the other, uncomfortable under her detached gaze.

"Look, I – I really don't know how to say what I've come here to say. Perhaps I should start by telling you who I am." He attempted a small smile, which faded and disappeared when Annie did not offer one in return. "My name is Clarence Camden. The Lamont Limelight is my company ... my uh, my newspaper."

Still no response. He sighed and plowed ahead. "I'm afraid I have some bad news, Mrs. Kelly."

For the first time since she had opened the door, Annie appeared to hear what he was saying. Her chin lifted slightly, and her eyes widened. "You've seen Jack," she whispered, and again he almost did not hear. "Is he all right?"

"I've seen him." He hesitated then asked, "May I come in, please? This could take a few minutes."

Turning, she walked away without a word. Since she did not close the door in his face, he followed. Motioning him toward a worn sofa, she perched on the edge of a straight-backed chair across the room. Still she said nothing, only waited in dull silence.

Clarence spoke slowly, uncertain where to start. "I found your husband ... uh, well, sleeping ... in front of my office three days ago."

"He was drunk, of course," Annie said, a touch of bitterness coloring her voice. "You don't have to be afraid to say it, Mr. Camden. I know all about Jack's drinking problem." She closed her eyes briefly, with a sad little shake of her head. "Poor Jack. He took this whole thing much harder than I would have expected."

Suddenly those vivid blue eyes flew open and stared directly into his.

"Did he tell you our baby girl was kidnapped five weeks ago?"

 Vintage Romance Publishing offers the finest in historical romance, inspirational, non-fiction, poetry, and books for young adults. Visit us on the web at www.vrpublishing.com, and to stay-up-to-date with our newest releases, subscribe to our newsletter on our homepage.

If you liked *Copper Star*, be sure to check out more of our inspirational historical romances at our website and available now at Amazon.com, all major online retailers, and your favorite bookstore!

Also look for our new list of titles coming the fall of 2007 and spring 2008!

Printed in the United States
99375LV00001B/16-39/A